Indecision

Books published by The Random House Publishing Group are available at quantity discounts on bulk purchases for premium, educational, fund-raising, and special sales use. For details, please call 1-800-733-3000.

Indecision

A NOVEL

BENJAMIN KUNKEL

RANDOM HOUSE • NEW YORK

2006 Random House International Edition

Copyright © 2005 by Benjamin Kunkel

Published in the United States by Random House, an imprint of The Random House Publishing Group, a division of Random House, Inc., New York.

RANDOM HOUSE and colophon are trademarks of Random House, Inc.

Originally published in hardcover in the United States by Random House, an imprint of The Random House Publishing Group, a division of Random House, Inc., in 2005.

LIBRARY OF CONGRESS CATALOGING-IN-PUBLICATION DATA

Kunkel, Benjamin.
Indecision : a novel / Benjamin Kunkel.
p.   cm.
ISBN 0-8129-7651-7
1.   Young   men—Fiction. 2.   Americans—Ecuador—Fiction.
3.   Decision   making—Fiction. 4.   Unemployed—Fiction.
5.   Travelers—Fiction. 6.   Jungles—Fiction. 7.   Ecuador—Fiction.
I. Title.
PS3611.U54I53 2005
813'.6—dc22   2004062894

Printed in the United States of America

www.atrandom.com

OPM   9   8   7   6   5   4   3   2   1

for n+1

"Willing too is merely an experience," one would like to say . . . *It comes when it comes, and I cannot bring it about.*

Wittgenstein, *Philosophical Investigations*

Indecision

Not until my ears popped and the plane was coming down over the winking lights of Bogotá—or really it looked like any other city at night—did I raise my eyes from the page I'd been puzzling at and begin to think of the girl, or woman, the friend or acquaintance, Natasha, whom I was flying so far to visit. That's how it was with me then: I couldn't think of the future until I arrived there.

Yet everybody always remarked on my apparently re-markable, indestructible Dwightness that was immune to time and place. "Dwight, dude, you're ex*actly* the same, man!" an old friend from school would say. Or "So lovely to have seen you, Dwight, you haven't changed a bit!" a friend of mom's would say. Even mom herself would sometimes say this. And I knew these peo-ple had to be on to something, since otherwise you would have to imagine either a) a conspiracy or b) a radical col-lective incompetence in matters of personal identity, both of which possibilities I tended to reject as someone who'd majored in philosophy in college and adopted, as the best of bad options, a pragmatist view whereby what most people *said* was true probably actually *was* true, or close enough. I never looked into this or other philosophical problems any deeper than was necessary to rate a B aver-age in an era of runaway grade-inflation, but a pragmatist

I was all the same. And not only did my dispassionate investigations reinforce this position, so did my whole agreeable personality that had always made me so popular with others.

I'm sorry to begin my narrative of important life-changing events so abstractly, especially when the story includes, as well as some sex and many drugs and my final prescription for what the whole world needs, plenty of specific sense data. (There were babies crying in the cabin as the plane sank down, and the guy in the seat beside me annotating in blue ink, with frantic circlings and passionate underlinings—"STRATEGY," he wrote, and "IMPORTANT!!!"—an article on Colombia in a business magazine.) But *abstract* is how I felt, up in the air, on the plane, at the time. Other people might feel I stayed the same from place to place; but to myself I always seemed totally steeped in my environment, or dyed in local color, and now because in transit I felt suffused with utter nowhereness, and therefore like I might turn out to be anyone at all.

Only five hours before I'd still been in New York. I'd lived there for four years plus, mostly downtown on Chambers St., with three other guys and also occasionally another one, who still had a key and sometimes crashed on the less structurally degraded couch. I wasn't leaving the city for good, of course—just ten days, was all. I think I'd left my bed unmade to increase its air of being there to be returned to. Besides, I had a reunion to go to when I got back, which was how the whole thing with Natasha got started.

Like Natasha, I was more or less popular at St. Jerome's, where we went to prep school together, admittedly along with hundreds of others, and when long-awaited senior spring arrived for us in 1992 I was elected Form Agent for the Form of that year. (Rumors circulated that some satirical votes had been cast along with the serious ones, and I can acknowledge that the recount may have taken an afternoon, but in the end the results were certified, and I came out on top.) Being Form Agent meant being in charge for the rest of my life of fund-raising, reunion-organizing and the like, and in this surprisingly burdensome capacity I had recently sent off a mass email reminding everyone to come to our tenth reunion or else be thought a total loser afraid to show his face. Or hers. Some people wrote back with regrets or other news, the one who stood out being Natasha, who said she might or might not go.

My sister Alice happened to call right after I received this tremendous communication. It was nice that Alice was willing to talk to me again, and as a reciprocal-type gesture of renewed openness between us I read her the message in which Natasha could be construed as genuinely inviting me to go visit her in Quito. "Where is Quito?" I asked. "Because I'm thinking I could go."

Quito (pronounced Key Toe, for the uninitiated) is in Ecuador, in South America. Alice told me so and I began telling her—not, she claimed, for the first time—about the fixation I'd harbored on-and-off for this younger acquaintance of hers. Al interrupted me: "What honestly is the deal, Dwight, between you and foreign women?"

It was true that Natasha was Dutch. And Vaneetha did hail from India. And Vaneetha *was* someone I'd been sleeping next to for a while, without us, however, all that often *sleeping together*. Lately other bodies tended to really bring home to me the famous other-minds problem, and I never felt like a woman I knew was more unknown to me than when and if we were kissing, not to speak of outright actual *fucking*. "Um, when they're foreign . . ."

"Yes, Dwight?"

". . . then it makes more sense that they're foreign."

Alice, who actually looked a bit like Natasha, if you

thought about it, which I refused to, snorted with semi-
indulgence. But then she called back an hour later mys-
teriously saying, "Go. I'm insisting, Dwight. Go!"

"Are you sure? Wait, let me find the coin," I said as I
went hunting through various pants pockets in search of
one of the very special unspendable coins that mom had
given me for throwing the I Ching, which I never did, for
ancient Chinese guidance. The first toss came up heads.
So that plus Alice's blessing had me feeling I should go.
Yet I flipped again, then a third time. I knew a larger
sample size would make the stats more accurate. Should
I really go? But how do you ever know until you've gone?
Alice was still on the phone for the fifth flipping. "You
are mentally ill," she said.

"Not for long," I assured her, and had my reasons.
"Toss number five . . . is heads," I said, "and so—"

"You really fucking do this?"

"So I go."

Yet in the five days after I purchased the ticket to
Quito through Bogotá, I'd gone from apartment to deli
to multiplex to restaurant to park, all the usual places
minus one, namely my former place of work, and as I'd
made my rounds somehow it hardly occurred to me to
think of Natasha at all.

There had been the email. Then the coin toss. Then I
got fired, from Pfizer. The upcoming trip made even
more sense to an unemployed person, presently hungover. It was like this little vial of purpose I could unstop-
per and sniff from in the morning. I really didn't know
what to do with myself next, once my savings ran out,
closely followed by my overdraft protection, and possibly the reckless expenditure on last-minute airfare existed in the darkness of my un- or sub-conscious as a
way of speeding up the reckoning. Or else I may have
felt like the answer to what to do next hovered beyond
me as a kind of Platonic form, and that I might bump

into some approximation of it—and maybe Natasha was even it—during my time with her down in Ecuador.

The landing gear unfolded over Bogotá with hydraulic wheezing and a thud.

I guess the thing I'd always admired about Natasha from the start was her easy adaptability to anything. That's what it had seemed to me and the other guys when she'd arrived as an incoming Fifth Former and played the Iroquois/WASP game of lacrosse like it was in actuality a Dutch thing; when she'd shown up at a seated dinner wearing the same sort of little black dress the society chicks from Manhattan wore; when she'd gone out to the Freaky Fields and taken 'shrooms with us, laughing and joking and dipping into drug-profundity like she was some veteran of the Dead show circuit; and above all when she spoke to us in her fluid, fluent English with hardly any accent to it even. Only pretty rarely could you detect a trace of the Netherlands—almost as exciting as if her dress had ridden a couple inches up her thigh.

But despite this way with fitting-in I never heard anyone accuse Natasha of *conforming,* which everyone at St. Jerome's unanimously considered the unpardonable crime. (Myself, I was considered innocent, I was so preppy already: from time immemorial I've worn my wavy brown hair in this kind of Bobby Kennedy way, and I showed up at the rectory, first day of school, wearing the same style thin-waled Levi's cords and Brooks Brothers shirt I still wear now in larger sizes, and even as a new boy I possessed, thanks to Alice, a respectable collection of second-generation Dead tapes.) But about Natasha: in spite of the whole adaptability thing, somehow she remained dignified and aloof. She was popular but belonged to no group, and had very definite and surprising opinions, particularly on euthanasia, legalized prostitution, and methadone. And as far as we knew she'd never more than kissed anyone.

Senior spring at St. Jerome's I would conjure up as a time of underage drinking, anticipatory nostalgia, and skinny-dipping in ponds across whose surfaces there floated all these gossamer blobs of milkweed pollen like miniature clouds collapsed and dragged down to earth. One time Natasha and I sat on the dam by Long Pond as water ran between and around our thighs and we passed the prohibited flask back and forth. We agreed how we might like to know each other better. Then we graduated, Natasha going off like Alice had—and like I did not—to elite Yale University. (My diploma, cum nada, from Eureka Valley College in California, doesn't hang in dad's office as Alice's via Yale and then her PhD from Columbia do.) In any case from all I heard from Alice or imagined by myself, Natasha kept up throughout her college years too that whole remarkable combination of participation and aloofness together, and still was not kissing many people.

Alice said—this was still on the phone—"Obviously the girl's a lesbian."

"Or she could just be shy."

"She never *seemed* shy, Dwight."

"Well I don't seem shy either," I said by way of refutation.

Somehow the thought of Natasha always tangled me into self-contemplation.

Now the tires struck the runway with a little squeal of swallowed hurt. The asphalt was smoking with steam and covered with little dribbles of red and white light. I looked around nodding at everybody in happy acknowledgment that our luck had held.

"Glad to be back on the ground, huh?" said the besuited dude in the seat beside me.

We would never meet again so I felt we could talk

freely. "Actually I hate indeterminate places." I'd meant to say *intermediate* but hadn't used words all day.

The guy frowned noddingly. "I guess Colombia is kind of . . . yeah. Good country to invest in, though. People want jobs. No problems with the unions."

"That's nice." I was so nice then too! "How come?"

He made a gesture signifying a little of this, a little of that. "Good luck to you," he said as he got up to retrieve his briefcase from the overhead bin. I noticed how he opened it carefully, prudently. Because it's true what they say about the contents—they can shift during flight.

Soon the emptied seats had filled up with passengers going on to Quito, and the flight attendants were reciting their spiel again, first in English, then español. I'd never learned to habla español even a poquito. I guess I'd studied French instead because it seemed like the thing I would do. In about an hour I was going to be completely at the mercy of Spanish-speaking Natasha.

Or the Joker, as we'd also called her back in the day. She had this incredible smile, a deep cartoon crescent in the parentheses of dimples, and somebody—actually, okay, it was me—once thought to call her the Joker. The name stuck, and we, the guys, would sometimes call her this affectionately and to her face. She accepted the nickname with grinning equanimity, just like she seemed to everything else.

But now as I buckled the seatbelt low and tight across my waist, and made sure the tray table before me was in a secure and upright position, I felt kind of bad about having coined the Joker. After all it was only me who'd stayed close to Natasha, if close could ever be the word there. And I was sure that when I showed up at our ten-year reunion my recent visit to Natasha van der Weyden would flash from me like some badge of pure prestige. At least I'd have *that* to show off to fellow Formmates with their professional accomplishments and spousal acquisitions which I knew all about as if they'd been tattooed on my brain in your-name-on-a-grain-of-rice-sized writing because it was my job, as Form Agent, to send in to the alumni magazine quarterly batches of these and similar boastings.

Whereas I was recently jobless and had not much to be proud of beyond not having gone bald. True, my hairline might have receded some, but at one point looking into the mirror I drew a kind of line in the sand, and past that point it stayed firmly put. Arguably much more of a problem was the insane (if blond) hairiness of my neck, back, chest, legs, buttocks, and arms. Somehow the women who saw and even handled me naked never seemed to mind my being covered all over with a light downy pelt. As the jet lifted off from the Bogotá runway, I wondered again why they didn't mind. Maybe I seemed to them like a missing link?

Suddenly, back in the air, it occurred to me what a coup it would be if I were to *go to the reunion with Natasha.* If I could persuade or even seduce her into doing it, what pride I would feel—as Form Agent and as man. This was great: now it was like I had come to South America for a reason! Also I hoped that after ten days with her I'd have something new to say on the whole Natasha subject. Maybe I could say to Stratton or Bill T., as I nodded toward her in the distance, where she would stand on the lawn in a sundress, "Man we were so clueless calling her the Joker, because actually the thing about Natash, and it's not elusive at all, is—" And here I'd slip in what I'd learned. Meanwhile everything I'd just thought about Natasha was something I already knew. It was like when I'd taken a trip to some foreign land and everyone asked me about it when I got back: my accounts would grow similar, focusing on this impression, that cool place, a certain funny anecdote, until there was just the one account, which then substituted for my memory. Remembering this tendency, I felt an honest fear. It was the familiar fear, made honest through sudden intensity, that once all the sensation had evaporated from my life the residue would be a cliché. I'd die, St. Peter would be like, "So how was it?" and I'd say, "Great place. I liked the food. I was sick for part of it. But all the people were really nice." And that would be it.

I looked out the window to the perfect star-free blackness. And I resolved to say something new about my visit each time anybody asked, not repeating myself once, much less twice or three times. And if there were unpleasant things to say, I would consider saying those too—because the world could be a painful place, the nation of Colombia very much included, as I'd learned since becoming unemployed a few days earlier and having found time to read the paper. Unfortunately my roommates and I had recently abetted Colombia's long-running civil war by buying and snorting cocaine. I wasn't very psyched to tell Natasha this. Yet because I hardly knew her I would need her to tell me everything, and in fairness I'd have to spill my own guts too. I just hoped she wouldn't ask me who in my opinion ought to win the Colombian civil war. Weren't there terrorists on both sides? Then again maybe it was getting to be about time to stand up for terrorists of the better sort!

Soon the plane landed without incident. Two for two. So that felt good. And as we taxied toward our gate all the babies started to stop crying. Have you noticed how they never do this without a few little grunts of totally babyish reluctance, forcing out a few last sobs before they let the new mood in? It's like they won't admit that whatever was upsetting them might not be that bad, even in war-torn Colombia.

But this wasn't *Colombia*, I reminded myself as I walked down the aluminum stairs, and stepped out onto the tarmac. This was *Ecuador,* a terra incognito I knew nothing about. I'd looked at those *Let's Leave!* and *Tough Planet* guides they have, but unable to choose, didn't buy one. My only real knowledge was that the air here—always amazing to be *here,* no matter the place— was cool and smelled like wood smoke. Maybe with a faint tang of sewage too? I wondered if I was distinguished in life by a sensitive nose and for my next job should take up wine criticism, drinking for a living and insuring my nose for a fantastic sum. Then maybe I could fake a smell-debilitating brain injury, and become very rich.

It felt so shameful and exciting, not knowing what to do with myself.

As I watched the carousel for my bag I noticed I was trembling: the DTs. DT she'd also been called, for Dutch Treat, which meant that anyone at St. Jerome's who had a crush on Natasha was said to have *the DTs.*

So had I maybe been in love with her all these years? Only she had never before shown any return interest? And now that she had gone so far as inviting me to Quito I could finally admit things to myself? Sometimes in spelunking the psyche your little headlamp goes dim. Anyway I was trembling. After all here was a new place, therefore new life, and hence an occasion for some quaking at the prospect of your freedom to do right away, if you want to, and can make up your mind, a wide variety of things in this world.

I hoisted my backpack onto my shoulders and stepped out through the gate into the sala de esperanza. Naturally a tall blond woman stood out among so many heads of glossy black hair. Even if she wasn't as tall as I remembered. Or very blond. At all. Yet a positive identification of me was vivid in her eyes as I maneuvered toward her calling "Hola! El Joker!" However the answering smile I got wasn't the one I recognized, and immediately I became horrified, not by the nature of her change—she still looked pretty fine to me—but the extremely drastic extent of it. When from her surgically-altered face she said, in a low lovely voice issuing from collagen-swollen lips, "Hello, Dwight," it was all I could do to smile through my intimation that a long strange trip was about to begin.

"Natasha has gone to the toilet," the woman said, and my relief at the news that this stranger was a stranger—not Natasha at all!—caused me to hug her tightly to me, saying, "My God, so good to see you!"

The woman and I were still laughing when Natasha arrived. "Look! Already fast friends!" She sounded more Dutch than I'd expected, or remembered. She was still Natasha, but it's true, a little different. She looked weird, anxious—kind of like how I felt. Then she flashed the famous smile. "You see, Brigid, Dwight is like I told you. Right away he belongs to everybody."

Part One

A week before Quito I was sitting up in bed in New York, the edges of my awareness lapped at by traffic. I was sitting there with one hand holding open the book I was reading, and the other hand placed above the head of sleeping Vaneetha. There I was, pinned in space and time like a specimen in a box.

Vaneetha had turned away and slid down the bed so that nothing of her was visible except for the dark disheveled Vaneethian hair from which the lamplight was extracting all these twisting strings of a greenish iridescence. I wouldn't have figured that even the darkest hair could react to light in this way, and the discovery blinked in my mind as just the smallest, quietest symbol of the multiple discoveries that could still be made between us if we—unless it was mostly me—weren't so ambivalent about making them.

Once a week had become more like two times, and on our nights together I was usually awake like this for an hour or so while Vaneetha slept and breathed beside me. Sometimes she'd twitch like a dreaming dog, and in part due to my intense feeling for dogs, shared by my entire family, this would induce a shiver of tenderness in me. Yet exactly because I experienced this tenderness I wondered if I shouldn't stop showing it when we were both awake. It could lead to us feeling, harmfully, that we were together. And as our relationship was predicated on not wanting to be in a relationship yet, that seemed unlike the best idea. We were both in agreement that contemporary courtship was far too accelerated these days. That was how Vaneetha explained why she'd had so few partners, and how I explained why I'd had seventeen or more. Nevertheless it eventually became up-in-the-air and unspoken whether we were sleeping together brother-sister style and mostly refraining from outright sex except when drunk because a) we weren't courting each other or b) we were, only slowly, just as these things should be done and never are.

In any case it often seemed at night that I would make a better dog owner than boyfriend. It wasn't apparent to me how best to treat Vaneetha, each woman being so different. Whereas every dog, in spite of the really incredible variety of the species, required more or less the same regimen of food and water, walks and affectionate pats on the head. However in the city it actually exacted a lot less responsibility to have a girlfriend than a dog. And I really wanted one or the other, since like any person, or dog, I too craved affection. Hmn.

It was almost a type of peace to arrive each night at the same mental impasse. Plus I felt at home in the quiet, like a local. I was sensitive and weirdly sympathetic to that moment when the refrigerator kicked in and began to hum. Then the groans of a garbage truck would as much confirm as interrupt the hush. And there was the bonus sensation of authority I got as the last one up, the presiding mind.

So I would return to certain issues like hands to a notch on the clock. It would always dawn on me, late at night, that life is made of days—and your life isn't likely to pick up whatever your days pass by. Granted, this was really a postmortem analysis of the given day, carried out when it was already yesterday or tomorrow, depending on point of view. If it was one of the nights that Ford (roommate one) and his girlfriend Kat were spending downtown with us, they would have finished giving one another the business to the accompaniment of frightened bedsprings. And if it was past two then Sanchez (roommate two) would have gotten up out of his humid sleep to shut off the TV he'd equipped with a hot cable box transmitting pirated pay-per-view sporting events, feature films, and porn in an endless jostling stream. And Dan (roommate three) might or might not be around, since more and more he moved very quietly through the world, subsisting on snacks and growing thin and spiritual and haunted-looking, and only occasionally briefing us between classes and lab at NYU med school on what he was learning there. Lately he'd expressed the opinion that general uremia must be the least painful way to go in the end, and had assured me and Sanch that there was little to no scientific evidence linking coffee, even my six cups daily, with cancer.

Sanch said, "Yeah man fucking Hugo Chávez drinks *sixteen* espressos a day. And that's after his staff weaned him down from twenty-four."

"Amazing!" I was really impressed with this man. "Who is Hugo Chávez?"

"He's, like, a revolutionary."

"Sounds like it," I said.

Sometimes Dan could be found in his room poring over a textbook while listening through his headphones to terrifying music by Austro-Hungarian composers. But his whereabouts were erratic, or I couldn't do the algorithm, and anyway he stayed with us only due to low rent. It wouldn't have been so low if the walls to our rooms had gone all the way up to the ceiling. Instead we lived in pasteboard cubicles and weird dorm-style intimacy—which kind of enforced an obscurish connection between my home life and my days at Pfizer, where the cubicle was also the unit.

Anyway Ford, Sanch, Dan, me—that was Chambers St., and was going to be for five more weeks, until our lease ran out. Other friends lived scattered around the city in ones and twos, and this had allowed us four to provide, in the welcoming squalor of our living room, a kind of community center for the school-days diasporae. Poker was played, friends were entertained, TV got watched and color-commentated. Out of everybody we knew our immaturity was best-preserved, we dressed worst and succeeded least professionally—and at times I could get into feeling that for the old crowd to set foot on the scarred linoleum of our kitchen must be like entering this circling, slow eddy in the otherwise one-way flow of time. Outside was the streaming traffic, the money bazaar, the trash-distributing winds with their careerist velocities. And here inside Chambers St. was this cozy set of underachievers. We even had a fireplace, though it didn't work, and housed the stereo instead. At times I gained control of the remote, and the drowned-sounding post-human electronica that was our usual aural wallpaper, making me feel like words might not apply to our condition, and freaking me out if I got stoned, was replaced by the bright fine stylings of the Grateful Dead, just as if Jerry'd never died.

But Jerry *had* died. And soon our lease would be up! And so would I end and die too! I tried not to be reminded of the eternal endingness of everything by Ground Zero down the street. I really preferred for the reminder to come, more gently, from philosopher Otto Knittel. In the months before Ecuador I was all about *The Uses of Freedom*—or *Der Gebrauch der Freiheit* if you're German. Late at night I would look at the words of this very deathocentric book, and on that Saturday night with Vaneetha (which had so far failed to distinguish itself from many of the Saturday nights preceding it) I was looking again at the words, with one eye open and the other shut since I'd taken out my contacts and otherwise couldn't focus on the lines. "Procrastination is our substitute for immortality," went the first half of the sentence I was rereading; "we behave as if we have no shortage of time." I read the book at maybe two pages an hour.

Yet I felt more slow than stupid, and suspected it had always been thus with me. Maybe my slow temporal metabolism wasn't equipped for the efficient digestion of modern—or postmodern life, as it had apparently already been for some time. Sometimes I felt like I'd never catch up with even the little that had happened to me. There had already been too many people and places, and the creaking stagecoach journey or straggling canoe ride by which one location might observe, in olden times, how it became the next (and one Dwight, the next, uncannily similar Dwight) had been supplanted by the sleight of hand of subways and airplanes, always popping you out in unexpected places.

At least at night the phone didn't ring. My feeling was, the soul is startled by the telephone and never at ease in its presence. Often on a midtown street someone's cell would ring and half a dozen people would check their pockets to see if it was them being called, and I'd glimpse a flash of panic in one or another guy's eyes. Myself, I kind of felt like I needed my news delivered by hand—to look out the window as some *courier* appeared in the field, coming from a distance so my feelings had time to discover themselves. But instead people were always calling and asking me to do things, and since only pretty rarely was I really sure I wanted to, my system was to flip a coin. "Hold on let me check my . . . yeah sounds cool but hold on . . ." I would say in the Chambers St. kitchen or if someone called at work. But I didn't have a date book and was actually consulting one of the special coins. Heads, I'd accept—whereas tails, I'd claim to have other plans. I was proud of this system. Statistically fair, it also kept my whole easy nature from forcing me to do everyone's bidding; it ensured a certain scarcity of Dwightness on the market; it contributed the prestige of the inscrutable to my otherwise transparent persona; and above all it allowed me to find out in my own good time whether I would actually have liked to do the thing in question. By then it was invariably too late—but everyone agrees that knowledge is its own reward, and so do I.

A night alone meant I could get a jump on *The Uses of Freedom*. At this rate there was every possibility of my finishing inside of the year. "Why don't you just *write* the thing," Dan said. "It would probably be faster."

"But how would I ever come up with Der Unternehmungsgrund der Individuums on my own?"

When I first read about this *ground for the individual's action,* I could at last put an unwieldy and foreign name to what I had felt had been missing from my life ever since puberty struck and my prep-school days commenced, more or less at once, and I'd begun to proceed unsteadily from day to day as if I were on a bridge swaying in the wind while both sides of the canyon—I mean past and future—disappeared in foggy weather. Suddenly I'd lost the sensation of there being either a source or an end to my life, an original birth or ultimate death, and was therefore amazed at how everyone seemed to consider me a solid reliable young man. Otto Knittel, I was learning as a much older young man, was *way* into forests, so while reading him I would imagine decamping from the city and going to live in the woods in Vermont. With a dog. Or several dogs. The idea was to inhabit a cabin, baking bread and hardly even watching TV, petting and talking to the dog, or dogs, and drinking tea instead of so much coffee. Sunlight, wide floorboards, caller ID for the phone . . . And old friends from the city could drive up to admire my aura of wisdom and calm benevolence that I would be too egoless even to notice. I felt that in these circumstances the *ground for my actions* might sort of percolate up through me in this slow molten way, and a prayerful clarity of consciousness would finally pop into my brain. Then I would know what to do. Then I could return to New York, and do it.

But in the smaller of the hours I could get to feeling bad that I hadn't even looked into doing "it" yet. And the feeling was worse if the night ended with the warm smooth length of Vaneetha at my side, as she slept and breathed beneath my not-so-clean cotton sheets. There were starting to be signs that a serious attachment to me had been formed, by her, so that not only would I need to slip out of the city to go let my truer understandings avail themselves of me—I'd also have to extricate myself from someone else's life.

One good thing was that at least I didn't have a lot of furniture to take. However first I would need to find a town in Vermont, and a job there. Yet I was full of hope that the new information-based economy might really spell the end of geography and I could do tech support from the woods. Then again this hopefulness was *so* 1999, and now it was May 2002—late May already. In any case I had a to-do list (more a list of good intentions) and before finally going to sleep I would get up to write down—after GROCERIES! or MOM RE: CHURCH!! or VANEETHA? or PAPER TOWELS or COST OF SHRINKS?—LOOK INTO VT. OPTIONS.

So it would be late at night before I fell asleep. But don't worry: I got plenty of sleep. Not only was I an excellent sleeper, but I had no functioning alarm clock to disrupt my Cimmerian rhythms. Of course when the relevant button broke off, I'd put it on my list to get another clock. But then at work they—or Rick, the manager—

made an announcement, which was that although we who worked at Pfizer in the Problem Resolution Center were already only subcontracted, we were still considered *in house* for the fairly inarguable reason that our office was housed in Pfizer headquarters. Soon some guys in Mumbai, India, were going to be doing our work for less of our pay. "You sayin we getting outsourced here?" my colleague Wanda asked. Rick was saying that, and adding this sick little smile all his own.

The effect on morale was not good. In my case I saw that globalization was for real and declined to replace my alarm clock. What did I have to get up for if my days at Pfizer were numbered anyway? Now I usually just woke around ten, yawning and stretching, replenished with ignorance. Work was officially beginning but I would go out and get an everything bagel—impossible, otherwise, to choose—and come back and toast the halves and slather one with pesto and the other with Nutella. Yum.

So far my main accommodation to Vaneetha-Dwight domesticity was to keep little jars of both condiments at her place in Carroll Gardens. "I still *can't* believe what you'll put in your mouth." Her dad's various ambassadorial postings had caused her to be educated in British-run schools, and she pronounced *can't* like as in philosopher Immanuel Kant. "But I'm touched you're moving in, after your fashion." Morningtime fun could be had if she was game and would feed me a mystery bagel half while my eyes were closed. "To have no idea," I would say, "when both options are so equally good!"

Then I rode the F train, if from Vaneetha's place, or took the 2/3 to Forty-second, and on the way would look at *The Uses of Freedom*—such a different book in the daylight, and so much less credible.

A philosopher of Knittel's caliber or even your average educated human being such as Vaneetha might consider it stultifying to sit in a cube farm all day saying "Hello, and thank you for calling the Problem Resolution Center. This is Dwight speaking," then patiently listening to the user's complaint, then suggesting the obvious solution, then waiting for the next user's call. But often when I was at work, feeling relaxed and unfree, overqualified and airconditioned, it seemed to me that the plight of the low-level corporate drone was unfairly maligned by believers in social justice and human potential. It was true that the pay was low, the benefits nonexistent, the question of upward mobility moot, and the institutional neglect of our hidden talents virtually complete. But what a tremendous, almost vegetal peacefulness there was in working for das Man! (As Knittel would say.) At night I might feel bad about colluding in my mediocrity—but somehow while seated before my terminal as I swiveled slightly back and forth in my standard-issue office chair, I felt that if I just kept working, with due diligence, at this time-serving American job that after all *someone* had to do, then whatever happened to me or my country wouldn't be my fault.

And I did work hard, or hardish, since Rick kept competitive stats of our individual call times and personal pride insisted that I keep my average low. It was something I liked bragging about to mom or dad whenever I saw one of them. Plus the sooner I told somebody how to translate a file into a new format, the sooner I could resume downloading for personal use free audio software from the web, or Google myself and discover again that Dwight Wilmerding was also a high-school basketball star, his team's top rebounder, in Ashland, North Carolina. Or I could ask Wanda to school me even deeper in the lyrics of Mary J. Blige. "Aw, that's some awesome shit she sings!" I'd say.

"Language, Dwight." That would be Rick.

Or else between calls I'd just go blank and white

noise would brim in my head. Up on the fifth floor in a huge padlocked cage was the server farm, filled with all these refrigerated Liebert cabinets—hundreds, we're talking—and also containing a superpowerful AS400 IBM mainframe, and at times I almost seemed to be *inside* these monster processors with their chilly emanation of a loud blank seething sound. I'd feel myself swoon and slip away into the world of information like a snowflake signing up for a blizzard. And if no user (Wanda called them *losers*) needed me, it would take the promptings of my stomach for me to recognize it was lunchtime.

Usually I ate lunch by myself so I could concentrate on the food. But then one semifateful day I went to meet this old Formmate of mine named Alexandra in the postmodern-seeming cafeteria attached to her place of work. Curvy walls of blue glass, opaque like they were pleated, surrounded kidney-shaped tables of brushed steel. And half-encircling the tables were these deep leather banquettes, and seated on this material was the ass of possibly one straight guy for every four women.

This was the headquarters of an enormous multinational media empire. Yet it more closely resembled some ideal and futuristic all-girls high-school cafeteria. I was wearing my trademark cords and frayed Brooks Bros. shirt as I sauntered out of the food course with my loaded tray, and already sensing that to dress not so well might seem in these environs like the trait of an authenticish heterosexual man. I'd heard this situation—where, as among water buffalo at the pool, the male of the species is seriously outnumbered, and in a pretty good position to choose among mates—was known by animal behaviorists as a *lek*. Not that I did choose, or mate, or was offered a choice. But I felt pleasantly like the object of some romantico-sexual attention as I sat down and

Alex introduced me to someone and somebody, and somebody else, and then Vaneetha.

(Now in bed on that Saturday night a week before
Ecuador, Vaneetha turned to one side, nestling against
my thigh, and grunted softly in the inquisitive way of a
sleeper.)

Some fairly technical trendspotting talk appeared to
be in progress, over lunch, so mostly I just nodded my
head and listened, occasionally weighing in with lay-
man's observations on matters of style. At one point I
caught somebody who wasn't the one called Vaneetha
looking at the one who was, then indicating me with her
eyes. As always I pretended not to notice what I'd noticed. Then the non-Vaneetha looked at me. "Nice shirt.
The tarnished prepster look? It's totally coming back."

"A stopped clock is right at least twice a day," I reminded everybody—and wondered if these women, now
laughing, would have been so friendly in a situation of
more sexual parity. Not so friendly but friendly still, was
my tentative conclusion. But to deduct the supplemental
friendliness from the rest was not a doable operation, so
I became uncertain as to their true feelings for me and
was reduced for the rest of the conversation to having
made this last remark.

I'd already set my tray on the conveyor and said goodbye to Alexandra when Vaneetha reappeared. "Good
meeting you," she said.

"Likewise." I had already pressed the down button on
the elevator. "Completely." Thankfully I speak slowly,
with a marijuana drawl left over from St. Jerome's—
otherwise I might at times sound nervous.

"Will we be seeing you again?"

"I really couldn't judge the likelihood."

"Well we could arrange something."

I was either titillated or afraid. "All of you?"

"All of . . . *me*?"

"You—I meant plural, all you girls."

"It might be easier if it were just you and I."

She was right there in front of me; I had no recourse to the coin. Yet her invitation suggested she thought I could say more than one laughable thing—and that the horrible indiscriminateness of my interest in all the women hadn't been apparent. So that was good. And letting the venerable philosophical category of the Good easily expand to include this tall, dark, and handsome woman, with a narrow nose flaring at its base, a diamond stud in one nostril, and serious-seeming plum-colored lips presently unveiling a smile, I said, "How about Monday? Didn't one of those girls back there say Monday was the new Thursday anyway?"

She agreed to Monday night as we stepped into the same down elevator. "You don't work upstairs?" I asked.

"Oh no. I'm on 52nd. I'm not one of these . . ."

"No," I assured her.

"I hate people whose inner lives are trends."

"I know, don't you think it would be much nicer to have an inner life where everything was very still?"

"I wouldn't know. I'm quite impulsive"—with a note in her voice like this was a brave and pleasant lie.

"So what do you do for a job?" I asked her on the street.

"In fact it's not entirely unrelated to trends. I'm in FX."

"Wow. *Very* cool. And it's nice you don't have to be in LA for that. I can hardly wait for *The Matrix* sequel—I was really impressed with what they were able to do there digitally."

"I don't do *special effects*," she said. "I do *foreign exchange*."

"Oh."

"Currency."

"I see." We started walking west along Forty-second, toward the flashing, scrolling, looming trademarks of all the various corporations—not the direction I needed to go in, but I didn't want to end on a mistake, or begin. It occurred to me that Alice might not like me dating a woman in foreign exchange—I remembered her being upset about what the lack of currency controls had somehow done to either Thailand or Taiwan.

"I work at Pfizer," I said. "But I don't come up with products. I just keep the computers running. I'm pretty neutral."

We paused at the mouth of the subway station. "Monday then?" Vaneetha said.

Suddenly I remembered something. "Oh you know what's going on on Monday, which I totally forgot? My roommate Ford—it's his birthday party. But you should come. I was going to suggest some date restaurant, but this will be much better. This way you can see me in context."

"Do you promise I wouldn't be intruding?"

"No, we're very accommodating on Chambers St."

"This isn't Tim Ford by chance—Tim Ford who went to Dartmouth?"

It did seem like a small world, after all, when you belonged to the exact same demographic and all lived in New York City. "No, yeah, that's him. You went to Dartmouth? Damn, you must be smart too."

"Too?" She took out her palm pilot to punch in the address. "Do you mean that in addition to Tim Ford I'm smart, or that intelligence is in addition to some of my other traits?"

"Let's just say both for right now."

"You're really too much, you know. I can't make out your tone—it was like that at lunch as well."

"Well you only just met me."

"Later on it becomes clear? In context?"

"That's the idea."

Walking back down Forty-second I felt extremely pleased to have invested my life with a certain short-term narrative interest. And in fact one thing led so directly to another that on the night in question, a week before Ecuador, and seven months after meeting Vaneetha at lunch, I'd found myself seated across a table-cloth from her as on certain other Saturday nights. She'd been telling me, just a few hours earlier, that when I started looking for a new job she would conduct mock interviews with me. "I don't mean to be ambitious on your behalf—but you need to think of what you want from a job."

"But largely what I want is just so basic. I want shelter, warm clothing. I want food . . ."

"But you've hardly touched your food. Here—" With her fork she speared a slug of gnocchi and poked it toward my mouth.

I chewed and swallowed. "But see, my desires are so minimal. It's good I live in New York, because just food and rent take up all my income. If we lived somewhere else I wonder what I'd spend it on. I mean in New York it costs a lot of money to be satisfied with so little."

"But clearly you're *not* satisfied. It's not a fulfilling position you've had. Your talents are languishing."

"I have a certain talent for modest contentment."

She smiled with friendly cruelty. "You know what I think of when I come by Chambers St.? Nineteen ninety-three, the boys during freshman year. The greasy hair, the deliberate aimlessness . . . And Dwight you *have* been smoking—"

"Come on," I said, "Sanch is unemployed—he shouldn't always be getting high by himself."

"But look at you in your flannel shirt. It's May, *dude*."

"It's a pretty light flannel. Here, touch." She demurred.

"The other day I caught you listening to Nirvana."

"Pavement," I corrected—though I too could remember the days when fellow college students had listened to Nirvana, dabbled in heroin, gone on Prozac, and with a recession on and the job market looking bad, developed the fad of wearing mechanics' uniforms with blunt proletarian names stitched in cursive over the heart. It had been cool and in some circles apparently mandatory to be unkempt and pessimistic. Meanwhile I'd gone around just being as chipper as my nature insisted. Only around now did I seem to have become, way past the point of cultural appropriateness, the unambitious and flannel-wearing holder-down of a totally dead-end job.

"You're living a cliché," Vaneetha had said. "It's not even a fresh cliché."

I knew she was right. It wasn't very unusual for me to lie awake at night feeling like a scrap of sociology blown into its designated corner of the world. But knowing the clichés are clichés doesn't help you to escape them. You still have to go on experiencing your experience as if no one else has ever done it.

That was my time-honored conclusion, and I'd just come to it again—and shut for the night my edition of Knittel with its piece of handsome shoelace sewn into the binding, and patted Vaneetha's deluxe head of hair, and made to turn off the bedside light, and wondered again whether I really might move to Vermont, and considered the variety of possible dogs I could get—when out of nowhere the neat isosceles triangle of a paper airplane sailed over the bedroom/cubicle wall, and glided to rest on the floor.

The sharpness of this event, in the midst of eddying

thoughts, astounded me. And getting out of bed I saw that Dan, clearly Dan, had written on the plane in fluorescent highlighter *Par Avion* and also *You up?* What a great question! Just to be asked it was to know the answer.

TWO

At one point no one knew what Abulinix was and neither did I. Obviously these days you can't open a magazine of the waiting-room genre without seeing one of those ads with the guy looking into the mirror at his multiheaded self displaying various facial expressions without a smile between them. That's before. The after, on the opposite page, along with the fine-print warnings, which tell you how safely you can ignore them, has the same guy restored to just the one head and beamingly meeting his simplified gaze. Moreover he has shaved. But back then I had just walked into Dan's cubicle, an innocent in flip-flops, boxers, and a tee shirt, not even having heard the drug's name.

Dan was sitting in his broken and faded La-Z-Boy, a proud trophy from trash day on our street. He had a cigarette going in the ashtray while meditatively, with thoroughness, he was eating some Combos, or miniature hollow cylinders of pretzel injected with orange squirts of cheese product. "Snack?" he asked. Waiving the offer, I pushed some papers off a milk crate and sat down.

Dan marveled at me in his jadedly-imitating-his-grandmother way. "The boy's hairiness I can never get over. A prodigy. So healthy."

I looked at my legs, blond and hairy as I'd left them. "Why am I here, Dan? And not asleep?"

"Why are you here? That's why you're here."

"Please, no fucking with me." I was wary, due to having been fucked with before. One fucking-with operation had even lasted several years, starting in 1995, night after Yom Kippur, when Dan had expressed some surprise that I hadn't given him any presents. He'd told me how it was traditional since the middle ages for gentiles to treat Jews to dinner once the atonement-making Jews, or kippurim, had finished their fast. Immediately I was abashed at my thoughtlessness, and offered to take him out for the most lavish available meal in Eureka Valley, an offer I renewed and that was re-accepted every following year as I grew increasingly outraged by the negligence of my fellow gentiles and more and more impressed by the extreme reserve of other Jewish acquaintances and friends, not one of whom had ever sought this special treatment to which they were all entitled. Not until September '98, when I asked Dan what he typically atoned for, did he tell me that one thing was the deception of a good friend.

"I'm sorry," he'd said. "Crafty Jew, dumb goy. So unfair to us both. But it proves what I say—they should teach people lies. Except in medicine. But as far as history—fucking *lie*. If we thought people had acted better in the past we would try and maintain that false standard. With only slight deteriorations. It would all be so much better."

I'd asked how we would then explain the reported widespread contemporary prevalence of things sucking so much for so many people through poverty, nihilism, and other ills.

"Blame everything on the immediately-preceding generation. Cast them as evil usurpers of a long-standing righteous regime. Then we kill them."

"But I like my parents."

"But you wouldn't, is the thing."

—So I asked Dan again why I was there, in his cubicle. We were whispering in order not to wake anyone up, which kind of conferred a conspiratorial feel.

"Choice," he whispered. "You remember our conversation about choice." He reminded me how I'd told him about what I considered the admirable prominence of the category of *choice* in Otto Knittel's thought, and how he'd then noted that when the occasion of an important choice had arisen in Knittel's own life Knittel had—whoops—moved to Eastern Germany where the government forced him to mate with a beefy Olympic swimmer who, in the opinion of most philosophic observers, he didn't truly love. Dan reminded me of this as he went rummaging through his desk.

"Sure," I said. "Knittel made a big mistake. But like I said last time—just goes to show how important choices are."

"Right." Dan the medical student had found a yellow legal pad and a ballpoint pen. "So my first question is this—do you feel you have trouble making choices?"

"If there's no trouble is there a choice?"

"Fair enough. But would you say you experience what might be considered uncomfortable hesitation in the face of a decision rarely; occasionally; sometimes; frequently; or often?"

I tried to think of whether my hesitation was uncomfortable, or if instead, considered from another standpoint, or vantage area . . .

"I'm going to mark that down from my own observations as a *frequently*. All right. Number two: do you feel you have a strong predictive sense of where you'll physically be in nine months' time?"

"I don't know. Americans are such a mobile people. Did you make these up yourself?"

"Are you hesitating now?"

"Well I don't know if it's *frequently* that I do."

"You don't know. You can't decide. And isn't that the official position on certain other issues? Such as the Vermont-Vaneetha nexus of questions?"

Reluctantly I nodded.

"Do you know what abulia is?"

"Ah-boo-lee-uh." I tasted the word like a dog testing a vegetable dropped on the floor, to see if he will eat it. "No—no idea."

"What it basically is, is the impairment or even"—Dan took a drag on his cigarette and let the suspense hang and dwindle with the blue smoke in the air—"or even finally the *loss* of your ability to make decisions. But now there's this new drug in phase-one clinical trials. Meant to treat this very issue. And it's called . . ."—in a listless voilà tone, as he tapped some ash into the souvenir ashtray from Pompeii—"Abulinix!"

My mood totally altered. Doesn't everyone dream of a magic pill? And wasn't this, come true, but with an ugly name, my own personal dream? Yet in order to seem like an appropriate subject for study I wanted to counterfeit a certain uncertainty. It could be that Dan took a scientific in addition to a friendly interest in my case, and that a trial participant's decisively expressed desire to be cured of indecision would disqualify him right away. "I'd like to think about it," I said. "Assuming I can even make up my mind. Can I get back to you?"

"Sure." But he'd produced a little orange prescription bottle from his desk and now tossed it my way. "Scored from the lab. And there's plenty more where that came from. You can start the course now, or you can think about it. Once daily with food is the indication. You know, the pharmaceutical industry doesn't come up with a treatment for chronic indecision every day."

I quickly outwitted the childproof top, shook out one

of the sleek two-toned blue and white capsules, and held it like a gem up to the light. The diagnosis and the cure all at once! I understood it didn't always work that way. Yet only now that I held the panacea in my hand did I recognize abulia as my major basic overriding problem. Previously in my mind I'd been floating candidates more along the lines of

- ambivalence
- laziness
- bad faith
- good family
- suggestibleness (regarding ideas)
- resistance (regarding events)
- indiscriminate breast fixation
- together with a weakened libido
- not having found the right person
- not having *been* the right person
- sociological sense of one's life (shared with so many others)
- inconsequence of the self (except to itself)
- early exposure to drugs
- early exposure to other persons
- especially one's parents
- divorce of those parents
- their marriage beforehand
- the whole Alice issue
- a little learning
- not near enough
- moderation
- immoderation
- lack of funds

and/or

- lack of Der Unternehmungsgrund der Individuums

and throughout this whole time I'd been unable to see all of these for the mere epiphenomena they only too obviously were! I felt like inside the pill I could see all these little magic grains of velleity adding up, maybe, to a *will*. I stood up and shouted. "Gimme a Combo!"

From his cubicle Sanch whimpered aloud in a sleep-blurred voice. "Dude . . . dude . . . shut fuck up . . ."

"So," Dan whispered, "I take it you're not at all curious how this shit works."

"Right." I sat back down. In my eagerness to make decisions I had forgotten my great love of knowledge.

"That, in your hand, is one of the *grails* of pharmacology. Turns out chronic indecision is a complaint for a huge number of ostensibly normal people. Of course the argument could be made that indecisiveness is precisely why they seem so normal. They're tractable—they're putty. But what these people are telling us, very consistently, is that chronic indecision is no picnic on the inside."

"No."

"Number of complaints is huge. Growing. At least among the sort of people who have doctors to complain to." Dan paused, took a drag. "Not to mention the hard cases where you have to be institutionalized. Or should be. That's who's officially enrolled in the trials. These are people with serious pathologies on both the macro- and the micro—I mean, these are people who literally they can't decide between paper or plastic. On the other hand these same people will go on dangling for years in front of *one major choice*. Often to do with employment or love object."

"*No.*" I was seriously aghast.

"In some cases the patient will have been *about to decide* whether to leave their job or spouse, literally right on the cusp, we're talking the fucking teetering *verge*, every single free moment"—another drag, while I waited, appalled—"for like several decades."

Naturally I thought of poor mom. Who used to come down the hall and sit on my bed asking how I thought I'd fit in at a new school if she left dad and we had to move. Finally it was me who went away to St. Jerome's while she stayed put. And after twenty-seven years dad was the one who called a lawyer. The horror of any condition would seem somehow to implicate the method of its cure, and with an inner grimace I put the pill away.

"These are people," Dan was saying, "who they couldn't deal with TV *before* cable, before TiVo. Now they're getting fucked from all sides. They can't look at a menu, can't even *en*ter a supermarket. These are like people who want to move to Communist Romania, but now that's all gone. And don't even try saying the word *internet* to them—millions of these people. And why?"

It seemed like you could start, if you wanted, with Eve's teeth poised a little iffily on the apple's unbroken skin. Eve who must have had very nice teeth . . . Or probably not, lacking orthodonture.

"Why? Mainly the problem's in the medial forebrain bundle—the part of you where you experience so-called 'pleasure.' And what you've also got going on in the MFB is essentially protracted civil conflict. On the one hand you've got the nerves that go *from* the ventral tegmental area *to* the medial forebrain bundle and these carry excitatory neurotransmitters. You know, make you happy, make you want to do things."

"Like what, for instance?"

"That's the thing. Some people don't know what to do. And if it's difficult for them to decide that's because in the medial forebrain you've also got the nucleus accumbens—that's where the *inhibitory* neurons from the locus coeruleus feed in. So when you take cocaine or speed—"

"I don't *take speed*." I was scandalized. "Mr. Ecstasy. But wait—" Something almost incestuous had occurred to me. "It's not Pfizer, is it? Who's making this thing? I hope Pfizer helps me decide to quit Pfizer."

"Sorry dude—Bristol-Myers Squibb. And what Bristol's done is create a drug with a *mixed agonist-antagonist profile*. So Abulinix acts *antagonistically* toward the receptors which would make you feel speedy or confused. But there's also a molecule bonding, as an *agonist,* to the specific receptor that has to do with decisiveness. Iron-clad resolutions. And so forth." Another drag, then he stubbed out the cigarette, totally resigned and blasé. "The idea is that the drug should foster feelings of capability in the face of conflict. Naturally I thought—Dwight Wilmerding."

He pulled his knees to his chest. The lecture was over. At one time Dan had been a chem major and played bass in a bright droney band called Haiku d'État. But what had *he* decided to live for, for now? His heavy-lidded and darkly bright eyes struck me as not dissimilar from sunglasses. He was wearing the green pajamas, same color as hospital scrubs, that he usually wore at night. He was the most catlike person of my acquaintance—efficient, aloof, compact.

"So what's your motive here?"

He smiled. "Humanitarian intervention."

"Come on."

"I think of you as humanity, Dwight. You're one of about four people I think of that way. I include myself." He just looked at me with zero expressiveness from those lacquered brown eyes.

"There must be risks. With abulia. I mean Abulinix. Side effects maybe? Or dangers?"

He shrugged. "Minimal so far. Some stomach upset. Some satyriasis."

"Meaning—?"

"Meaning excessive desire for fucking in the adult human male. Also it's a potentiator with regard to alcohol. One drink will equal two. Two plus two will equal five."

"I'll save lots of money at bars."

"Ignorance will be strength."

"Except I don't like bars—I don't like standing up. It's the same with rock shows and museums. Don't you feel like that? I feel like we'd all be much more receptive to things if we had more contact with the ground." Or maybe this was the Knittel talking.

Dan lit up another Marlboro Light, as I note because without smoking myself I know that smokers can perform characterological analyses of each other by means of brands, and frankly Dan sometimes mystified me. Ignorance will be strength? "I must warn you," he was saying. "I do have one concern. So far no one has gone nuts—or more nuts than already. But I think the possibility must exist. What if the id—to use outmoded terminology—but what if the stalemate between id and superego in the medial forebrain is what's preserving civilization. Decency. Homeland security."

"Yeah," I said. "Right . . ." I suffered a vision of myself charging up Madison Avenue in a rented gorilla suit, grabbing at the asses of wealthy female shoppers and looking for flower planters to overturn. "I would hate to run amok." I saw myself driving through Nevada in a stolen red convertible with a rocket launcher in the trunk, occasionally stopping to take out a billboard. "I wouldn't like to go berserk."

"But I've thought about this. You're a highly socialized person, Dwight, you're very polite—"

"Thank you Dan."

"Nice. Kind. Whatever. Even Mr. R thinks so." Mr. Rorschach, or Dan's dad, had on several occasions shaken his big gleaming head at me and pronounced me the genuine article. Somehow my not knowing what he meant seemed particularly to confirm him in this impression. "So I would hazard that you pose less of a risk than another more or less 'normal' person. At the same time Abulinix may affect you more powerfully than people whose abulia is more truly pathological. I've given you the lowest dose. Twenty migs. Should be interesting. You understand"—he stubbed out his second cigarette—"I'm committing a serious breach of medical ethics."

"Thanks, man. It's good of you."

I borrowed Dan's bathrobe and we crept out of the apartment, going down to the street to buy at the corner deli another pack of Combos and some Jiggy Juice (I refer to the popular if controversial caffeinated malt-liquor beverage) so as the better to solemnize my first swallowing of an Abulinix. "Someday are they really going to have a drug for everything?" I asked.

"For everything, yes. For everyone, no."

He always was a riddler. Possibly he should have been called that: the Riddler. And then wistfully I thought of the Joker, as I did every so often in those days and late nights before I received Natasha's email from Quito and then became far too excited to think of her at all.

"I'll regret my intervention," Dan was saying, "if you end up in Vermont."

"That's like the sweetest thing you've ever said to me. You're not on Ecstasy now are you?" Dan had remained a big proponent of Ecstasy and a downplayer of its neurotoxicity even after we'd all taken it about nine months previous on the night of Ford's birthday and the eve of a pretty seriously bad day.

"If I were on E my pupils would be dilated."

"Are you depressed Dan? Because sometimes I've wondered."

He was spared from answering by the appearance right in front of us of a jostling cohort of drunken pros-

perous young men in shirts of probably superhigh thread-
count. A bar had just released them into the streets, and
one dude was looking kind of askance at me in the
bathrobe—which was thick as a carpet, maroon-colored,
and classily monogrammed with Mr. R's initials. Really
I had nothing to be ashamed of.

"Happy bathing!" the guy shouted aggressively at us
while another was like, "Happy Fourth of July!" These
were the guys who basically owned the neighborhood
on weekend nights.

"I wish those motherfuckers would die," Dan said.
"Not in a terrorist attack of course. Some other mass
death."

I too was offended. The regular alliance of happiness
with idiocy has always been for me as a happy person
one of the world's more painful features.

Inside the deli I went searching for something besides
Combos. There was something else that I wanted, now
and always, and often I devoted several minutes to hunting out this phantasmal snack. Mr. Youn no longer asked
me whether I needed help when he saw me retracing my
steps through the aisles. "You a patient shopper," he'd
told me. "Not so hurry. Live long."

At last I gave up and went to fetch Dan where he
stood cradling two fat torpedoes of Jiggy Juice by the refrigerated beverage bank. "Tomorrow, man, I'm going
to come in here and I'm going to make a beeline straight
to—straight to whatever it is I'll have decided I want.
This is so exciting, Dan. When do you think I make my
first Abulinix decision?"

Dan frowned. "I should have told you. No effect for
five to ten days—or could be two weeks. There's like a
nine-day window there where you may not know if it's
affecting you yet. Sorry." He smiled a nonsmile. "The
look on your face Dwight . . ."

A minute before, all the commodities on the shelves

had seemed to brim and gleam with imminent disclosures. Whereas now they were restored to being things that are only themselves. And with them still them, me still me, the world still the same world, except a minute older, everything looked really barren, and under the nervous rods of fluorescent light, just so nakedly so. "What will I *do* tomorrow?"

"What would you have done anyway?"

Sometimes Dan could laugh a pretty sinister laugh.

THREE

I woke up to the smell of frying eggs. Also to some hip-hop cranked on the stereo going *thug-a-thug-a-thug-guh—guh—guh—thug-a-thug-a-thug—guh—guh* and which I identified as "Electric Chair" off Quality of Life's *Embarrassment of Bitches* CD. The album was in my view their most superlative outing yet, and now the cheerful obnoxiousness of the music melded so thoroughly with the yellowish eggy smell from the kitchen that each seemed an expression of the other.

There was still a ghost of heat and indentation to the other side of the bed. But when I got up yawning and stumbling to go check by the door, I saw that Vaneetha's tall black boots were gone. I was also able to assess, via standing up, that I'd contracted a serious hangover from my forty of Jiggy Juice the night before, plus the half I'd drunk of Dan's in my disappointment at the nine-day-window thing. Age sure takes its toll: back in the day at St. Jerome's I'd been able to stay up late drinking shot after shot of cut-rate vodka before going off in the morning, feeling fresh as newly baked bread on a truck, to study French and later on practice baseball. Now a little caffeinated malt liquor and I felt like next time I'd wake up with a tag on my toe.

"Hello, Sanch," I said to the broad back hunched over the range. But I'd lost out to *Bushy go to Yale / like*

*me I go to jail / I think tha's really fair / cause I think
tha's pretty funny / you be laughin in the chair / whi'
they rakin up they money.* I went to go tap him on the
shoulder. Meek and giant, Sanch started. "Sorry about
the music, man. I figured ten o'clock rule."

" 'S cool. As long as I get some mess." There was pain
in my head.

Sanch had gotten us to relieve him of regular cleaning
duty by volunteering to cook on Sundays what we all
called eggy mess. More and more this was looking like a
good deal, for him anyway, since Ford was usually uptown on weekends, and Dan—I went to go check his cubicle. Nobody home.

All the evidence corroborated itself: our communal
life was breaking down. For months Ford had been
mostly lost to Kat and the higher standard of living cou-
pledom seemed to exact from you, if you were in a couple, or an official one. Meanwhile Dan had become
more evasively himself than ever. And as for Sanch, his
absenteeism—more of the spirit really than of the pretty
considerable flesh—could probably be dated from
around when the medical information website he'd gotten in on the ground floor with had finally collapsed,
causing him to flip out, smoke weed for a record twenty-
six days in a row, at last find a temp job, and then apply
to nine different grad schools in four different subjects.
He still couldn't decide between the places he'd gotten
into, and so had semi-impoverished himself by paying
commitments to all three.

I went and sat down on the saggier, more forgiving
couch. Pointlessly I reached into my boxers, weighed my
balls, and let them go. I wondered what the Abulinix
would assist me in deciding to do once our lease ran out.
Vermont? Really? Truly? Or maybe Dan and I would get
a place together in the city. In which case we ought to be
looking right now. (I got up and went to find my to-do

list.) Or else I should probably begin contemplating the harrowing but low-cost possibility of moving in with mom for a while. Even dad . . . However there didn't seem to be much purpose in thinking along these lines until the drug kicked in, and all I wrote down on my to-do list, standing over it and foully burping, was PATIENCE!

One of Sanch's potential subjects of knowledge was American Studies, so I went up to him and asked about Quality of Life. "We ever find out if these guys are white or black?"

"Supposedly they're black guys pretending to be white college students who act like they're black. They all wear blackface."

"But they are black?"

Sanch nodded. "Infinite regress has gone mainstream. Supposed to be a think piece about it in the *Times*."

From the landing I fetched the Sunday *New York Times*, four thick pounds of information. On average I read only maybe two ounces or so. Yet I felt excused in this by our whole collective ownership of the thing, and simply by the nature of Sunday as that recurrent day whose tremendous potential seems much more enjoyable than any actual use of it could be. Usually if the weather was at all iffy I'd just sit inside idling, fueling myself with coffee, and looking out the window at the shoppers and brunchers going by, the terror-tourists headed down the street. I'd sit inside and luxuriate in the impossibility of mailing out overdue bills, or sending anyone my résumé, renter references, or questionable credit report. Alice had warned me that soon the Postal Service would be privatized, and I wanted to savor this sabbathy pleasure while it lasted.

No sooner had I settled with the *Times* into the battered bamboo satellite dish of Ford's papasan chair than the phone started to ring. It was ringing, terrifyingly, in my hand. Apparently I'd picked it up under the misleading impression that it was the TV remote.

"Chambers St.," I said in my best fear-dissembling voice.

"So are you on your way, Dwight? Or what are you doing?"

"Al!" My beloved sister Alice! "I'm so glad it's you."

"Dwight . . ." From the note of constraint in her voice I could tell that she was with mom. And from a glance at the old homeroom-style clock that we'd nailed to one wall it was also possible to know approximately what both Alice and mom would be wearing at this hour. And even to remember that I'd forgotten to reply one way or another to mom's suggestion that we all three go to church together. "Fuck." It had been a to-do list item that I'd carried over from day to day like some indivisible remainder. "I'm on my way now."

Two clean shirts were available, and after closing my eyes in order to pick one, I buttoned up the blue oxford cloth, stuffed it, along with my hairy legs, into some presentable khakis, then threw on my seersucker blazer and ran out the door yelling to Sanch, "No eggs for me, man."

"Who am I cooking for? I'm already fat, Dwight. You fuck!"

I had just reached the bottom of the stairs and stepped outside to the street when I knotted and centered the floral-print Liberty tie that made me feel, once I did this, on the very same page as the weather. I sighed. The spring consisted on our block of warm blossom-rinsed air and some pear trees in leaf. So that was nice. Nor did I even feel like I would puke as I dashed to the corner to hail a cab.

I found Vaneetha standing off the curb with a brown deli bag in one hand as she waved with the other hand at a slowing yellow taxi. "Hey lady," I said.

She took a step back. "Remind me not to look at you again in natural light. Are you well?"

"I'm confident that in the end I will be." I piled into the cab after her.

"But where are you going?"

I knew where *she* was going—to some relative-arranged and parent-appeasing brunch date with some literally Brahmin, like *Indian*-Brahmin young man.

"Church," I informed her.

"Ah. Mummy's new initiative."

Vaneetha wasn't a huge fan of my mom's. This may have been because mom pronounced Vaneetha's name—like she did all girlfriends' or potential girlfriends' names—with this delicate indulgent condescension as if it were, à la *Mademoiselle* or whatever, some honorific in a foreign language. "Vaneetha . . ." she would say, like that. "How are you finding New York?"

The second time, Vaneetha was like, "It's certainly hard to miss." And what a real little shiver of lust it turned out you got the first time a love object was, behind the joking tone, a little bit bitchy to your mom.

To our cabby's neck I said, "Um, just to the corner of Eleventh for me."

A sense of largesse is what I always experienced in taking a cab, and cheerfulness from running late, as my whole being sharpened toward the point of arrival. Equipped with these feelings, I swiveled to kiss Vaneetha.

"You smell of . . . Is it Jiggy Juice? Did you go out drinking with Herr Knittel once I was asleep?"

Vaneetha was a little sensitive on the subject—the many subjects, really—of *The Uses of Freedom*, and had even complained not completely in jest that I cared more for Knittel than for her. Admittedly I did feel I had more to learn from him.

Usually if you ignore one question you will be asked another—and now Vaneetha had switched to her default question of what did I feel like doing on such and such a fast-approaching date. "I'm free on Wednesday," she was saying. "Or late Thursday might work."

"I'm thinking," I told her.

It bothered Vaneetha that I couldn't produce too many clear pictures of our shared pleasant future activity. And when I'd suggested that she was such a special person in my book that I despaired of finding any matchingly special context, such as a really nice restaurant, or one we could afford, she'd accused me of sophistry. I liked it that she knew just the word to wound me.

"Dwight?" Vaneetha asked.

"Still thinking," I said by way of an update.

The streets were Sunday-empty as we shot up Sixth Ave. like a drug through a vein. Sunlight falling from the east splashed across Vaneetha's knees snug in black nylon, and I discovered I was glad to be hungover. Sometimes a hangover really helps—otherwise simple mental operations are so easy to carry out that you disdain to perform them. But right now the easy question of Wednesday night seemed ideally suited to my present level of mental competence, and unhesitatingly, with an air of unshakable certainty, I produced two words: "Cambodian Cuisine. Let's go get Cambodian cuisine in Brooklyn. On Wednesday night *or* late Thursday. That's what *I* want anyway."

I'd always been impressed by Vaneetha's basic clarity of will or lucidity of desire (except regarding our relationship), and had aspired to emulate it. But I could really only sham the thing, and usually it wasn't until it was too late—and I was eating dim sum while pining for gnocchi, or swallowing some gnocchi while jonesing for dhosai—that I could locate in myself a genuine preference for one restaurant or another, something that was a crucial skill in New York and evidently an important contemporary venue for personality-expression. Yet in order not to behave like one of those wishy-washy males whom I joined everyone else in deploring, I would affect some insistence on—well, in this case, Cambodian food. And this was genius! Because not only was there just the one Cambodian establishment known to me, but it was also fairly cheap and was called, with tremendous forthrightness, Cambodian Cuisine. Pick the food and you'd chosen the place—which more than compensated for my indifference, palate-wise, to fried triangles of tofu.

"Cambodian cuisine!" I said again, and it did sound good, because at least it was food, and I hadn't eaten any breakfast. Nevertheless I saw with dismay that you can hardly get more conscious of your arbitrariness than by pretending to be free of it. And as I looked at Vaneetha with a big smile meant to cover up my shameful condition, I was also looking sort of *through* her—and through the brick buildings knocking past with their zagging fire escapes, rainbow flags, and dazzled streaming windows—to the time when the Abulinix would come and intervene in my brain.

"I adore your cravings," Vaneetha said. "It's as if you're pregnant." She put a hand on my thigh.

I put a hand on *her* thigh. Soon the two of us would have to decide whether to become, or remain, or cease to be a couple. The anticipation of this event was such a foretaste of shared punishment either way that I wanted us to enjoy things while we could. So I took hold of Vaneetha's hand in this very romantic heartfelt manner—even if to do so might mean prejudicing our ultimate decision in favor of continued physical contact, a choice that seemed to be, on balance, and all other things being equal, probably the worse or worst of the options. After all she'd gotten to know me as an abuliac, and people who know you have a way of regulating your behavior to make it conform with your incoherent past.

"So what's this about Vermont?" Vaneetha asked out

of the blue. The question alarmed me—Vermont was not a state we had discussed.

"Don't look at me like I'm mad—I saw your great big note to yourself, VANEETHA, VERMONT. It was lying in plain view on the dresser. I'm not sure when you're thinking of, but you know I have two weeks in August. Hint."

I squeezed her hand. "Hint taken," I said—and immediately postponed thinking about Vermont in August until the Abulinix kicked in.

"I'm going to kiss you in spite of your breath," Vaneetha announced.

"Go crazy," I tried to say.

FOUR

The cab released me at Eleventh. "Call me," Vaneetha said, and I said, "Defin'ely." I started running toward mom's place past the brownstones and the mixed generations of cars, past all the twitching leaf-feathered branches, past a concrete elementary school with aluminum window frames and a primary-colors paint job. Normally I didn't pay that much attention to New York. It always seemed weirdly *pre-perceived,* with other people already on the job. But it really was a nice place, if you looked in the right neighborhood, and imagined people more like yourself and your friends living there. Mom had relocated to Eleventh St. just a few months before, when she and Dr. Hajar broke up for the second or third time. It was also around then that she'd gotten way more interested in the Church.

The new apartment was inside the one brownstone disguised with scaffolding and dark netting. Originally mom had moved to New York to be closer to us kids, and if you did the geography she had been getting closer all the time, living at first with Mrs. Howland up on the Upper East Side, then sliding down for a while into Dr. Hajar's place in the rich little district it seemed like she was the only one still calling Turtle Bay, and finally renting this apartment on the same block as St. Vincent's like a month before the walls of the hospital became this horrible mural of 9/11 missing. Then there seemed to have been some terrorism-induced backsliding with Dr. Hajar—a nice guy with a sense of humor, an orthopedic practice, very hairy arms, and sinus troubles—and now she was alone again and spending the days I didn't know how. I got the impression that the landlord assured her that work on the façade was nearing completion much more often than any worker dudes came along to bear him out. And I resented him and those delinquent guys for prolonging architecturally the whole transitional phase mom was already going through as she tried to set up a life without dad involved, and organized around something else.

These church excursions with the kids were the latest addition to her single-lady routine. In fact her Episcopalianism had revived to the point where she was threatening to go all the way and get ordained. Mom was full of ideas on how the Church had gone astray. She had even been shopping around this manuscript called *The Episcopalian Vegetarian,* copyedited by poor Alice. According to mom, new ethical commitments needed to be made by the Church, along with new dietary restrictions imposed, if it was ever going to recover the big-time relevance it arguably never had. This was the notion that led most directly to last Thanksgiving dinner where she served—to me and Alice and Dr. Hajar, plus the visiting ex-archbishop of Cleveland and his wife—an enormous golden-colored tofurkey, or tofu turkey, as what I guess you would call the pièce de résistance.

"Hmm . . . Mmm . . ." the guy's wife mused with that special warm falsity of certain rich-ish women. We were sitting in mom's dark dining room that was paneled in dark wood and made even darker by the workmen's eternal veiling of the building's façade. There was no art or other décor in the room except for this white rectangular panel attached perpendicularly to one wall with a

Christian cross cut out from it. And in two cages in one corner, standing on their perches, you had Budge and Gordon, mom's parrots, somehow like souvenirs from a more tropical period of a person's life.

Now I stopped jogging, caught my breath, and realized that Charlotte Bell's was the buzzer to push, since mom had reclaimed her maiden name. I leaned on her buzzer while fixing my hair, so much like hers, in the reflection in the window in the heavy wooden door.

"Excellent tofurkey, mom," I'd said back at Thanksgiving, and really it wasn't so bad.

"I hope it was a *free-range* tofurkey," the ex-preacher said, and sipped his wine like it savored of his wit.

"I think humor is good for the Church," Alice said so dryly that except maybe to me she seemed in earnest.

Everyone wanted to show Dr. Hajar how we didn't have anything against Arabs, especially if they were wealthy physicians, and the former preacher asked him delicately how things had been since . . . over the last few . . .

"Oh not terribly bad. I'm still being allowed to live in a tall building."

The Episcopalians looked uncertain over whether it wasn't too soon for jokes. I tried to help them out and keep things solemn by expressing the hope that Dr. Hajar, who was wearing a bandage over the bridge of his nose, hadn't been roughed up by some patriotic Turtle Bay thugs.

"Dwight," mom said sharply.

Dr. Hajar chuckled. "No no. It was simply my sinuses that had begun to overwhelm me."

"Felix is a very sensitive man," mom assured everybody. "We cried so much after the—And that can't have helped."

"Crying frees the sinuses in fact," he said. "If I could have continued crying things would have been fine. That wasn't the trouble. At any rate my daughter is now accusing me of having gotten a Lebanectomy—as she calls it."

Alice smirked. "A Lebanectomy . . . Isn't that what the Israelis tried to do?"

"Yes. Well . . . With local assistance." He swished his wine kind of ruefully.

"The Middle East seems *so* troubled . . ." Mrs. Ex-Archbishop said.

"But we mean to help them," her husband said.

"Yes," Dr. Hajar said. "I feel that in coming years each side will help the other to be more as it wants to be."

"Right," Alice said. "Terrorism as a form of flattery. It's the sincerest form of flattery. 'See? *that's* how free and good we are.' "

Mom didn't like this. I was confused. The ex-archbishop and his wife were looking deep into their tofurkey. Mom said, "What I propose is that we go around in a circle and each say what we're thankful for in America. I know for one thing that we're all thankful to have people like Alice to keep us honest."

Now I heard Alice and mom trotting indistinguishably down the stairs. Formerly Alice hadn't trotted very much or generally moved around our old Lakeville house in any way implying that she consented to live there, and it had been a regular feature of the old days for mom to scold her for being *on the warpath*. But these days mom was very gentle with all animals including humans, and didn't scold much. Now she got along fine with Alice, who lived just a few blocks uptown. Relations were less warm with dad, who mom and Al blamed in the divorce. My own sympathies were more with him, if only because in deserving them less he obviously needed them more.

It was good mornings and cheek kisses all around and

then the three of us went heading off toward the Church of the Ascension. "Dwight's looking a little green around the gills, don't you think?"

"Bristly too." Alice brushed her hand against my cheek.

"You wouldn't want to go to church without sins," I said.

"We're not *Cath*olics, Dwight."

Alice took my hand and we began swinging our shared fist in time with our stride. This was something that despite its cuteness I still liked doing—even if any physical touch from Alice put into my mind the fear that the obscure pact between us would be lifelong, and end up with our comforting each other in some mutually lonely old age of unmarried Wilmerdings.

Mom, looking very nice in a pale green suit with a light iridescence and some sharp angles to it, greeted people as we walked into the church and started down the nave with the organ going full bore in its somber/joyous registration. Alice was dressed more simply in a light yellow dress, and looked very bridesmaid. Unfortunately the days were gone when she'd worn the awesome costume of a dog collar, black leather pants, and a pink Izod polo shirt with an angry ball of shirtfront stuffed under the fly. "What *are* you trying to dress like?" mom had asked. "Um . . . a punk WASP bitch?" It was one of their more notorious exchanges. I'd just stood on the sidelines, half in love with crazy Al and actually, physically clapping.

We settled into our pew. The doors shut and the light withdrew. And now the rector and the other ones, the acolytes and choristers, strode down the aisle in their whispering vestments and carrying those colorful heraldic pennants they all have. I do feel that the Episcopalians put on a good show. And as always I was enjoying the borrowed solemnity of sitting in church. You could feel like the wood itself had grown dark through meditation and that even sunlight became semithoughtful sliding through colored glass into the incense-marbled air.

The sermon began but I didn't pay any attention. Although it was not impossible to fool me, I had never believed for a second in God. So I thought not about Him and his Son but about Abulinix. And yet in listening without listening to Reverend Withrow I adopted the look of pious and unhungover contemplation his voice encouraged among more earnest-type congregants, and before long I found myself actually praying. *May I discover,* so I prayed, *or otherwise locate, during this, my limited time only, and even ideally in the next few weeks, before my high school reunion—and with or without the aid of pharmaceuticals—such clarity and justice and stillness of heart as have so far eluded me during my dark but not uncomfortable sojourn here, while I wasn't looking for them, at least under those exact names, though I mean to embark, very soon, on the pilgrimage of starting to.* Then I realized that praying for stillness of heart wasn't such a good idea. I added, *May my gist nevertheless be made plain.*

When the time came mom got up to take communion, and I watched her walk away in her fancy suit, with her neat, bobbed hair. "Mom looks swank," I said.

"Dwight do you realize what's going on?"

"I'm sure in part I do."

"Our mother has become a de*vout* Episcopalian—she's an Episcopal nun."

"But I thought there weren't any—"

"Exactly. Charlie"—dad called mom Charlie, and so did Alice—"Charlie's a sect of one."

"That's not good? It sounds kind of good."

"Why do you think she's so careful to be pretty?"

Al had been mad at me for a while and I wanted to say whatever she wanted to hear. "Um, because we live in a superficial media-driven culture? All of whose products are converging toward a pornographic norm?"

"Shut up. She dresses like that in order to assure herself that *celibacy is her choice.*"

"I don't know, Al."

"Well if you thought about it you'd know."

Whether my own mother ought to be having sex, and how often, and who with, and in what positions, employing what toys or lubricants, really wasn't something I wanted to think about. But Alice is a brave person unencumbered by politeness or most taboos.

She said, "We have got to get mom eating meat again."

"What are you saying?" Because it was Alice's sullen anemic picking at even the cruelty-free portions of our family dinners, while the rest of us scarfed up dead flesh, that had probably struck the first blow against the omnivorous patriarchy run by dad. "You always used to complain you could never convince them of anything, and now that mom is veggie . . . You should be happy, Al. You and the animals should be happy."

"Mom has become an *ascetic.* That's why she's vegetarian, okay? *I* have nothing against pleasure."

"Like which particular ones don't you have anything against?"

But she just glared and shook her head a tiny little bit.

To wrap things up churchwise a hymn was sung— "Morning Has Broken," as immortalized by Cat Stevens—and when mom returned to our pew I stood up to add my wobbly tenor to the unmistakably white-person chorus. I couldn't help wondering whether this song had been a suggestion of mom's and thus another device to trick kids like Al and me, weaned on classic rock and known to include vegetarians, back into the fold. She'd always tried to keep from losing us by dabbling in our interests. She was all right with books but not so much with the music. A few months after Kurt Cobain had died his epochal death her first comment— or momment, Al would say—was, "I saw a photograph of the poor young man. He seems to have had just *terrible* posture."

At the time Al and I were creeping out of our classic rock ghetto, had semi-grungified ourselves, and therefore wanted to defend the musical genius of our own best substitute for the rock-and-roll casualties of the parental era. Alice in the passenger seat had turned to mom as we drove to the supermarket: "Kurt Cobain was like a Beatle-and-a-half, Charlie. He wrote *masterpieces*."

I remember the foliage had turned, and everything was decked out thrillingly in tragic colors.

"All right, Alice. What might be a song to start with?"

" 'Rape Me,' " Alice said, and indeed it was in my opinion the last album's most exciting song.

Mom repeated the title as a scandalized question and said, "I think that's terrible."

"But it's a protest song."

Even from the backseat I could detect mom's sharp cross-examining smile. "And what is he protesting darling?"

"The culture," Alice said.

Mom's eyes met mine in the rearview mirror.

"Yeah," I said, "the whole culture."

"And what don't you guys like about our . . . culture?"

"We're exposed to so much violence," I speculated.

Alice said, "We hate the blasé cynicism."

Poor mom! I always wanted her to have some other, better kid. But I wasn't willing to become that kid myself or capable of convincing Alice that she should do it. Alice was an excellent student who didn't, however, get very high marks in the attitude department, whereas my geniality, while genial enough in itself, was also pretty transparently an attempt to ingratiate myself with parents who would otherwise punish me for the underexploitation of my alleged mental resources. Mom was never able to secure a single ally in her bid to reform us. We'd given up sibling rivalry early on, committing ourselves to mutual defense, while dad had contented himself as a parental figure with this separation of powers whereby he took part in legislative decisions regarding Al's and my conduct but played virtually no executive role in the distribution of demerits or awards. Plus he regarded us as unreformable, same as he did everyone else, including himself.

Yet mom wasn't asking that much of us, especially Alice, who she only wanted to be happy and heterosexual, and to dress like a happy heterosexual too. Instead Alice had instituted her punk-preppy style, she'd made remarks such as "So I sleep with girls and boys. So what?" and when the Cold War finally ended, and it stopped seeming like we'd been brought into the world only to be incinerated here, Alice still continued fulminating, becoming a Marxist right around '91 and reassuring dad that while she felt that socialism should be tried *one last time,* she had no intention, when the revolution came, of executing him personally or encouraging her New Haven comrades to do so.

"Come on, Alice," dad growled. "Show some spine. A diffident revolutionary is no good. I'm a commodities trader. If you don't kill me, who will you?"

This was one of the rare things that made Alice cry. She'd spared his life, and he mocked her. Then she swore off meat and therefore game hunting with dad. Not that there wasn't still the horned head of a taxidermied ibex from their last trip to Africa—really, an *ibex*—mounted above the bed in her apartment. In fact the creature seemed to bear some kind of glass-eyed witness to some aspect of family relations which it might be painful to picture any more clearly.

We had followed mom through the receiving line and come to Reverend Withrow. The nervous pink-faced glad-hander slapped me on the back with vacant game-show host affability, and told me how pleased he was that my sister and I were showing a renewed interest in the Church.

I was barely sustaining myself on stale Jiggy Juice fumes as we escorted mom back to the apartment. She mentioned again how she was seriously thinking of going to div. school and getting ordained. "The last thing I'd like to become is one of those aging Village ladies tottering around with their grocery carts in between going to the latest what-have-you. Creaky bohemia is not my cup of tea. Don't you think, Dwight"—she turned to me on the street—"that in New York you can become more inert than you notice. You can mistake the city's commotion for your own."

"Yeah," I said in order to seem like someone who participated in conversations and responded thoughtfully to questions. "I wouldn't want to become one of those like balding solo guys walking around in tight jeans and a leather jacket with a cute little dog poking out."

"It's like I said mom. Dwight is gay. It explains everything."

Mom wouldn't have it—she has a *need* for grandkids. "Dwight is very masculine," she told Alice.

In accidental confirmation of her thesis I let loose a ripping burp.

Mom groaned. "The Episcopal disease."

I felt bad. The likelihood of my seeing mom and of my being hungover were both markedly higher on Sundays—a meaningless statistical convergence that nonetheless could create a false impression. I said, "If I really drank too much I wouldn't be hungover now, mom. In fact I'm a lightweight. I should really drink more—or at least more steadily."

On the north side of Eleventh Alice and I kissed and hugged mom and said our see you soons. I looked for a moment into mom's splintered blue eyes and saw there that love was so strong in her that she feared the thing. I think she guessed accurately enough what it was like to be somebody else (such as her husband or one of her kids) that the guess freaked her out and so she kept from making it. In fact I could see how one might do just that, avoiding sympathy out of an excess of it. "Love you," we said to each other and let go.

Mom had latched and unlatched the little clinking metal gate and gone beneath the scaffolding when she turned around. "I hope you kids are off to do something fun. Come here Dwight, let me give you some mad money." I went up to her as she pressed some bills into my hand and folded my fingers back. "Take your sister to the movies. You know she studies all the time." She drew back. "And buy yourself some breath mints."

I returned to Alice and asked if she wanted to see a movie. "Maybe there's some documentary? About exploitation?"

"Just take the money."

"Come on, Alice. Obviously the last time we hung out was pretty weird. I'm sorry that I acted inappropriately."

She didn't say anything. And indeed we hadn't really talked that much since the fall.

Then she said, "So are you seeing anyone yet?"

"What do you care? You're a nun like mom."

"It's more likely that I'm single because once upon a time mom wasn't."

"What is that? That's like nonsense. Was that like translated from French into professor talk? You're like a Communist nun."

"So I'm a nun because—?"

"I hope you don't say any hurtful things that I think you'd want to take back right away. It was a trying day for everyone."

"Fine. Don't worry about it. So I asked you a question. Are you seeing anyone?"

"What do you mean—shrink or a girl?"

"Girl. Woman."

"Kind of. Yeah. Vaneetha. Still."

"Kind of," she repeated. "All you are is kind of."

"I'm feeling some real tension between us, Al."

"What is this way you talk, Dwight? Everything you say is in quotes."

"Everything everybody says."

"I'm not going to stand here arguing with you on the street."

"You think mom can see out? From behind the, like, shroud? Because I really don't think so."

Alice told me to take the money. I tried forcing it into her hand. Then she pushed the small sheaf at me while I yanked my palm away. The two twenties dropped and fell facedown on the gum-spattered sidewalk.

"Pick them up," Al said. "Mom will see."

"What kind of Communist are you—"

"Of course I'm not a *Com*munist—"

"—if you don't think somebody's going to pick some money off the street. Those aren't like injured *people* lying there. Without health care. It'll take like two whole seconds."

"Pick up the money, Dwight."

"You, Al."

"You're such an idiot."

"No, that's not it." And with my new knowledge of myself—indecision was my problem—I turned on my heel. Alice did too, on her heel. I'd made it about half-way down the block before I turned around to see if she was following me—she wasn't—or if the money'd been snatched up. It felt very distressing to leave forty dollars lying on the street and I considered running back for it, and then after Al. I mean the money was basically mine, and I also knew that in some way Alice still really liked me—even to the point of hopeless, because familial, love.

Someone had come out of the pizza place on the corner and was bending down plucking something up off the sidewalk. Forty dollars! Gone! I turned and went on a few steps, then stopped to lurch and vomit up some acidulated and foodflecked Jiggy Juice. This made me feel temporarily better about everything. Yet in fairness I couldn't expect a similar attitude from the thin fiftyish bald dude in clamdiggers, leather flip-flops, and one of those guayabera shirts, who had emerged onto what I have to presume was his own stoop while I was engaged in puking and retching. "What"—he practically shrieked it—"are you doing in my new trash can?"

I looked up again at the guy. "I'm sorry—I have abulia." Somehow this made me start laughing my head off. I felt sorry toward the victimized homeowner, but not excessively, and with occasional glances back over my shoulder I went running off in a crapulous zigzag down the sidewalk. I was glad to be on the road to recovery and felt like a convalescent should be granted some leeway.

But I'd barely reached the next block, and stopped running, panting, before I was completely dismayed again by my somewhat preliminary life that I was constantly starting all over again. I felt very upset to have to wait between five and fourteen days before learning what I would decide about Pfizer, Vaneetha, and my living situation. Plus sad or bad moods employ a deductive method, and always look around for data to confirm them—so I couldn't help noting, in terms of sad facts, that here today was Sunday, formerly the main family-togetherness day, and all four of us were apart from each other and probably from all other non-Wilmerding humans too. What solitary people my family were! It amazed me that two of its members had ever gotten together to produce the others. But then solitary people pretending not to be—that must be how many families start up, and how the race of the lonely has grown so numerous.

FIVE

My concern over Dan's poor diet plus my liking to cook had recently combined into a tradition of shared Sunday dinners, and I'd just finished sautéing some spinach and mushrooms when Dan walked in the door. "You should be a Jewish mother," he said. For an instant there flashed through my mind the possibility that under the influence of Abulinix I would have a sex change and then a bat mitzvah. Then I realized that despite Dan's dry tone he was kidding; that I could never bear children; and that possibly I'd just endured a crazy person's thought. But these were concerns which I folded without comment into the dough I was rolling on its way toward spinach pie.

Later on we sat in the living room under the three splayed fingers of the ceiling fan and ate our food in the rosy/sooty light of 7 PM. "Nice pie," Dan said between bites.

"Thank you," I said.

"Dwight, would you let me know when you start feeling the effect? Because we should really start thinking about our living situation. I see my own options as follows: either we find a place together, or I look for a studio in deepest Brooklyn, or I move into NYU housing with the other geeks."

"Do you have a preference?"

"Eh," he said. "I live with you, I eat better. I live by myself, I live by myself. Mr. R used to tell me, he used to say, 'A young man wants three things in this life: he wants one good sports coat, one good pickup line, and a one-bedroom in New York.' Of course, he meant a one-bedroom in Manhattan."

"Cool. Well I'll just weigh my options until—until the Abulinix puts its finger on the scale in which I'm weighing them. Meanwhile I should do some research. On Vermont."

"I believe most researchers have found Vermont to be a state populated by hippies, yuppies and farmers."

Once the evening had drained all the way out of the room, Dan got up with our plates and placed them unrinsed in the sink while I went to my cubicle to check my email. Opening my inbox I found that upwards of twenty Formmates were sufficiently unembarrassed about checking their email on Sunday as to have written me regarding the reunion. Of course the correspondent who stood out, as in a certain way she always had, was Natasha, who said she might or might not go. Moreover in a postscript she seemed to be inviting me to visit her in Quito!

Excitedly I lay down on my bed and then stood up again. What an opportunity of some kind this must be! Certainly there was no law saying I couldn't go to Quito! (Unless this city or town happened to be in Cuba . . .)

Suddenly—it was always so sudden—the phone rang. I picked it up and waited to hear who it was before committing myself. "Hello?" Alice was saying, "Hello?" and, once I acknowledged this was Dwight, telling me a) I was paranoid b) I was annoying and c) she was sorry to have talked harshly to me earlier that day.

"It's okay," I said, pleased by this news of her contrition as well as by the exciting development regarding Natasha, which I related right away. "I mean maybe I should go. Nastaha's such a nice, thoughtful person—"

"With such a nice, thoughtful body—"

"So? She also always seemed very wise. Didn't she?"

"I haven't talked to her in ages."

"And it might be good to be with a potentially wise person in kind of a nonaligned country—Quito's not in Cuba is it?—so that I could gain some kind of objectivity when I'm thinking about the decisions I'll be making once the drug—I should tell you about the drug—once the drug kicks in." It was then that I told Alice about abulia and the drug designed by careful scientists to treat and cure it.

"You're not serious. Can you really think that abulia even *exists*?"

"Oh yeah. Whatever else may not be real, abulia definitely is."

"Just like social phobia suddenly exists, even though it was created by the pharmaceuticals about four years ago. Like neurasthenia used to exist but now somehow it's died out."

"Maybe the people who had it didn't reproduce."

In Alice's and my arguments she often played culture while I played nature, and though you would suppose nature to be the stronger force, I usually lost. It was hard not to when Alice was a trained anthropologist—whereas all I had for anthropology was introspection. Yet it was introspection above all that proved the reality of chronic indecision. "For instance I can't decide whether or not to go."

"Then maybe exercise some caution."

"Maybe is the key word there."

The next few hours I spent alone in my room, paralyzed with the maybes. Then I received Alice's second call. "You're right, Dwight." Apparently she'd been thinking about it. "You should go. It's just like what you said— you should be in some neutral country when this ridicu-

lous drug takes effect. God knows, if you're in New
York you might ask the first woman you see to marry
you. You'll see a cop on the street and you'll enroll in the
police academy. At least if you're in Ecuador you can't
do anything rash. Natasha's not going to marry you,
and there are no jobs in a country like that."

"We don't know about Natasha."

"So go find out then. Go to Ecuador, Dwight. It'll do
you good. You're completely provincial anyway."

"How can I be provincial? I live in New York City."

Aphoristic Alice was like, "A cosmopolitan provin-
cialism is the worst."

In the end I referred the question to the reliable and
impartial coin-toss method. I have reported the results
in the Prologue, and they were still the same as then.

The next morning I went to work at the Problem Resolution Center, just as on thirty-four of the previous thirty-
five Monday mornings. Which meant that I still had one
week of vacation time available. Yet it was uncertain to
me whether I was really allowed to take time off on such
short notice. So I called Alice from my desk to ask for
some advice.

"I didn't say you should call me every day," she said.

"You called *me* yesterday. Twice." Then I presented
her with my dilemma.

"Family tragedy. It's obvious. Say there was a death in
the family."

"All right." I turned around to make sure Rick wasn't
eavesdropping. "But also I'm going to need to say
something to Vaneetha."

"Lie to her. Better to lie to other people than yourself."

In some way I had always imagined maybe the opposite was true. "Really?"

"Listen, lying is incredibly important in developmen-
tal psychology. Telling a lie is the child's way of separat-

ing its world from that of the adults. It establishes your independence, it's how you mark off your own private area of the truth."

Alice could be so helpful when she wanted. "I don't see why you can't still be my shrink, Al."

"If you had a real shrink they would tell you why."

"Not that I haven't lied. I don't want you to think I can't lie."

"But not well. Not with that face." It was like with her tone of voice she was pinching my stubbled cheek. "Now *I* know how to lie."

I emailed Natasha with the fantastic news of my likely visit—an action that made me feel so guilty that immediately after hitting SEND, I called up Vaneetha at work and told how vividly I was looking forward to seeing her on Thursday and eating some Cambodian food.

"Lovely. You know if you're so much looking forward, we could do it a bit sooner. I've hardly seen you."

I said I had plans. And it was true. That evening I visited a travel medicine center where I spent hundreds of dollars on all these shots and prescriptions for pills that I certainly hoped weren't contraindicated for Abulinix users. But that seemed like the least of my worries. The information the nurse gave me on various Ecuadori dangers made it seem amazing that anyone who went there didn't pitch off a cliff in a bus while reeling from dengue fever and nibbling at some piece of hepatitis-soaked fruit as a scorpion crawled up his shorts.

"But what about spiders?" I asked the nurse. "I hate spiders—if something's going to bite me, I want it to roar at me first."

The nurse flipped through some papers. "Nothing here about spiders."

Faced with the reality of Ecuador's many perils, I felt almost frivolously morbid to be devising the death of a fictional relative whose fate of not existing I might soon be forced to share—and then I wouldn't take it so lightly. Still, the next morning I asked Rick if we could speak in private.

We went out into the hall by the vending machines.

"But a whole week?" Rick said. "This is extremely short notice."

"He was my favorite uncle."

"I'm so sorry. What was his name?"

"Um . . . Dwight. I'm named after him. His name's the same as mine. Spooky."

Rick nodded his head. "But are you sure you need a full week?"

"Well see the ceremony is in Quito. That's in Ecuador. But first you have to fly through Bogotá. I could show you a map online. Anyway they have a very humid climate down there, so it's important that we get there by next week. At the latest."

"So the funeral—I take it that's what you mean by the ceremony—the funeral's in Quito?"

"He was very close to the land down there."

"And what did your uncle do in Quito, Dwight?"

"Middle management," I said.

"And what did he manage there?"

"It was a medium-sized concern. Import/export. Obviously we weren't *that* close. But still I'm pretty bereft, all the more since now I'll never get to know him."

By now Rick's scattered previous suspicions had fused into a hard point of skepticism, a look of real forensic dubiousness.

"What did your uncle die of, Dwight? If you don't mind my . . ."

"Um . . . We're kind of keeping that under wraps." Things, having gone unplanned, were also going badly. The awkward scene aggrandized itself into a representative instance of my flawed approach to life, and as Rick folded his arms and stared at me I felt Natasha slipping out of reach like a dream-discovered formula fumbled from your mind the moment you wake up.

Suddenly a strategy emerged from my distress. "You know, Rick"—I met his eyes—"I feel I can be honest with you. I mean, you're my manager. You watch over me. My uncle had been sick for a long time with . . ." I sniffled without even planning to. "With abulia. It's been a real embarrassment for the entire family."

Rick granted me my week.

"Hello and thank you for calling the Dwight Resolution Center. This is Problem speaking." Over the next two days I delivered correct and incorrect versions of these statements over and over again into my headset. Pfizer was completely the same as before, but contrasted with the upcoming novelty of travel, now much more so. In fact now that I was allowed to leave, I finally began to feel sick of the place. Between calls I stared into my cubicle's gray carpety divider and saw a wilderness of tedium there, and all day long, as I swiveled back and forth on my chair, I sipped cold coffee that seemed to come from some primordial pot brewed and scalded long ago.

At one point I tried to keep boredom at bay by making my first ever subversive remark to a user. "Sounds-like-you-may-be-having-a-bit-of-a-problem-with-the-Sherman-antitrust-processor-but-I-think-we-can-fix-it-in-a-jiffy—" Thus I alluded quasisubliminally to the antitrust act that Microsoft was in the business of flouting in order to foist its inferior product all over the world. At the same time I recognized that if Windows didn't suck so much I wouldn't have a job.

"I'm sorry?" said the middle-aged male voice, no regional markers. "Would you mind saying that again?"

Then I began actually to help the guy. People upstairs generally seemed humbled by software failure, or else they may have heard a note of doom in my young man's allegedly tech-savvy voice, unaware that—not even up to speed on Java—I was getting surpassed in my own right. But for now nothing more difficult was required of me than to lead the user through a step of six keystrokes to get his vital document to return from the false oblivion it had landed in. Then he thanked me, whoever he was, and I made a report and sent it to the database called UTOPIA. It wasn't really very utopian, being a repository of every problem any user had ever had.

Wednesday passed in this way, then half of Thursday. Thursday at lunch I walked down to Times Square where there was a Belgian frites shop whose product I admired. Then I walked back to Pfizer wondering if flying off to meet some hardly-known person in a foreign country was really the ideal decision-making procedure. (I had booked my ticket online but still had four hours left to back out.) If it turned out that Natasha was everything I hoped and dreamed and was into, then what would she want with me? And if she wasn't, then what would I want with her? And why even ask these age-old questions that must have had all the nutrition chewed out of them long ago? I fed the mayonnaise-limp frites into my teeth one by one, and when I returned to my cubicle I deliberately spilled a little leftover mayo into the cracks of my keyboard, just in order to make the corporate world a little more soiled and grimy, more in need of being replaced for a week by a trip, however ill-advised or well-considered, down to Ecuador.

" 'Sup?" Wanda asked me when she got back from lunch herself.

"Wanda, I have a question."

"You know I got an answer."

"You notice how all the users—"

"The *losers?*"

"—yeah, how they sound so guilty on the phone? It's

weird. It's like they're ashamed of themselves that the software doesn't work."

"Damn straight they're ashamed. These are business-people people. They believe in Darwin, baby, *and* the computer. They can't use a computer, they feel like they got no business bein alive."

Rick appeared out of nowhere and said, "How's it going, people?"—his way of telling us to get back to work.

"It's going very well, thank you," Wanda very crisply said. "How are you this afternoon, Rick?"

It wasn't long after a suspicious and disgruntled Rick had wandered away that the fatal email popped into my inbox, addressed from CEO William Starboard to CFO George Bailwater. I'd hardly started reading the document—many, many numbers, and big ones, were involved—when I heard Rick saying my name as his quick little steps approached from behind. Pressing CTRL A and CTRL C, I sent the thing to my clipboard and turned around with an innocent expression.

"Dwight, were you just sent a document?"

"I was. I started reading it but it didn't seem meant for my eyes. Should we delete the file together?"

He watched me delete it. I said, "What you don't know can't hurt you, right?" Sometimes I couldn't make out the tone of my voice.

Rick looked peevish. "Dwight, I'm sorry about this uncle of yours—"

"No, it's okay, no one is very sorry. My uncle was avuncular, I admit. But that was really it. He had no other characteristics. He was just this kind of mediocre, redundant, blank sort of dude. Then they let him know he was dead." Tears of suppressed laughter or misplaced grief sprang into my eyes while, on the other side of our divider, Wanda began to laugh out loud.

"What is going on here? Story hour is over, people.
Just—"

"Okay," I said as Wanda in similar tones of quick
submission also said, "Okay."

And in order to elude suspicion, I decided to wait
until the next day before retrieving the document from
my clipboard.

SIX

I came up from the subway in low-buildinged Brooklyn, into the breeze-soothed air of an irresolute spring evening with Venus, aka the evening star, hanging out over New Jersey. I was on my way to meet Vaneetha at Cambodian Cuisine. Later on we could take in a movie if she didn't hate me by then for having chosen to go to Ecuador to see another woman, an aspect of the trip I was debating whether or not to bring up.

Soon I was undeniably within sight of the restaurant. I instructed myself to tell the truth to Vaneetha, because she would never buy it that I was going without any reason or Spanish to spend ten days in Ecuador by myself. Maybe I could just request that she not feel threatened by Natasha. After all I did feel vaguely committed to her (Vaneetha), and possibly I wouldn't so much as touch Natasha even if she (Natasha) encouraged me to. Or else I could just leave the facts bare, letting Vaneetha take offense and dump me. Or maybe I could somehow imply by a rare suave tone of voice that I was only behaving in the way of all sophisticated people who always leave all their romantico-sexual arrangements undefined. Moreover, presenting this third option casually, as a matter of course, might force or otherwise encourage semisnobbish Vaneetha to go along.

Vaneetha was standing outside the restaurant. She

was wearing a gray cotton skirt and one of those short-sleeved button-down white shirts inside of which her breasts strained to be released like Superman inside of Clark Kent. And slung around her shoulder was this shiny green handbag whose contents, at this point in the possibly expiring relationship, I could more or less guess.

We kissed, then walked hand in hand into the restaurant for our date with destiny.

The one hundred and twelve menu alternatives made my head swim. People on dates often went to restaurants—and suddenly this seemed so misguided of them. It seemed like really terrible mental training for love to go to restaurants where they hand you a menu, because the personality of a person would seem to show in its indivisibility every sign of being more of a prix fixe deal. For instance I was always thinking to myself that I liked Vaneetha's affectionality, but didn't care for the clinginess, and that I liked her sophistication, but wished she'd be more crude, like she was some list I could pick from. . . .

"What's good here?" she asked.

I'd read my horoscope that morning and learned today's lucky number. So I said, "55 I could recommend. The Chicken Ahmok?" And with still more self-assurance I ordered us two copies of the largest available beer.

Then I reached across the table to hold Vaneetha's hand, and gazed profoundly into the bright wet surface of her anxious eyes. Whenever it seemed like Vaneetha sensed, correctly, that my affection for her was flagging, I was always at pains to demonstrate how wrong she was.

"Is something going on," she asked. "Or are you just being Dwight?"

"I think maybe we should just take a second to look kind of longingly into one another's eyes." I hoped she would see in my face, and remember once I'd wronged

her—if that's how she would consider it—that I felt
nothing but tenderness for her urbane, semiopaque and,
come to think of it, somewhat deer- or antelope-like person.

Another favorite and inexcusable method of relationship management was always to accuse the woman in
question of doing exactly whatever you suspected yourself of doing, and I was on the verge of asking Vaneetha
whether she hadn't been avoiding me lately when a phone
rang, close to us—almost *in* us—and I jumped. Vaneetha
fished it out of her bag and looked at it, smirking. "It's
you ringing. It's Chambers St."

She handed me the device and I passed it back like a
hot potato.

"If you want I'll answer. But you're *here*. Surely it's
not for me."

The phone kept up its panicky sounds of abandonment and distress while fellow diners glared.

"It can't be *for* me," I whispered. "It's *from* me. There
must be some mistake."

Vaneetha rolled her eyes and went out to field the call.
After a few seconds she beckoned at me from the sidewalk. Oh I did like being beckoned by her—but not this
time.

Into the phone I was like, "Hello and thank you for—
or, no, this is Dwight."

"What'd you do, Dwight?" It was Sanch calling.
"You did something bad, man. You're in big trouble."

"I hate being in trouble." It reminded me of being a
kid—which reminded me of being in a family.

"You know some guy named Rick?" Sanch was enjoying himself. "Who might be your manager? Because
he's called like four times. He in*sisted* we track you
down. Finally I figured, right, Vaneetha."

Vaneetha took pen and paper from her bag and allowed me to write down Rick's cell number on the im-

provised drafting table of her nice Pilates-strong back. What was or (if the word was plural) were Pilates anyway? *Goodbye back,* I patted her between the shoulder blades. *Possibly goodbye.*

When I reached Rick he shouted, "Christ, Dwight, where the fuck have you been? Don't you own a cell phone?"

I knew what had happened. I knew it was all over. I knew I had nothing to lose. "Hey, Rick, man? Dude? I don't think so much profanity is appropriate when you're asking me, during this extremely difficult time for me and my family . . ."

Vaneetha raised up her eyebrows and smiled at me. She looked tolerant, skeptical, and amused.

"Coming in late," Rick was saying, "I could let that slide. But listen here you lying little—the theft of private documents is a class-one felony."

"Yeah well—" I couldn't think of any very tart riposte just yet. "Well you and everyone else can tell it to the judge. Because here I am right now with an attractive female muckraker who's hungry for a scoop. And I'm revealing to her in every filthy detail whatever was mentioned in that document that I was felon enough to steal."

"You better not, you—"

"Done. Done. Already done." But I was feeling some sharp regret at my negligence: how could I have stolen important corporate secrets and failed to look at them, and also, to be frank, failed even to steal them? Now I said, "Imagine the enormous liability! The share prices tanking! The horrible gloating competitors!"

"Don't you dare come to work tomorrow, Dwight. We'll send you your shit in a box! I hope you understand, you—"

"Make sure you include the pocket watch." I couldn't think of any possession of mine being at work besides a pretty thoroughly stained coffee mug. "You better include the watch, which is like an heirloom from my dead uncle. And that I'll otherwise sue in small-claims to get back." Wow, lying—you could really get on a roll.

Rick was still screaming when I pushed END.

"What uncle?" Vaneetha asked. "Which watch? Were you just now fired?"

"Um, yes. I was just now fired. From Pfizer. Wow. Pfired! So I'm pfucked!" But the *p* was silent so no one laughed but me. I looked at Vaneetha. "Don't worry about my uncle. He doesn't exist. So he's fine."

We went back inside to our expectant steaming dishes. Losing my job had evidently given me an appetite for even this wobbling Khmer Jell-O of a chicken I had ordered. "Chicken Ahmok!" I dug in.

I explained to Vaneetha what I had done and not done with the scandalous document. Meanwhile I realized that Rick, by firing me, had placed a very heavy burden on the Abulinix, which now I would need not for deciding the simple binary issue of Pfizer or not, but for the vastly more complicated problem of where else to work—and at what? If only I'd actually *read* the document, and been able to secure some renown and maybe even a career as this corporate whistle-blower. . . .

"I suppose," Vaneetha said, "we should get extremely drunk?"

"Yeah. I think that's what you do. When you're fired. Yeah . . . But like I said, we were getting outsourced anyway. Where the fuck is Mumbai anyway? I never heard of it."

"Bombay. Mumbai. You know that. It's simply the older name."

We raised our glasses to toast. "To Mumbai!" I said at the same moment she said "Bombay!" Then in order to accommodate each other we switched names and like two polite people trying to let each other pass in a hall-way, we wrongfooted ourselves again.

Half an hour later we were leaving an excessively large tip and deciding to skip the movies. Arm in arm and jostling each other between tongue-heavy pit stops of affection, we walked down the dark cool streets toward Carroll Gardens. "Well you're free," Vaneetha kept saying. It sounded wistful. Maybe she was afraid my freedom wouldn't stop at unemployment. Or maybe she feared that as my savings dwindled and I didn't find work I wouldn't be able to go out to dinner anymore, or otherwise keep up the false illusion of our salary parity. I wondered how committed she was anyway to socioeconomically-based assortative mating, or dating.

"I am pfree," I said, "but also pfucked." And it had stopped being funny.

I imagined handing out at the reunion an itemized list of life-sized excuses: 1) Child of divorce. 2) Fired for an act of conscience. 3) Duties as Form Agent overwhelmed me. Maybe then my Formmates would take pity on me and the vaunted old-boy network would kick into action. I certainly hoped our country wasn't yet the meri-tocracy it was pledged to be. "Thank God Bush is in office."

Vaneetha ignored me, kissing me, while this sullen corporate hipster passed to one side. "Get a room."

I yelled out our extenuating circumstances. "I'm un-employed! She's an immigrant! You shit-sucking Repub-lican fuckwad!"

Vaneetha clamped shut my mouth with her fingers, then lips. In this way, if delayed somewhat by occasional mutual crotch-grabbing, pretty soon we were passing the Smith St. subway stop. As on other nights, a certain homeless black guy rattled his cup of spare change at us. "What," he asked, smiling but without too many teeth, "is the very finest nation in this world?"

The correct answer was *donation*. But Vaneetha and I enjoyed one-upping one another with wrong or random answers. "Uzbekistan?" she'd ask or I'd be like, "Uruguay?"

That night Vaneetha said: "I know, Ecuador!"

I choked on my own identical answer and dropped some change into the cup without a word.

Vaneetha squeezed my hand as we walked away. "What's the matter there?"

"*I* was going to say Ecuador."

"Always have a backup. I do—always. Come on." She led me away towards her apartment, where we burst through the door, disrobed our way through the living room, and collapsed into her queen-sized bed. And what happened there all felt very good, in the medial forebrain bundle, where I experienced pleasure, but not quite so much in the conscience. I couldn't believe I still hadn't said anything about the trip. Worse yet, I could *totally* believe it.

Afterwards I got up and went to look at all the pictures marshaled on the dresser. In years past she hadn't been so pretty, so Manhattanized, and had allowed lots of pictures to be taken of her with her not-so-cool college friends, many of them also foreign students. Whereas now she was this incredibly put-together person—who right at this instant was probably getting an eyeful of my incredibly hairy ass. It occurred to me that Vaneetha's and my relative values on the love market weren't necessarily always going to be equal—that right now I might even be selling high, and she low. Good time to get out, then.

"It's probably time to ask what you see in me," I said.

"It will help if you turn around."

I turned around and shielded my crotch as in a penalty kick.

"You're certainly a very *curious* person," she said.

"Except that's not true! I didn't even read the document! I wonder what it said."

"I don't mean curious that way. I like you because you're you. A dozen reasons. You're Dwight Wilmerding. And now that you're free to take a better job, I think you're going to feel much more fulfilled."

Vaneetha fell asleep as I whispered some sweet nothings into her ear. Probably their sweetness was rivaled only by their nothingness. Then a few myoclonic jerks told me she was asleep, and I got up to go take a leak. Seeing myself in the mirror I shook my head. "You again." I always did that—a habit.

I started gathering up my clothes from the floor. Then I sat down in a chute of streetlamp glow to compose my little valediction or whatever:

My dear Vaneetha,

I am flying to Ecuador—can you believe the coincidence?—on Saturday. Sorry if this comes as a shock to you as well. But there is no stopping me when I must learn from my mistakes. I am going to South America mostly in order to do some thinking. Here in New York I have been mistaking the commotion for my own.

It is also the case that there is another woman in Ecuador. This is Natasha, but only a friend. She speaks Spanish and can keep me from being misunderstood or deceived. However I make no guarantees involving my conduct with her. I feel it would be unphilosophical to do anything but submit to my freedom.

My provisional conclusion is I should have waited to attain a state of higher personal and professional development before endeavoring to be a suitable partner for such a fine woman as undoubtedly and really very impressively you are. For now I could only be the hindrance I always was.

I promise I will suffer for this. Hope you won't.

Thank you for everything. Maybe there will be more. If you want. Which I doubt. You know how I feel. XO,

—but instead of signing it I folded it up and put it into my pocket as an ambulance siren blared past and then wavered away. (Ultimately I would use this note as the rough draft for an email I sent from dad's house the next day.)

Then I was out on the street, in the TV-screen blue of the night. In front of a deli a man was hosing off the shining sidewalk. He had this particular kind of dark and steep-nosed usurped prince's face that later on I would recognize as a basic Andean type. At that time I just saw him as foreign. He shut the nozzle to let me pass, and offered with a lowered head just the breath of a smile.

SEVEN

The train pulled out of another quiet white-painted town and recovered that slack regular ratcheting sound of all trains. I was on my way to see dad, to play some golf, to sip some scotch, and then in the end, or somewhere in the middle, at an opportune moment, before it slipped past, or maybe, on the other hand, right away, the minute I saw him, first things being first, and just in order to get it over with—anyway I was on my way to ask dad for some money. I had every intention of telling him I had lost my job, and in the context of my resulting penuriousness I would request a loan. Or ask him to take me in for a while once I got back from Ecuador. Or both things, actually. That would make the most sense from an economic point of view, at least if I could deal with the psychic cost of living with him for the first time in fourteen years, and without mom and Alice around to parry him and distribute throughout the household their various counterpointing moods. It would be interesting to see what I decided to do, always assuming I did decide, which I shouldn't necessarily do. Today was only Abulinix day six.

We arrived with sighing brakes at the Wassaic station. I stood up and followed a few fellow passengers down the aisle and off the train. There was dad waiting for me in the parking lot inside his fancy new car.

Suddenly it seemed possible that I would just return to the city, tail between my legs, without saying anything about money. Besides, a plea for funds must gain something in urgency when made from a sketchy third-world country. And yet I really didn't understand this personal bankruptcy thing of dad's if he could buy himself a new Audi, fully loaded and lustrously painted with the extract of crushed oyster shells. The vehicle was already notorious. Alice had called it "his new car that's like painted with the crushed fingernails of illegal combatants" and mom had snorted and said, "We should all be so bankrupt!" I hadn't had any opinion until now, when I discovered my feeling to be that if that shiny white machine was dad's car, I didn't see why I couldn't be made a small loan.

Dad released the dogs from the backseat before even acknowledging me. They trotted forward snorting and wiggling, sneezing and wagging their tails, first Marshall, a glossy half-Rottweiler mutt, three years old, who leapt like a deer from all fours, and then our half–Rhodesian ridgeback, Frank, chubby and blond, who liked sniffing and rooting with his nose like a pig. One dog a deer and the other one a pig—it was strange. But stranger to me still was this new dog hanging around all timid and small in the neighborhood of dad's pant cuffs: a yellow lab puppy, by the look of her.

Marshall was squirming with frantic happiness, licking shyly at my hands. I knelt down to pat him while Frank laid his muzzle against my thigh, and dad came up to me with the puppy slipping in his arms. "Cave Canem," he festively said—Latin for Beware of Dog.

"Hey, dad, man."

He set the puppy down while I stood up. Then we squeezed the breath out of each other. Ever since roughly the middle of Clinton's first term, when hugging seems to have become acceptable mainstream practice among straight or straight-acting men, we've always hugged upon greeting and saying goodbye.

"So who's the new dog? Why didn't you email me? I mean a puppy—that's an event."

"Nothing I could have written would be like Betsy in person. Isn't she just a little—aren't you Betsy?" Dad dangled his hand near the puppy's mouth and little miniature Betsy leapt up to chew on it with her clean new teeth.

"Doesn't look like a mutt," I said. Usually it was only mutts—the only true dogs, according to dad's former idea—that he rescued from the pound.

"Sometimes, Dwight, you reach a certain age—you just want a yellow lab. You're willing to buy one. You've worked all your life, you've raised two ungrateful children." The friendliness of his cynicism was the nice, but not the consistent thing about it. "You've at last divorced the woman you love. The woman well-lost . . ."

A serious reader, dad had gone through many volumes in his office, and from his tone of voice more than from my own strictly limited erudition I could sometimes tell when he was alluding.

"I've lost something too," I said, or more mumbled it maybe.

Together we drove to the club, dogs and puppy panting away in the backseat. And probably here is the place to explain that when I was a kid we had another dog: a large fit golden retriever named Mister, very regal in the face, with a pale coat flaring in cowlicks all across his back and an attitude of stoical sadness that only being played with or petted could placate for a while. Mom and dad were physically shy with me and Alice except when spanking us, and we were also shy with each other, unless sumo wrestling or playing karate, so that all of us

showed Mister an affection that was plainer and more
extravagant than anything that passed between us actual humans except in times of crisis. Yet this attention
to Mister seemed also to be the emblem of our basic mutual filial thing, implying as it did what large volumes
of love-grade emotion must get trafficked invisibly between us if this was how we treated—I mean, nice as he
was—*our dog*. Our feeling for Mister kind of took the
measure of our hearts, is my guess.

"Only nine holes," dad assured the dogs when we left
them with windows half down and a biscuit each.

Out on the links, typically we'd discuss which club for
me to use, then I'd whack the ball. Then dad would hit
his own ball. Then we would walk in the direction of the
errant ball and the well-placed ball, discussing things in
general, such as money, sports, and current events. I
think one time we used Tiger Woods for all three.

Though I didn't golf so well, I did enjoy dressing golf-
style, since to me all uniforms—and, in this particular
case, some pistachio-colored pants and a pink-and-mocha
sort of argyle sweater that had fit me a lot better in the
Third Form—seemed to loan the body a rare sense of purpose.

It was a nice morning, heating up, with voluble birds
happy in the trees. You could distinctly feel our whole
part of earth easing itself down toward summer.

First hole, dad peered weirdly—stagily—into the little
cylindrical hollow. Before scooping out the ball he said,
"Burns spared this one," and chuckled. I wasn't sure
whether I should know what he was talking about.
When he made the same enigmatic comment at the next
hole—"Spared this one too"—I was like, "Huh?"

"*Pardon me,*" dad said, because he and mom—one
item they agreed on—didn't like it when I'd say *huh?*
They considered it a shame to waste all that money on a

young man's education if he still put his elbows on the table and said *huh?*

"I mean what. Regarding Dr. Burns?"

So dad related the scandal. Burns had been a community fixture ever since his days back during Nixon as an enthusiastic Valium prescriber, and now apparently the doctor had been caught a week or so before, literally with his pants down, defecating into the fifteenth hole.

"Ew"—because this is something I don't like about my parents. Their conversation around me frequently runs to the scatological, and this I find infantilizing—this and my mother's habit of peeing when I talked to her on the phone—since you don't have to be a freelance psychoanalyst to feel that making these procedures a public matter between parents and child must be a way of reinforcing an inappropriate intimacy way past the deadline. "I'm really not into hearing this, dad."

"As a result of this incident," dad was saying with serious relish, "Burns has been suspended from the club. For a year!"

We were walking toward the islandy clump or copse of trees in the direction of which I'd—whoops—hit my ball. Once when I was seventeen I'd deliberately knocked my ball that way in order to duck into the dappled shade and take a hit off of this little one-hitter I'd carried with me at the time, since I was then in the grips of a conviction that weed made you see things more truly, clearly, and that was how I wanted to see dad, in order to check out whether, defamiliarized a little, the guy still was basically a good guy or what. On that occasion when I exited the trees disguised by Visine and breath mints and those aviator-type Ray-Bans we all used to wear, he'd struck me as just some bluff pink-faced ghoul of a commodity-trading genius who had chosen the main features of his life in order to make himself into some weird

totem of his social position, instead of—I don't know—
following the mad, barking dictates of his soul wherever
those might have led, like possibly to Vermont or else
northern California. I mean, how could any free person
choose, from the whole universal range, to be this dad
and moneyman and golfer, a resident of northwestern
Connecticut walking around in WASP casual, going to
the reunions, belonging to the clubs, and describing
himself—still, or at least then—as a Rockefeller Repub-
lican?

But now in light of my own recent actions and, even
more, my damaging reluctance to carry them out, I tried
experimenting with the conclusion that dad's scotch-
and-golf-oriented generation wasn't so different, in terms
of courage, from my more weed-and-rock-climbing one;
that it was a pretty unusual life that didn't travesty the
better nature of the person inside it; and that dad's very
dad-like knowledge about many things, and intermittent
basic decency, and astounding handiness, made him not
such a bad person at all, despite any reservations I may
have had about the rate of his scotch drinking, and any
sorrow I may have experienced at having become, thanks
to him, and along with Alice, another child of divorce.

"What makes it all particularly amusing—" he was
saying.

"Yeah but do I really want to know this?"

"—is that Burns had just been quoted, in the *Times*,
about ten days before, as one of the last physicians pre-
scribing Croxol—"

"So would you say seven iron here or—"

"—despite a certain frequent side effect. Of explosive
diarrhea! Which he said—in the *Times*—had been exag-
gerated!" Explosive laughter.

"Dad, man."

"Can't you just picture him because—"

"I hate this. Don't you know that yet?"

"Because what is Croxol prescribed for?" He waited a beat. "For morbid embarrassment."

"Hmm . . . The gods' sense of humor." This was in order to suggest that my education hadn't been totally for not. Or is it naught?

"Precisely! Precisely right. Just how to characterize it."

It was touching—he was proud of me. I wondered if I should seize this opportunity to make my confession. But it was turning out that the story of Dr. Burns's come-uppance was only the overture to a much longer conversation about the role of pharmaceuticals in our American society.

Dad had raised his eyebrows and was tapping his index finger on his cranium. "This," he was saying, "is the new frontier." The Croxol fiasco notwithstanding, he had decided to make pharmaceutical concerns pretty central to his recovering portfolio and he felt it was one of the smartest things he'd done.

"But aren't you bankrupt, I mean . . . ?"

"I was." He stopped walking and looked off—I did too—into the hazy distance. "I was, as you say, bankrupt. Had to put the house in your mother's name. True. But no one in commodities made it through 2000. You know that much."

I did know but never, even after lengthy explanation, did I get exactly why. I knew money had been managed for institutional clients, and that it had been invested at high risk, generating high returns, in gambles on foreign-exchange rates, actual commodities, interest rates, and so on. You took an average directional movement of this, and some relative strength indicators from that, and figured in some four-day average true ranges, and you fed this stuff to the computer until arrows came on-screen telling you to get in or out, and this meant being, until 2000, a hero among commodities traders, profiled in *Barron's* and elsewhere, and a mystery to your wife and kids, all of whom liked complaining that you weren't a good listener but then turned into, like, hypocrite deaf-mutes the moment you tried to explain to them the baroque system your semidipsomaniacal genius had devised one evening when you were supposedly in your office reading literature books.

Dad said, "I'm speaking to you as a private individual now. The drug companies are the place to be."

It was like I was being taken into his confidence as a potential investor in my own right. Dad's confidence in the pharmaceutical industry gave me some faith that the Abulinix might be starting to work and I said, "There's probably, dad, something that I should—and that might be of interest on a somewhat different, but also related—"

"People have so much money these days, Dwight—have you noticed this? They've really bought up most of the goods they're going to want." This was the place where Alice would have noted in chilling tones that it was in fact a tiny minority of the global count that dad was including in his category of *people*. And I would have said, "You know what he means, Al," because it just seemed like too much for dad to have *two* kids who felt that the best response to the available pleasures was a constant awareness of those unable to enjoy them.

"But that's outer goods," dad was saying. "There we're sated. Consumer electronics, SUVs. In fact this is one reason the economy's so sluggish. There's a lot of excess manufacturing capacity in this world, this"—he pointed to my golf clubs with one of his—"this world of what you and I would call physical *things*. But the market for what are essentially inner goods—this has only begun to be tapped."

Dad and I often had these very zeitgeisty conversations—they seemed to be an aspect of the father-
son relationship. For a couple of years whenever we
went golfing or skiing he'd initiate dialogue about how
nice it was that we'd won the Cold War. It was like we'd
chipped in together. "During the Cold War you felt like
you had a reason to get up in the morning. Now what
have we got?" The words had seemed to imply a certain
sympathy with me, since my own reasons for getting up
in the morning were unknown to us both, hence I was
studying philosophy at Eureka Valley, in order to learn
them.

We proceeded from hole to hole underneath the low
Connecticut sky. "Ten years," dad was saying, "and
people won't be so suspicious of drugs. Sure, the Arabs
might be. But we're chemistry. That's what we are. We
just have to wait for this realization to trickle all the way
down. Food, exercise, sexual intercourse, warmth—all
these things function like drugs. They modify your mood
and perspective. That's how it's always been. Mark my
words, this distinction between natural and artificial,
when this is your brain but then it's your brain on drugs—
that will frankly come to be seen as so much twentieth-
century superstition. It's a last hangover from the—don't
tell Charlie I said this—but from the old religious concept of the 'soul.' "

"But you and mom were always worried if *my* brain
was on drugs."

"Well Dwight"—and here he sailed a long straight
beauty of a shot down the fairway. "Would you look at
that." If I'd been on mushrooms there would have been
the lovely fading arc of a tracer in the air. "Well marijuana is not exactly a performance-enhancer. I trust
you're not still using that stuff."

"Very rarely." We went off to the rough to fetch my
ball. "It can be pleasant and relaxing." The phrase en-

joyed a certain currency in our family. When mom had
come into my adolescent bedroom one night to tell me
what sex was, and how it would be okay if eventually I
had it with someone I loved and even, when desperate,
with myself, she let me know that it could be *pleasant
and relaxing.* This was the same phrase with which dad
had defended himself against Alice's accusations of excessive drinking. And even Alice herself, during the great
Lesbianism Scare of 1992, had suggested with heavy
sarcasm that the girl-on-girl lifestyle could likewise be
pleasant and relaxing.

"Marijuana can have an effect on motivation, you
know. Would you say you smoke the drug once a fort-
night?" dad said, a pretty accurate guesser.

"More like in a blue moon."

"The point is, to think of the person without thinking
of chemistry is like thinking of a house without archi-
tecture. There's no house that's simply a house you go
home to, then you add or remove the design. The design
is the house."

I could see this was a case you could make and knew
that disbelief in a person's innate character had a serious
intellectual pedigree going at least back to Scottish philosopher David Hume. But it was also true that mom and
dad had always encouraged me to be *true to myself*—
a phrase actually used—and seemed to have an idea of
what this kind of fidelity should entail. So it was kind of
disturbing to have dad wiping the human face off the
mirror as casually as a smudge.

I started to say it seemed like people would continue
to subscribe to a certain vague regulatory notion of health,
that this would have a conservative effect on would-be
psychonauts, and that in fact the somewhat scary effort
to reengineer the whole human personality was one of
the reasons I was kind of down, these days, on Pfizer,

where, in fact, as I really should have mentioned earlier—

"Clearly you haven't seen what the pharmaceuticals are investing in R & D."

I wasn't getting through. A lot of times it seemed like I'd been well enough educated to be considered a decent audience for dad, but not a qualified interlocutor. If I brought up something he hadn't thought of before, he ignored me. But if I said something he already knew, he'd say, "Sure. I know." Like many men, he was impregnable.

He was reciting statistics when I interrupted him. "I wonder if anyone's looking into a cure for the kind of mild, low-level autism that's become such an epidemic in this country. Especially among white suburban males. And that's been linked to lots of—"

"Well I don't know Dwight. I hadn't heard of that problem."

"But now you have."

He regarded me with some sort of dim suspicion. "And where did you read about this, this—"

"*Wall Street Journal.*" I met his gaze. "Pretty small item." I shrugged.

"Since when are you taking the *Journal*?"

"I think maybe is it Bristol-Myers Squibb? major Pfizer rival? that's been looking into this, um, MLLA—"

He began to taste the concept: "Mild, low-level—"

"Right, autism. This like mild inability to recognize the basic mental reality of others. Total potential cash cow, they're thinking. I think. Because it's definitely an issue out there."

Possibly he couldn't tell if I was fucking with him or had instead given him some valuable information. Unfortunately an online consultation of the *WSJ* archive was likely to settle the matter.

"Could be I read it somewhere else," I allowed. "There's *so* much information online . . ."

He threw an arm around my shoulder, and when I looked to my side I saw up close what relatively hairless knuckles dad has—just some blond downy sprigs alert above the crosshatched flesh. "Well, thank you, Dwight." I looked in the opposite direction, at the thin silky thatch of hair and the nose tipped with red like that of a kid come in from the cold. With his free hand he visored-up his shades, and there were the old periwinkle eyes, squinting and innocent. "I'm serious here. Thanks for the heads-up. That's a very interesting piece of news you've given me. Old Bristol-Myers, eh? Because I have noticed just that problem, the problem of the low-level—"

"Yeah."

"Even in a place like Lakeville. Salisbury . . . So the scientists are referring to a kind of inability to make what we would consider psychological contact with, with—"

"Bingo."

"With others. Hmm. Old Bristol-Myers . . . Certainly sounds like they're back on their game. Because what you're referring to can, I think, be quite a serious problem."

Dad returned the sunglasses to their position and there I was in them, reduced and convex, smiling and also beshaded—a huge friendly insect. He turned away and released me. "Hmm. And this low-level, this very mild form of autism, it afflicts Caucasians and males in greater than average numbers? Did the *Journal* suggest why?"

"It was a short item. I can't honestly remember where I read it. I think the scientists must still be at an early phase."

Around this point I began to feel a little cruel. I recalled mom's accusation that efforts to get through to dad were often met by a busy signal, and how a year and nine months before, when she'd been screaming out near the pool, wielding a pewter candlestick and making some threatening gestures, he'd displayed great calm and an impressive talent for mimicry by making just the sound you hear when someone else's line is engaged.

"I think we've all noticed this problem," he said. "Even you have, I'm sure. Well, good for old Bristol. That it attacks who it does. Because that is precisely the target market. Isn't it? White suburban men. I'll be damned."

Now I was feeling pretty sad. "It's really a pleasure to play golf with you, dad. Maybe if we play more often I'll get better."

He barked out a laugh. "Sounds logical."

Next hole, he turned to me and let me know that he was very proud of my being employed by Pfizer. Apparently this disclosure was the hole toward which he had driven his earlier, more speculative shots, and now he was just putting his way in. He said the pharmaceuticals were doing fascinating work, just as I'd indicated. "A vanguard industry."

"You're serious?" Things were feeling kind of tragic.

"Sure."

Or maybe it was me getting fucked with now? But I told myself probably not. Besides, the stable behavioral patterns of your parents seemed important to believe in.

I reminded dad that I was actually only subcontracted to Pfizer and in point of fact employed by another firm providing tech support. "And the rumor is that pretty soon some guys in Mumbai . . ." Meanwhile I wondered if he was trying to win me over to his camp as opposed to mom's with his ingeniously contrived praise of my (former) employer.

I told him I had some vacation days coming up, and that in part because New York interfered with my mind by its abundance of advertisements printed in a language I could read, I was considering going off someplace more quiet, less legible, to do a little thinking. "I hope I'll have enough money, though."

"You're not intending to do some thinking about Pfizer?"

"Possibly about them. It. About us."

"We are not about to enter the Zone again are we Dwight?"

I experienced a flashback to a childhood Thanksgiving. Probably dad did too. I'd loved cranberry sauce, the savory stuffing, and turkey itself with such equality of love that after a gabbled grace I'd been unable to begin eating, and the more ludicrous the spell of indecision became, the harder to break. I'd been salivating and paralyzed in front of my plate, plunged in what later came to be known as the Zone, until finally dad raised his fork at me saying "Eat! Eat! Dammit, eat!" So I'd shut my eyes, loaded my fork with mystery, and raised it toward the cave of my mouth. The tart surprise of the cranberries I could remember still.

"Also," I was saying, "there's a girl I'd kind of like to see. Natasha van der Weyden?"

A good way to suspend conversation with dad was always to bring up something personal. Very dad-like and typical, I know, but true all the same. It seemed to be part of his syndrome, just identified, of mild, low-level autism.

Golf resumed.

I wondered if dad remembered Natasha. She had visited once upon a time with a large delegation of other kids from St. Jerome's and her presence had notably coincided with the escape of my mom's favorite parrot from the cage which dad in his negligence had left open. The bird was discovered jabbering anxiously in the crown of the huge elm on the lawn. I was afraid it would fly away and this would mean dad becoming guilty of one additional thing. A horrible recidivist, he proceeded from crime to crime through twenty-seven years of marriage. At best he was on probation. "You didn't!" mom would say—but usually he had. He was super-absentminded, and so an unlocked car got stolen, or the trash bins weren't wheeled down to the road, or ice cream got returned to the pantry, later flooding in slow stages down through the shelves of dry food. My theory was that the more mom complained of these atrocities, the more absentminded dad became, as he more and more mentally took leave of their shared daily world with its vehicles, trash, and foodstuffs.

But so on that long-ago day Natasha had stepped and shimmied up the tree with simian agility, then coaxed the bird onto her shoulder as we family members and Formmates all watched from below. "She's something else," mom said. "She's from Holland," I said. I couldn't think what to say. She was more Alice's friend than mine. Dad said, "I suppose in a few minutes we'll be calling her parents in Holland." "She's saving your ass, Dun." Delicately Natasha had worked her way back down the trunk, while the wind picked up and all around her the leaves broke the sky into glitter. Down on the ground again, Budge began to say, just as I'd taught him, "What's up dude? What's up dude?" and everyone laughed, family happiness restored.

But not for long.

I wondered if I myself would ever marry.

"Is there something on your mind?" Dad was handing me a new club.

"No, no." I shook my head. "Not yet."

We knocked off after nine holes and went to have lunch at the clubhouse. Two double scotches arrived in advance of our food, and we toasted, clinking, without either of us proposing an occasion.

"Very peaty," he said.

"And smoky," I said.

"Peat-smoke, I think"—an admirable synthesis. He looked at me. "It's important to stick to something, you know."

"Pfizer, you mean."

"I can be taken to mean that."

I said I would bear that in mind. I felt bad about having spoiled his paean to pharmaceuticals by expressing ambivalence about the job I had already lost. Meanwhile I was pondering the tragic irony of Croxol with regard to morbid embarrassment—and wondering whether it might be, in a similar irony, that Abulinix would force me to decide that my entire personality boiled down to neurochemistry, and I only flattered myself in believing I possessed a free will in need of regular exercise. Then why would I do anything at all? Once you decide you're only an animal, how do you keep from becoming a vegetable?

Suddenly dad said, "What do you know about Australia?"

"I don't know, convicts, Aborigines. Marsupials. Just the clichés."

"Because I've met really a very nice woman."

It was a rude shock. "A woman!"

"Yes, a woman. That's not such a rare thing. And as it happens she's from Brisbane. I've been thinking I might fly down there and pay her a visit. Fascinating country, Australia."

"What if she was like Bulgarian? Just as a thought experiment—"

"Well I'm sure she would be a very different person then, Dwight. Australia I imagine as being something like the US in the early sixties. Still open. Kind of raw. New."

"Dad, man, I thought the whole point of you di-

vorcing mom—which, I mean that's a serious thing—
I thought the whole point was you were *an essentially
solitary person.* That's what you said and I quote." I may
have raised my voice at this point.

The waitress had showed up with our sandwiches.
"Veggie burger and—"

I pointed. "The carnage is for him." And when the
waitress had gone I said, "An Australian woman!" Some
guy at a nearby table turned his head.

"Frances," dad said, "happens to be an interesting
woman about whom I have simply entertained the possibility she and I might enjoy meeting face-to-face."

"You did *not* meet her on the internet."

"Listen now, no cause for alarm. It's not as if I'm
considering relocating to Australia at this point. We'll
discuss this at home."

"Home!"

"You aren't usually like this, Dwight."

"Thank you."

"Let's talk about these things later on."

"So if it's urgent it can wait? Dad, man"—I had to say
it—"I've lost my job. And I have basically zero point
zero in the way of cash. And I have no skills!"

Dad looked confused.

"And what I *do* have is abulia."

"Abu—what do you have?"

"I *know.* It's probably hereditary!" I shook my head,
bitter and sad with a foretaste of what I might feel when
more drunk.

Dad's reaction to my unemployment news was the
same as Vaneetha's—to order more drinks. And immediately after saying "Christ, Dwight, you've really gone
south, haven't you?" he said—tipsy, already free—"You
know I love you, you fogbound sonofabitch." Neither
the curse nor the blessing was such a common thing to

receive from him, and getting both at once, the far edges of my mind felt lit with feeling while the middle regions kind of sank away, and I hope I don't sound like a cry-baby if I say that in this strange state over my veggie burger at the club, my eyes went kind of moist.

EIGHT

Dad was driving the dogs and me back home on four scotches, too fast around curves and showing a new mood. "And again, what kind of little pizzle of a job was that at Pfizer anyway? Good to hit bottom, sooner the better. It's a fucking required event, in my book."

"Have I really hit do you think?"

"Bottomlessness—is that what you're suggesting? I suppose the world is at bottom a bottomless place. Fine point, Dwight. Well, good on occasion to tip out of your goddam canoe." He was swearing much more than I was accustomed to.

We passed by the Lakeville Lake, which flashed thinly like water tilted once in a pan.

"Don't imagine I haven't wondered. What can be done with Dwight? This isn't a new one on me. I'm familiar with your performance. On the other hand you've got a hell of a pure soul. If you were a girl we'd never have let you out of the house. . . . Frances—the Aussie—of course she asked, and I said, I wrote back to her, I said, 'My son's an innocent bastard, it's a remarkable thing in this day and age.' But I don't mean by calling you a bastard . . . Listen, I love your mother with an insufferableness of love that may surpass the insufferability of the woman herself. And look, Dwight, listen now, if I were to show to you, on a chart, how much

I miss old Charlie—a quarterly recap, if I plotted the graph—you would see one gruesome goddam shape. It's been spring outside. Still is. —But I sired you." He laughed. "I take full responsibility. Glad to do so. Kind of a nonperforming loan. But you turn out a good product. Innocence! Christ!"

"Thank you. I guess."

We were passing all the streaming landmarks of the family's life. There to the left was the silo I'd climbed and fallen from miraculously without injury as a kid. And next up was the turnoff to Factory Pond, where I got a puck in the face but scored lots of goals and even had a hat trick in one game.

"You'll turn out fine," dad was saying. He laughed again. "Unless you take after me!"

"Either of you." Mom was an Episcopal nun. "I've never heard you talk like this, dad." And now to the side of the road was the spot where Alice had been nabbed by the cops for spraypainting on the glass doors to the Millerton movie theater LOOK BUT DON'T TOUCH.

"Nice we're getting fucked up, isn't it? I believe that's what you and Alice called it—getting *fucked . . . up . . .* ?" He looked around with satisfaction at these words in the way that guys in a car with hip-hop blaring will look around while stopped at a light.

"There were so many terms," I said. "It was like the Eskimos with snow. Or I guess now they're called Inuits."

"Let me ask you then. Alice?—did Alice turn you on to marijuana? I've always thought we're a peculiar family. Because dammit if Alice didn't steal you from us!"

"No one stole me *yet*. Come on, dad."

"It might be we didn't drink together enough, father and son. Getting fucked up. Or perhaps the whole family—yes, I can see it now, fucked up as a family . . ."

Musingly he said, "Whenever I touch a drop I have the urge to call Frances. Thank God with the time difference I often don't. But she has a lovely voice, not brassy in the way of some Australians—"

"I think you maybe exaggerate the role of getting fucked up in me and Alice's relationship."

"Ah, but isn't it in the nature of getting fucked up—to exaggerate a little?"

"You're not going to marry . . ." I couldn't bring myself to say the Australian woman's horrible name. Frank, he'd probably call her. A year and nine months ago dad had been eloquent on the subjects of necessary solitude and marriage as one big mirage of false relation—and now he had a girlfriend.

"No wedding bells for me," he was saying, "not if I remain lucid and . . . Yet I'm too much alone, if you've noticed."

"That's like what you asked for!"

"Much too much . . ."

"Alice thinks you drink too much."

"And don't you think so?" Another barked-out laugh.

We pulled off Belgo Road onto our driveway and glided through the familiar strobe of leaf-crumbled light. The dogs stood up from the leather seats in the rear, whining in anticipation of being let out to do nothing. And here was the old lawn, green with new grass, a big circle of it enclosed by looping asphalt. And as we swung around to the front door, lurching to a stop in front of slim white Tuscan-type columns, everything looked so formal and pre-arranged that it felt like we should be met there and announced. But of course no one was home since dad had kept the house, while mom herself, feeling nervous and excited—"Like an actress," she'd said—had gone off to New York.

After disabling the alarm dad went inside to call

Frances. "Probably just getting out of bed over there. Down Under. Would you go out back and water my flowers? Then maybe I'll fork over some money." I could tell by his harsh tone that he would, and felt some relief at least in the accounting department as I took the dogs behind the house.

I turned the spoked knob clockwise and then stood with the hose above the flowers, waving the spray over the lilies and svelte irises, the blowsy pansies and banks of phlox, as if to soothe and somehow wake them at the same time. Then I turned the faucet almost shut and set the mild silver flow down inside the bermed bed where the climbing hollyhocks and orange heads of calendula grew. It really wasn't such a bad flower garden for a divorced bankrupt of a father to keep up.

You can eat calendula, so I stuffed some in my mouth. My jaw working, my palate receiving, I tried to do some thinking. Because I could feel there was a thought that needed thinking, or a decision deciding, and it even seemed connected in some way to the dogs or the flowers.

(As a kid I'd been convinced by dad's lectures about germination that I knew how it was to be a seed. That is, I felt I knew how it was when the seed first split underground and the tucked neck of its original shoot buckled up, tugged by the light while its roots strayed down, and then straightened out and began climbing up through loosening soil toward the open air and light. I was less sure of what the tiny consciousness of a plant went through as it emerged on the ground, paused, and kept mounting. And as for how it was in the end when the leaves came out and the actual colored flowers blew—I had no idea. By then I felt about a plant as I did toward other people. I mean, mom and dad and Alice—they were incomprehensible! One would never do what they did, or I never would anyway. Why had they chosen to be themselves? Dim as I was, and the youngest, still I could tell they weren't delighted with their choices.)

Flowers . . . Dogs . . . The whole fucking dogflower of it all . . . It seemed like the only way I had of thinking about anything was to think about something else. And this really ruined the procedure.

I shut the water off, and threw up my hands, and sat down drunk on the lawn. I was afraid that the shape my life wanted to take would never describe itself to me any more than I could ever accurately describe just the exact mild savor of all these calendula blossoms I had unconsciously started eating one by one. (Yet while I may not be able to say what these flowers tasted like, they did taste like something, and like nothing else but that.)

The grown-up dogs sat protectively to either side of me while Betsy bounded in and out of my lap. Then I heard the whispering of pant legs and turned to see dad approaching with a tumbler in one hand and a rakish look pulling at one side of his face.

"Poor woman." The smile tugged to one side. But on the other side he looked too wise for this.

"She thinks you like her?" I asked. "Like, *like*-like her?"

"Why do I call her poor woman?"

"Sometimes you seem like a pretty terrible guy." I must have been doubly drunk to say this.

"What can you do? The trouble with your mother and me is that we'd exhausted our illusions. As you grow up, and you'll find this, Dwight, you keep getting involved with larger and larger illusions that take longer and longer to fall away. The great hope is eventually to find a delusion that will outlast your life. You'll do well to marry a woman you won't realize you can't live with until you're both dead. Ha! But Frances? No I won't marry her. And yet when I think about her I sometimes feel . . . Frankly I feel a capacity for self-deception that makes me feel like a much younger man. I'm in pretty good health, you know, and could go on living for some time."

"How did you ever become a dad like this?"

"Very simple operation."

"Seriously, should cynics . . . father?"

"You're suggesting they should just masturbate in the public square? Along the lines of their founder?"

This remark bewildered me.

"Don't worry." Dad looked at me with this wicked charm that made you imagine his long-ago way with the ladies. "It's only lately that I've come to realize the vanity of . . ." He shrugged and sighed. "Of all my years of trading. Fathering. Husbanding. I had my system, the system worked, the system failed."

"You mean Commodysis?"

"Nor was the vanity all in vain, don't you agree? We've had our nicely appointed lives. We haven't added any material privations to the more spiritual varieties of our suffering. We've been able to address ourselves to pains other than those of social inferiority. That's been quite nice." I'd always admired the way dad could talk. "And I put you and Alice through those schools which—well, it remains quite prestigious that you went to St. Jerome's. Yet it does come to seem somewhat in vain. In a sense. Vita longa, ars brevis, is how you wind up feeling. You survive your rationale. But I shouldn't be saying all this—not to you I shouldn't." For a moment he looked genuinely concerned. "You can't understand what I'm saying on the cheap, Dwight! You have to fucking *do* something. Don't see the vanity until the end, all right?" He laughed. "Find a job, a girl! The Dutch one may do. Sure. Wasn't there some particular thing she did? This is the tall blond girl with the freakish smile? Am I remembering correctly?" He looked at me again. "But did they really never teach in your courses about Diogenes Laertius? The inventor of cynicism as it were?"

"I don't think they had us read that. It probably *would* be discouraging to the young."

"What books did you read, Dwight? All those god-damned schools . . ."

I began providing him with an annotated bibliography as, trailed by the dogs, we went inside the house.

Always the same, the smell of the house was always a surprise: cool and somehow mineral, with a sort of iron flatness beneath the pleading richness of dark wood and moist sense of venerable rugs. Not strong at all, still the smell was stronger if there weren't any cooking smells, as there weren't today in the swept-bare quiet and over-whelming bachelorhood of the place. The smell of the house took up innumerable lost and scattered moments of the past and fused them for a second. I got a sudden white blast of pure life—and then the flare was gone.

Recovered, I said, "So the question, according to Quine, is whether the guy is seeing a single, discrete entity that you and I would consider a *rabbit*—"

"All right."

"Or just a bunch of separate rabbit *instances*."

"For Christ's sake . . . One hundred thousand dollars . . ."

Dad settled in the big rolling chair on the far side of his desk and produced his checkbook from a drawer. This was in his office. Marshall and Frank each turned a semicircle, then sank on their flannel dog beds, while I sat down like an anxious—and drunk—loan applicant on the other side of the desk. Puppy Betsy scratched and licked at my hand, which I wiped off on my shirt before reaching for the check dad was handing me.

"Should tide you over until you find your feet. Ha!"

I folded it up without looking at the amount—I was

afraid it would cause inappropriate degrees of either glee or dismay. "Thank you more than I can say."

"You wouldn't think of doing graduate work in philosophy, would you?"

"Oh, no." The idea appalled me. "Never."

"Good." He poured out two or three fingers of scotch for us both. "I hope you've given up on that stuff. I blame myself for not directing you better. And for my influence." He gestured sweepingly at the books on the wall. Thirty years of evenings were stored between the pages somehow without taking up any space. "However, Dwight, mostly I blame you."

"That makes sense."

I sipped at my scotch. I'd kind of lost track of my mood. On the wall facing me was this darkly lustrous portrait in oils of mom as young Charlie. There was also a heavy clock—think captain's quarters—on the mantel above the fireplace, and beside the computer one of those high-tech crane-necked lamps with a weighted base. When I was a kid, and in fact up until right about now, the office had always seemed to represent a world of considerable ballast, not easily knocked around by rough seas. And dad too was impressively solid, thick through the chest and broad-shouldered, with the heavy-boned face distinguished by the long nose, faintly cleft at the end, that had been passed down through the generations until it stopped with him. (I had my mom's nose, and Alice had her own.) But now all the fatherous solidity seemed less so . . .

"Just sits there," dad said. "You just fucking sit there. Well I have one goddam piece of advice for you, Dwight. And I'm sorry I'm swearing so much. Obscenity has really lost its power don't you think? But—what are you looking at?"

It was the Dwight in the photograph on another wall, in black mortarboard and gown, looking into the camera with his head cocked to one side in this curious expectant way I recognized from somewhere.

"College seems like a long time ago," I said. It wasn't really what I was thinking.

"Listen, Dwight, I have a piece of advice for you. All right? There is no worse preparation for adulthood than having been a child. Do you hear me? Be a fucking kid and you get trained in that business and forget all about time. But listen, here is my fatherly advice. I suppose I ought to have dispensed it more often—and to a more plausible son." I sensed he was trying to be angrier than he was, and putting on a roar. "Don't make a career out of your childhood! Do you understand me? Don't make a career out of your childhood or you'll never adapt yourself to any other. Is that understood?"

"There are some decisions I'm really eager to make," I said. "Once the Abulinix starts to—"

"But you already know what you know!"

"What do I know?" I knocked back the rest of my scotch for courage, and smiled at him.

"Sonofabitch!"

He sent me ducking as a miniature stapler came flying at my head.

"Good! Good! Duck and cover! Cower and hide!" Suddenly he paused. "Do you know what I don't trust about those SOBs?"

I unshielded my face and looked at him. "Which ones?"

The box of a VCR head cleaner came flying at me and I hit the floor. "Great! Great! Good! Cower from the Great Satan! But let me tell you the reason I don't trust those Wasabi Muslims—that's the terrorist kind—it's for one single reason! They don't drink is why I don't trust them! If what you want is an education in human frailty . . ." He nodded at his glass and swished it around.

"If what you want is a humanizing tolerance for weakness and the varieties of failure . . ." He polished off the rest of the tumblerful. "I tell you what you do. Hell, there would be worse things for you to do than to set yourself up as the premier liquor distributor to the Arab world. Just do not *play dead,* you hear me!" At the words *play dead* Frank the dog got up, looked at dad with a look of put-upon exhaustion, and rolled over onto his back, legs straight in the air. I observed this noble, baffled obedience from my crouch on the floor.

"Oh come here, Frank, come," dad said with almost a sob, and when the dog got up and laid his muzzle against dad's thigh, he—dad—gently removed a little ball of sleep with his thumb from one of the creature's baleful, intelligent eyes. "There, you're a good one." Looking at me he added, "Take it from me, you lousy sonofabitch. Whom I love!"

He threw a heap of paper clips—they lightly rained on me.

"Listen: Thou shouldst not have been old till thou hadst been wise."

"What are you saying."

"For Christ's sake! You know what you are, you illiterate goddam . . ."

He shook his head while selecting the word, and from down on the ground I noticed something. That look, in the picture of me? It was the look of a dog awaiting a treat! I was filled with horror, and sprang up onto my knees in an agony of comprehension. "I'm a dog! I'm a dog! Oh no! That's what I know! I'm a seed that grew into a dog!"

Soon it became evident to me from dad's confusion that this wasn't what he'd been about to say. Nevertheless, still kneeling on the rug, I went ahead and said, "It's horrible! I'm always doing what the humans say. I'm always hoping my innocence will forgive me—it's so corrupt!" Was this the Abulinix I could already feel? "I admit it! I'm a dog."

"Nothing's wrong with dogs," dad said defensively.

"They're inhuman!"

At this Betsy launched herself at my face and licked me on the neck. Sunlight was falling slantwise through the south-facing windows, and the dust across the panes was lit up from the side, golden-ish, like pollen, and giving off an air of immense drowsy fertility, as I swayed with feeling on the floor. Maybe I was drunker than I guessed. I got up to my feet and sat back down in the chair.

"And what," dad asked, "do you propose to do with yourself, now that you're no longer a dog?"

"I want to start a new life."

"Ah you'll grow old doing that."

I stood up and went to the other side of the desk. I put my hand on dad's shoulder. He looked at it like he did not know this hand.

"Just don't eat any more of my goddam flowers," he said.

"I'm going to go up and pass out in my room."

I walked out of dad's office, blocked only once by the doorjamb. "Good night," he called out after me, the dogs all barking when his voice was raised. "Good night," he called again—it was five in the afternoon—as the dogs continued barking.

I paused at the foot of the stairs, with their worn blue runner still cascading in place through the years. "Glad we had this conversation," I yelled.

"About time!"

At the top of my voice I said, "Everything takes longer than you think."

"Not life," I thought I heard him grumble. Unless it was something about a wife.

The words were still ringing indistinctly in my ears as

the plane took off from JFK the next day, forcing my back against the seat and adding its torque of actuality to the fact that I was leaving. I sat in my seat and watched the fragile city dwindle to a model of itself—a touching sight, like there was no strength in numbers. And then there was nothing but the mirroring ocean down there, flashing and bright but also really dark.

Part Two

The driver relieved me of my backpack and threw it into the trunk like an abducted child. Natasha opened the right rear door of the taxi and motioned me in. She sat down on one side of me while Brigid—that was her name—came around and sat down on the other. There was kind of a kidnapping feeling going on as they pulled the doors simultaneously shut. "You're like double agents," I said. Because there *were* two of them.

The taxi lurched away from the terminal and Natasha leaned forward, looking across me to Brigid. "Dwight is very mystical. He has mystical ways of knowledge."

"Untrue," I assured Brigid, then turned to Natasha, who should know better. "That's not true."

"But how did you recognize Brigid was waiting for you? She didn't wave to you?"

"She knew me is how I knew her. Plus Brigid is white." I turned to Brigid. "I mean you are, Brigid. You're a white person, I mean—"

"Yes," she admitted.

"Not that the Ecuadoris aren't white. In part. Some of them. I understand. But—"

"Yes I confess. I gave him the secretive wink of all white people in conspiracy." Natasha and I were supposed to laugh, but didn't. "That was funny," she complained in her slight, unlocatable accent.

I was really curious who this Brigid person was, but it seemed rude to ask right in front of her. It struck me as possible that Natasha had told me all about her many years ago, or else in a recent email that I'd forgotten the moment I logged off. Of course it was just as possible that Natasha hadn't mentioned this other woman at all, and unable to recall whether Natasha was generally considerate and forewarning or not, I couldn't guess whether this was likely. Meanwhile I felt kind of disloyal in my divided attentions. Then again it was only fair since Brigid was the one inquiring how my flight had been.

"Good enough, I guess." I turned suavely to Natasha. "Since I'm here."

"Nice that we all are here. Next up Cuncalbamba!"

"This is a picturesque town—" Brigid began to explain. Was she going too?

"In a beautiful valley," Natasha added.

Brigid: "Very near the cloud forest."

Natasha: "But not nearly so wet."

"The climate is like an ideal."

"Everyone loves Cuncalbamba."

"That sounds nice," I said to them both; and I guess it did. But by the time the cab had deposited us on the steep empty street, and Natasha was unlocking a fourth consecutive door in order to lead us into her apartment, I was feeling more anxious than enthusiastic about my visit to this country, and in particular afraid that thieves or revolutionaries would set upon us the moment we went back outside through the four locked doors in the morning.

I put my pack down and walked to the window to take in the view through the bars. The city of Quito was laid out in glittery drifts down below, and moody-looking mountains loomed to what was possibly the north. Off in the distance a cloud dangled a single branching nerve of lightning. Despite the fact that my brain was prickling with dread, I turned around and was like, "So I'm very glad to be here Natasha."

"I know you're going to have such a great time."

I would have felt more convinced if she hadn't started to yawn.

"Should we—I don't want to offer you your own liquor—but shouldn't we have a drink or something?" Brigid had disappeared into the bedroom, and now that Natasha and I were alone I desired some quality time.

"It's very late, Dwight—it's past midnight."

"I know, same time zone as New York." I looked around the bare, unfamiliar room. "That's the strange thing."

She set me up on her couch, then left to join Brigid in the bedroom, whether because they were cousins, lesbian lovers, enlightened Europeans, or just two women in a place with one bed, who knew? Alone in the clean cold kitchen, I poured myself a glass of water—hopefully potable—to wash down the pills I was taking. The Larium was an antimalarial and the Abulinix, of course, was an anti-abulial. I gulped and swallowed the pills, and went and lay down on the couch.

Everyone always moves so insouciantly into the future, one foot in front of the next, that it seems as if they've already been there and liked it enough to go back for more. Only their total confidence permits me to follow without undue terror. Yet sometimes—such as when you read in the *Times* of certain weird and bad events, like the guy who heard a noise outside his sister's house, ran out the door to inspect, and then plunged into an old abandoned chalk quarry, just caved in, from which his body has never yet been recovered—you realize how the future is a place where no one has been, and from which you don't come back.

Plus the idea that I might not return here was somehow made more credible by the emptiness of the apartment. There was none of the clutter of living, zero in the way of personal effects, no furniture beyond the basics, and nothing on the walls but a few rectangles, pale as scars, where maps or posters must have hung. Natasha had apparently moved in so recently that it looked like moving out. It troubled me that two conditions so opposed could appear so basically identical. But I told myself not to get too overly freaked out—I knew that one side effect of Abulinix could be some mild initial paranoia as the patient's mind began assembling its new conditions of awareness.

TEN

"Morning, Natash!" I called out to the voice murmuring a tune in the kitchen. Sleep is so nice, I thought. Otherwise things would just add up.

"We go to meet Natasha at eleven. This sounds good to you?"

Because she sounded maybe more German than Dutch I said, "Ja." I had studied some German in college—they made me.

Brigid came out to the living room in a white tee shirt and these shimmery red-green harem pants. She sat down on the arm of the couch. She had drawn two braided plaits of her hair—which was rich and glossy like freshly turned black soil—back from above the temples to where they met in a broad barrette and fell with the rest to her shoulders, something possibly done to fit with her somehow equally old-fashioned face, with the forceful and diminutive nose, the beautifully high and wide-set cheekbones, and the skin so nice it was like the little patch of acne strewn across one cheek had been put there to point up the flawlessness of the rest. She was smiling as she extended a plate of toast. "With jam of tomate de árbol. What you would call a tree tomato."

"Thank you." I ate some bites. "Hmm . . . Delicious. Not that it tastes very tomatoey."

"More like a pomegranate," she accurately observed, her voice a precise, quick instrument, whereas the look in her eyes was vague and sweetly stunned like that of a girl who's just taken off her glasses.

"Does it at least grow on trees?" I asked regarding the fruit.

"Yes," she laughed. "So it is not altogether a lie. You slept a long time. Did you have some good dreams?"

"No dreams."

"I am the same when I travel. A new country is enough of a dream, don't you think? So there is no need for dreaming when you sleep."

I chewed my toast, considering this, and between glances at Brigid looked all around the room with equal attentiveness, just so it wouldn't seem like I was particularly fixated on her face (so sharp-boned and precise, but with a pleasant suggestion of former plumpness everywhere smudging it faintly with voluptuous life) and happily analogous body. Certainly she would make a welcome addition to any threesome.

"Is there a mosquito?" she asked. "Or what are you looking at everywhere?"

Soon the two of us had walked down the hill and were scampering across the street, then waiting in some strange paved-over median—"The tram was to go here, but the government has lacked enough money"—then making the dash again. It was like some 3-D version of that early-period video game where the frog tries to hop across all these increasingly murderous lanes of traffic until he loses his life—or one of three lives.

"That felt dangerous," I said, safe in my one life on the other side.

Next we were riding the tram where it did go and hanging from the straps like you still sometimes do on the subway in New York. We were on our way to where

Natasha worked as a volunteer in this Catholic home for underresourced children whose mothers had been thrown in jail.

"Really? She never even told me. Natasha's so modest. I guess that's part of being so moral."

Brigid said that often the moms had been locked up for stealing food to feed the same kids, whereas the dads might be working off the books somewhere in Spain or America.

"Yeah, so what's the scene here, like economically?"

"I would say it is underdevelopment with also an aspect of—what would you say?—*pillage*." And as Brigid explained (I've got it down now, though it was total Greek at the time) how the oil companies spirited the crude out of Ecuador, leaving behind just a few dollars for pipeline builders and low-level managers; how the IMF made its new loans conditional on a screamingly high general sales tax; how local industry had hardly been allowed to develop, dooming the country to the mere export of unfinished goods while *a sedentary comprador class squatted atop their rentier wealth in place of even so much as a minuscule national bourgeoisie*—during this furious primer on underdevelopment, delivered like it was for fun, I noticed, glancing accidentally down the brief tunnel of her tee shirt sleeve as she swayed with the turns of the tram, that Brigid didn't shave her armpits, a beautiful negligence in my opinion, and echt Germanic.

At the same moment that in spite of her somewhat dusky appearance I asked Brigid whether she might be German, she said, "So you are a philosopher?"

I laughed and said no, and she frowned and said, "How could you think so? Mostly I am from Belgium."

"Belgium!" When you have the good fortune of meeting a nice Belgian girl it really becomes necessary to con-

front her as a complex and unique being unlike any
other in the world, because at least in my case you have
no national stereotypes to understand her by. Or was
Belgium sort of like Canada to America's France, so that
an indefinable air of comedy clung to its existence and
its residents were noted mainly as bland and amenable
drinkers of beer? "Sorry. I'm not an ace with the ac-
cents."

"But do you like Germans?"

"Well, you know, their philosophers more than for
example . . . the *Nazis*."

Her dubious expression, as we stepped off the tram,
caused me to explain that I didn't like Nazis at all. "I
don't even like George Bush very much."

She looked at me with hard, mirthful eyes, and smiled
as she shook her head.

The streets were nearly deserted except for some
scurrying stray dogs, the ventral sides of the lady dogs
lined with swollen teats. We passed through an empty
square flanked by palm trees, a surprise to me at whatever high altitude we were at—and looking up into the
air I also saw this enormous winged statue crowning a
steep green hill like a hood ornament atop some fero-
cious engine's grille. "What is that?" I asked. "An angel
I guess?"

"Mary." And this was another surprise, because in
being dragged as a kid through all these European cultural museums, to the point where eventually I'd really
had enough of the Holy Family, and was even somewhat
tired of my own, I had also naturally encountered plenty
of paintings of the Annunciation—but here for the first
time it seemed like the announcing angel and the Virgin
had got confounded into one. Probably it was some Ecuadori heresy they had.

We turned up a narrow street running between signless bread-colored buildings. Burdened women were moving slowly by, and as we maneuvered through the solemn bustling crowd the air was thick with smells of smoke, fuel, waste, and meat. Before long a nun in her wimple had let us in through a metal door set in a wall of scarred plaster bearing the graffito ¡No al Plan Colombia! and immediately she and Brigid began discoursing in Spanish in this rapid worried way.

I just stood there like a cigar-store Indian until Brigid said, "Let me introduce you to the children."

"Cool. Where's Natasha?"

She ignored the question, shouting to the kids something in Spanish which included my name, and right away I became this virtual Santa Claus: all these beautiful Andean children, with their enormous smiles, a tooth or two short, suspended between high cheekbones, ran up to me, buffeting me with hugs as I waded through their ranks. Two brave little girls climbed up either arm to kiss me on the cheeks, one calling me guapo, evidently a term of praise. "Mucho gusto," was all I could think to say, an inadequate-sounding phrase when it seems you have hit by accident the basic human jackpot of love. I was really, really happy and wished I had candy or pens to distribute. Instead I just sat on a wooden bench giving and receiving hugs, and handing out from my wallet, as my only gifts, two quarters, three dimes, eight pennies, a nickel, a library card, several ticket stubs, and the business cards of acquaintances, friends, a drug dealer, and two unaffordable shrinks. I smiled with beatific incomprehension at all remarks made to me while the surrounding kids pointed, commented and laughed like I was some exotic friendly animal introduced into their midst. My delight in their response, and the fear that soon I would become boring to them, because simpering and unable to speak, competed so poignantly in my heart that I had one of my more emotional experiences since graduating from Eureka Valley and marching around to "Pomp and Circumstance," and felt I might cry.

I wondered if right then at the back of my mind I was deciding to one day have children—many, many children. With Natasha!

Brigid canceled my reverie: "Natasha has vanished." For some reason this absurd news caused me to stand up and smile apologetically at the nun, as if disappearing was something people like Natasha and me were likely to do. My awful immediate fear was that in crossing the street she had lost a game of human Frogger, and was now in the hospital—or worse, the morgue.

I shook the kids off, and turned from them waving goodbye.

Brigid had handed me an envelope with my name written across it in a script I recognized from notes slid under my door long ago at St. Jerome's.

"She wrote to the sisters also. And there is one for me as well."

But how would I ever get to know her after her suicide? Suicide—such an extravagant thing to do! Yet at the same time so discreet! I could barely unfold the letter for my shaking hands:

My Very Dear Dwight,
　　I'm afraid you will think I have played an awful trick on you. You'll think I am not the friend you knew if I have lured you to Quito and then abandoned you [If you WHAT?]. Abandonment isn't really the word, but still I am extremely sorry. Let me try to explain.
　　When I said you should come I assumed you were busy in New York and never imagined you would ac-

tually jump on a plane. So it wasn't really a question of my wanting you to or not. It was only that I was having a bad time here and wanted to convince myself otherwise, as if to say, "Come visit me in my wonderful life." And you have a very calming benevolent presence [Not me! You!] *so perhaps I also simply liked to* underline*imagine* your visiting.

I may even have become afraid of your visit because you are so well adjusted to everything [No!], *and I was afraid I would envy you, and maybe be angry at you for that. Things would have been hard, obviously through no fault of your own. Until yesterday I thought I might be okay. That's my excuse for not warning you. In fact I am writing this letter only* underline*in case*. *You arrive tonight. But I have a flight scheduled—I may or may not cancel* [She's worse than me! We should be together!]*—and if you are reading this I am on it.*

I turned to Brigid. "This isn't happening."

She looked guiltily useless. And not all that distressed. And not like Natasha! Not like Natasha at all!

Brigid is great and it's good that you two should meet. [Thanks.] *I have sung your praises to her.* [Thanks a lot, you fucking jilter—] *Hopefully you* [—you Joker—] *want to travel with her* [—you deserter, you Dutch treat, you—]. *If not and you go directly back* underline*please* underline*please* *let me pay for your ticket.* [—you casual crusher of long-standing hopes!] *I have plenty of money, because I am going home to my parents (no rent), and nothing here has cost very much. Ecuador is a very affordable country, as well as beautiful.*

"Are you a very slow reader?" Brigid asked.

When I see you again I want to be your old Natasha.

and she'd signed the thing with just her initial.

I looked up. "How long to the airport?"

"But this too is a free country. What can we say? 'Please suffer your crisis here with us'?"

"That's right. We'll offer some thoughtful advice. Clearly this was a very dash rescission." I meant a rash decision. "We have to go to the airport now!" I was being so decisive—I must finally know what I want—and just as it, just as *she,* was leaving . . .

Brigid seemed to be deciding something herself. Then calmly she said, "It is not even legal here."

To go to the airport? But I'd bought a return ticket! What kind of a country was this anyway? I paused and waited for clarification. Finally I had to say, "What? *What* is illegal here?"

Brigid scowled, put her finger to her lips, and glanced over at the grave sweet-looking nun. She walked off, sat down on a pale stone step, and waited for me to do the same. This seemed to mean giving up, and I could hardly do it. I looked down and saw that the trampling of childish feet had worn a shallow basin in the stone. It seemed like a pretty hard thing, asking me to give up what I hadn't even had. Still I commanded myself to sit, like I was my own dog—so then I sat down.

"Ecuador, you can see, is very Catholic. Abortion is prohibited here." My face must have confessed how I still didn't get it. "Maybe Natasha does not say this in the letter for you? Oh I am more blunt than our friend."

In the courtyard the kids were singing to the point of shouting, goaded on toward joyful madness by a woozy accordion.

"I think there is nothing for us to do."

She stood up and I followed suit, brushing off my seat—excessively. It was a gesture that made sense, so I overdid it. And then we were walking out the door, into the future, and I was saying "Gracias" to the nun, who blessed me with the sign of the cross—I blessed her right back—while Brigid was just like, "Adios."

Outside on the jostling crowded street I said, "So when'd she learn she was . . . ? And do you have any idea who the dude is?"

"Who who is?"

"The man," I said as some stranger bumped against me. "The inseminator!"

"I don't know these things."

I figured it would be impolite to ask to see Brigid's letter. But I wasn't going to be overpolite. "So who *are* you anyway?"

In a tone of strange flirtatious courtesy, like this was some sort of cocktail party gambit on my part, she said, "And who are *you*?"

"Yeah yeah yeah. But how do you know Natasha?"

"I am—or I *was* here to work on my thesis. But now, since two weeks ago—"

"And are you at all related?"

"Pardon me?"

"Do you and Natasha have any, like, recent common ancestors?"

She shook her head no. I asked her how long they'd known each other. Three months, came the shrugging answer. At last in exasperation I was like, "I don't even know your last name!"

"But I have learned yours. Wilmerding, no?"

It was like she deliberately mispronounced it. "It's not Vilmerding. We're not Viking." I shook my head. "None of this makes sense."

"Well. Amid this plentiful nonsense"—she kept up a slight, determined smile—"I am Brigid Lerman."

"Enchanté," I said sarcastically.

"Wait a moment." Literally she put her foot down, lightly stamping twice. "Natasha abscondating is not a fault of mine. Okay? Maybe complain to her about it—not to me."

She headed back down the street, and I followed after her toward the actually existing tram, as opposed to the one the Ecuadoris couldn't afford. Why, again, had I traveled to this shitty little godforsaken country of orphaned papists who couldn't afford another tram? I lagged behind Brigid feeling crestfallen, would be the word, that Natasha had abscondated. To have staked my heart on her would seem to have been a mistake. She was so confused herself, not to mention pregnant. Yet it also might be—or might *have* been!—that if you took two confusions and fused them, then the dialectical result would be a kind of lucid understanding otherwise unavailable to either party. . . .

Brigid and I stood waiting for the tram as a silent pinpoint drizzle materialized out of the air.

"I am sorry," she said. "You liked her very much."

I looked around and took in the dilapidated mudbrick buildings, the guilty-looking bedraggled mutts, the teenager in a soccer jersey carrying home some firewood, the palm trees with their shivering fronds—all in all, a much colder town than it appeared, like they'd shipped a Mexican town to Scotland by mistake. "What am I doing here?"

To indicate that this was my affair she made one of those *bof* sounds possibly common throughout the Francophone world.

I was blinking a lot and feeling dizzy.

"But still do you want to go to Cuncalbamba, Dwight Wilmerding?" (pronounced correctly). "I am indifferent. But I am free."

"Let me think." I continued thinking, or at least blinking.

"And this takes a long time?"

I glared at her.

"I am sorry," she said again. "You may think. Natasha says that you really *are* a philosopher."

"But doesn't this surprise you? The whole Natasha taking-off thing? Because you don't seem all that surprised. Or concerned. I mean, I'm pro-choice and all, but still, an abortion . . ."

"Oh she will be all right. Natasha is quite tough, don't you think so? And I suppose I am less than fully in sympathy because—because she is not a very constant sort of person, do you find? To leave us without warning . . ."

I was still feeling dizzy. Maybe I should have eaten more than just the one piece of toast.

"So I am surprised, yes," Brigid said. "But also not surprised. You can see?"

"*Totally.*" Except I didn't know if Brigid's familiarity-of-the-strange idea was meant to characterize a) Natasha, b) the world, and/or c) her own cast of mind. Still, one way to get on a good footing with people is to agree with them without knowing what you are agreeing to, and from there the rest should follow, or proceed. "So you're still cool with going to—"

"Perfectly cool." She shrugged with one shoulder. "I am free."

The tram picked up more and more passengers at each station until it became so extremely crowded that when the doors opened people yelled out to the hopeful faces on the platform, "No hay donde! No hay donde!" Even I got in on the action, once informed what I was saying. Then somewhere in Quito we stopped, and stayed stopped. The stillness of the car, combined with the rap-

idly changing circumstances of my trip, made for a
weird sensation. Then a loud kind of pluckily mourn-
ful song came on flecked with static over the speakers
above us, and everybody, very much including Brigid,
chimed in with the wailing female chanteuse. The passengers sang the song through twice, all mouths in concert,
wailing with happy expressions until the trip resumed.
Such a musical people, the Ecuadoris! I felt left out along
with the crying infants and sullen old men and wished to
learn right away this apparently national song. And when
Brigid and I were able at last to squeeze out through the
pressed bodies and raised-up arms into the thin cool air
of drizzling Quito, I requested a translation.

"The chorus? A love—that is deceiving me. My
heart . . . is in your hands."

"My heart is in your hands."

"I despair but lack for the courage to . . ."

I waited. "To *what*?"

"To leave you. My love."

"But that's so sad. And they all seemed so happy."

"Poor country, happy music—a correlation all over
the world. Have you been to India? But no more . . ."
She waved the noun away. "I should remember I have
abandoned my dissertation."

"Was your dissertation set in Quito?"

Standing hugging herself against the cold with goose-
flesh on her arms, she said, "Set? No, it more concerned
the jungle. But now two weeks ago I gave it up." Uncon-
vincingly she shrugged. Then smiled: "So I too have no
reason to be here."

We laughed and walked off rehearsing the song—
"un amor que no es amor"—to Natasha's abandoned
apartment. My dread from the night before appeared to
have gone away. After all I'd decided without reserva-
tion to learn the song by heart, just as I'd suddenly de-

cided to travel around the country with Brigid the foreign stranger, and in this second decision I was so blissfully free of even the most rational misgivings that I suspected the Abulinix must already be flooding my system and lighting it up.

ELEVEN

We were sitting pressed together on a torn vinyl seat, knees up high like overgrown kids, when the dirty diesel engine sputtered up at last; and yet even with the bus turning out onto the road, all these ragged entrepreneurial dudes still kept on boarding with sweet and savory things to sell, and bottled water.

"Here we have the great question of travel in Ecuador," my new friend Brigid was saying. "Does one prefer intense thirst or else the persistence over many hours of the need to urinate?"

Our ETA in the town of Baños was six hours away. So instead of H_2O I just purchased these soft fleshy beans bathed in clear liquid in a plastic sack. The beans looked appetizing and tasted that way too, salty, squishy, and with a definite tang of je ne sais quoi. "What are these things I'm eating?" I asked as we watched the last of the vendors scramble down the aisle, hop off the bus—which had by then attained a serious speed—and stumble headlong on the roadside, nearly biting the dust.

"I do not know, Dwight."

"Well they're excellent." With a pinching of the fingers I squirted the beans, or at least they *seemed* very fabaceous to me, into my mouth one by one. Our plan, excitingly pointless in the way of modern or postmodern travel, was to stay in Baños tonight; head to famous

Cuncalbamba with its ideal climate in the morning; and then wind up drinking rum-based cocktails on the dazzling Pacific coast, an aspect of the plan which in fact we never realized. "Baños . . ." I said. "Sounds like baths almost."

"Baños *is* baths—the word is the same."

"So I'm one for one so far. All right. Sure you don't want one of these—?" She shook her head. But even if she didn't know what I was eating, and very happily chewing, and kind of rationing a little, because they were so, so good, and how would I ever ask for them again, not knowing the name?—otherwise Brigid was this fount of knowledge and total information awareness. We paid for everything in dollars—right, *American* dollars, the familiar dirty presence of which only made the novelty of everything else that much sharper—and this, she explained, was because the government had wanted to halt the hyperinflation of the sucre, the venerable currency named after one of Bolívar's best officers, who had defeated the Spanish and secured Ecuador's independence in 1822 at the Battle of Pichincha, Pichincha being a mountain we were about to pass as we descended in this crowded rattletrap bus through "the avenue of volcanoes," as the great traveler Humboldt (whose fame never reached me) had called it. And the tall pale spotted trees with their waving islands of broad leaves? "Eucalyptus." And the men's felt hats that the Indian women in their rainbow-colored shawls wore tilted above their sharp handsome faces? "A porkpie hat, I think is the word."

"Damn Brigid I listen to you and I feel like what was I thinking, studying philosophy? I wish I could have studied just the facts."

"I have met many Americans, but you are the first who is what I always imagine a *true* American is like."

"Really? That's funny." I couldn't tell if I was being defensive or playful. "Because I'd been thinking how totally Belgian *you* are. Belgian as frites."

"As what is?" She laughed in this sharp way of hers that seemed to separate the comedy of laughter from the charity part.

"I think you heard me," I said.

"So . . . Do I seem to you a Walloon? Or a Fleming?"

"Yeah well just very *pan*-Belgian is how you seem—with your love of neat distinctions and precise terminology."

"You make me very impressed with myself! Because I am not born in Belgium."

"Oh." Nothing was seeming to be what it seemed today. Moodily I ate another so-called bean.

"Maybe I should have told you this. Only my mother is Belgian. Papa comes from Argentina, this is where we lived until I was five. I *was* Brígida until in Belgium they removed the letter and of course changed how to say it. However," she said with a certain residual air of defiance, "I would not allow them to spell me as *Brigitte.*"

"So you're half Belgian. Maybe you overcompensate and that's why you seem so Belgian."

"Not to the Belgians! Who care more about the family lineage than anyone. Every year the book on the aristocracy, *Le Bottin Mondain,* it sells very well. Bof—Belgium. You know the Belgian delicacy, les petites crevettes grises? So this is what my father calls the Belgians: the little gray shrimps. No Belgian I know is the least bit wild."

"And yet you seem so sort of proud—"

"Really it is of Argentina that I'm proud. And yet I have hardly a memory of Buenos Aires, so to me it comes to seem almost that I am merely pretending to be from another country, almost that I am being pretentious to feel that I am so unique a Belgian."

I told Brigid she seemed like a pretty complicated person.

"Really I am extremely simple in my—my . . ." She gestured vaguely at herself.

"Dans ta coeur?" I suggested. "Dans ton tête?"

She looked puzzled for a second, then said, "Somewhere, yes, I am a deeply simple person."

Somehow this tantalizing admission was the cue for us both to stop talking and look out the window, watching the world, or really the third world, pass by. Pale faces gigantic on a billboard looked down on the encampment of tin-roofed roadside shacks while on a dusty street two kids were passing a bald gray soccer ball universally between them. And beyond the scattered human stuff stood a green volcano terraced and planted with corn at the base and topped up above by a blank toupee of snow.

The bus stopped in Latacunga, where, feeling superthirsty, and with the idea that moisture must be good for a fluid decision-making style and a pro-growth mind, I bought a liter of water. And so all the way to Baños my bladder acquired a very stoical temperament. Plus I knew my suffering must be scandalously mild compared to being tortured and disappeared by a fascist regime, as luckily hadn't happened to Brigid's dad when the generals took over Argentina and he fled with his shrink-cum-wife.

Brigid looked at me as I took a last swig of water. "You will burst."

"Burst, shmurst." I offered her the lees. "Hey"—something had occurred to me—"are you Jewish?" She congratulated me on finally a correct guess (dad being half Jewish), and I asked her what it had been like being such a double foreigner in Belgium as a kid.

"I don't know really—I find it impossible, in a way, even to think—"

"Right," I said. "It's too close to home."

"To think about home? Yes it is."

Looking out the window, I commented that the Andes didn't look like the other mountains of my experience. "Jagged. Yet soft."

"Good way to put it."

"Hey where did you learn English, by the way?"

"In fact I was studying for three years in New York."

"Really? I wonder if maybe we passed each other on the street one day." I looked at her and doubted it.

"No," she said firmly.

"Yeah but you didn't know I was me then. So you weren't looking. You know, my sister's also an anthropologist and she teaches in New York, at the New School."

"Not really? Another anthropologist?"

"Yeah, Alice, Alice Wilmerding. I even have her book with me."

"You see—there are too many of us. Good that I quit, no?"

From my day pack I fished out *Consumer Survivalism*, n+1 Books, $18.95, paper. "I think the idea is how people buy more things than they could ever actually *use* in order to like secretly convince themselves that they'll live some absurdly long time. Like long enough to actually use all the stuff they buy."

"Not a problem in Ecuador."

"No yeah it's more about American garage-filling culture. See, in her appendix there are these inventories of select American garages that she prints side by side with—look—with all these actuarial tables. She says it proves dad hasn't read the book because he never complained about—see—that's a picture of his garage. She's like, 'That's another thing'—because everything always proves everything with Alice—but she's like, 'That's another thing, people like to accumulate big trophy books they'll never get to.' But I'm like, 'Dad reads *everything*, Al.' And she says, 'Except what *I* write.' So we're sort of at an impasse. In lots of ways actually."

"You don't share your sister's politics?"

"I don't know. Haven't finished the book yet. My opinion is that good books, just like bad ones—don't you think they're better if they're short?"

Life was short, I was thinking, a thought not original with me. But it got a fresh context as the bus hung and turned on a precipitous mountain curve. And looking outside I saw a clutch of Ecuadorians (as it turned out they were more officially called) peering from the road-side down a steep green escarpment to where some car or bus must have plunged.

"Yikes," I said to Brigid. She looked unsurprised. Or else it was just that she was a serious person, and there-fore a little sad and unsurprisable. Because the thing was that when her ready smile stopped, it stopped abso-lutely, with no leftover glee—and then all you had then was an impression of her close-kept sense of her own significance, which she seemed to carry somewhere hid-den on her person like diplomatic papers. The question was: did I enjoy her company, and what did I want with it? I had little to no clue, and this made me wonder whether I'd been mistaken in thinking the drug was working.

Arriving in Baños at dusk I dashed into the HOMBRES room of the bus station and stood pissing into the reek-ing urinal with fantastic mightiness. It did me a lot of good, releasing the suffering contents of my bladder. And as my pain gave way to half-happiness I thought of how I loved to piss, and in fact to sneeze, to shit, to re-move wax from my ears or snot from my nose, to ejacu-late or to spit, and even when sick to vomit—anything at all along those lines. I might never become a wise and decisive person, but at least an entire lifetime of excretion and other removals remained before me, and faced with the prospect of such cost-free, morally neutral, and abundantly available pleasure, how could I ever regret my disgusting life on earth? I am the poison that is in me, I thought, and I love getting rid of it!

"You are relieved?" Brigid asked outside on the street.

"I feel like a million bucks."

"That will buy you a lot in Ecuador. For now we look for a fifteen-dollar pensión." So we did, though my gaze kept lifting from the street to where on the far side of town a waterfall poured from the lush darkening mountainside, the spout so white it seemed to light itself by friction from within. Stars were coming out higher up, as well as the sound of insects all around.

Brigid told the stout hatchet-faced woman at the desk that we'd like a habitación matrimonial—a presumption that might indicate thrift, affection, we're-in-this-togetherness, who knew. It could be prelude to a seduction or a peremptory announcement that our relationship was to be deromanticized right away by the sharing of a toilet. Not to mention that Brigid too was a live and free creature who wouldn't necessarily know these things herself. Maybe I was going to get lucky, something which, I reminded myself, following her up the stairs to our room and giving her ass a good review, wasn't always a piece of unmixed luck, and shouldn't automatically be hoped for any more than feared. Did any of the world religions, in some of their sects, recommend the perfection of ambivalence as a spiritual course whereby the novice ensures that he'll never be completely disappointed even as he also disqualifies himself from any true satisfaction? I wondered this.

"Doesn't seem very matrimonial," I said about the

dingy yellow-painted room with bunk bed and single bare overhead bulb.

"No—they had no more left."

Brigid dragged her backpack into the bathroom. A grunt and a sound of wrestling ensued, and when she came back out she'd put on lipstick and eyeliner and a wrinkled beige dress. I wondered whether this was typical of Belgian backpackers in Latin America.

We went out together in the new dark and chose at Brigid's suggestion an Italian restaurant where we drank bad wine and ate pasta that was more like Play-Doh made from cornmeal and subjected to marinara sauce. "I am so sorry," she laughed. "It is like a copy of Italy after many many times through the machine."

I asked her if she had ever played the game of telephone, in which a whispered message circulates from ear to ear accumulating distortions as it goes.

She shook her head gamely. "But I will try."

"No. See there's only two of us. So we wouldn't be able to get enough distortion into our communication." I took another sip of the bad, effective wine that was like a libel against the whole Chianti region. "We're condemned to understand each other."

"Okay. Too bad." Then she smiled with a pleasant faux wickedness not displayed before all day. I could really see why alcohol is so heavily used in Western civilization.

But all we did later on was climb up to the gazebo-y or belvedere-ish half-enclosed room atop the pensión, and play three games of Connect Four. I got routed in the first two, but the last one I won. And then I felt so high on benevolent novelty that I declined a fourth game and went out by myself, making last call at one of those emailerías cropping up wherever backpackers go. After using primitive universal sign language to explain my desires to the proprietor, I was able to write Natasha:

FROM: wilmerdingansich@mail.fignet.com
TO: natasha@arenquerojo.ne
SUBJECT: Hola

Dear Natash, in a rush. Don't worry about anything
and do what you need to (the universal law). I
hope you are okay in terms of whatever crisis or
procedure or experience you may be undergoing.
All's cool down here. Like Ecuador a lot and enjoy
Brigid as well who is less sold on me. What did
you *say* to her? Just kidding. In Banyos. Nice
town—waterfall! Important thing: I love you.

I had never said this last thing to her before and didn't
mean it in any binding sense. But in light of the morning's whole Santa Claus–esque experience, plus being a
little drunk, I wanted to strew kindnesses throughout
the world. Sharply, strangely happy was how I felt (also
patient, restless, and free) as I strolled back from the
emailería along blue dusty streets, under the nearby rising moon.

However as soon as I returned to our room I had to
confront the problem of happiness's nontransmissibility—
from which I imagine very happy people must really suffer terribly. Because there was Brigid stumbling back as
she opened the door for me, and looking more or less
miserable with her lipstick smudged and the mascara
having run beneath her eyes.

"You wish Natasha were here. So do I!" She sat down
hard on her bunk.

I tried to console her for her loss. "No, it does suck.
Because Natasha's just so great."

"I know it."

"A fine woman," I said, although the whole concept
of Natasha had come to seem a little vague. "So don't
think I'm not commiserating."

"It's a disappointment without her."

"That's right." I wanted to emphasize this in order to seem to be paying less attention, or attention of a less lecherous kind, to Brigid herself in her shorts and little nighttime camisole. Next to the camisole, and presumably underneath it—except at the nipples, which would naturally be darker, though there was no predicting their size, much less their responsivity—Brigid had this nice pale olive skin that seemed touched with some old nostalgia for the sun. It was such nice skin that I looked away, and climbed up to my bunk. "Tomorrow Cuncalbamba?" I said.

She sighed. "Tomorrow again the bus."

TWELVE

We hoisted and donned our backpacks and set out toward the station. Glare rose off the dusty streets like dirt from a beaten rug, and there among the mountain-humbled buildings I seemed to feel purposefulness and good cheer bubbling up in me. Brigid however was still seeming a little sullen, possibly because she was still disappointed that I wasn't Natasha, or possibly even because she thought *I* was disappointed that *she* wasn't.

I was on the verge of trying to clear the issue up when a small powerfully-built teak-colored man wearing glasses, tiny running shorts, and one tall rubber boot, ran out of one of the dim shops along the main drag yelling "Brígida, Brígida!" like it was Eureka! Eureka!

Alarm changed to surprise on her face, and then delight, with maybe a taint of pity too, as Brigid shook off her pack and braced herself for the impact of this scrambling bowlegged man. They joined in a sort of two person huddle, demonstrating the strange custom of presumably some culture or other as they clasped shoulders and leaned their foreheads together. They talked for a minute excitedly in Spanish, then Brigid shoved the guy in my direction. He wore his black hair in a bowl cut that made you think of boys sent off to school, and had something shy and undefended in his broad-nosed face. Still he walked up to me with his hand struck out and introduced himself—that much I could tell—as Edwin.

"Estoy Dwight Wilmerding," I ventured. "Me han robado."

Perhaps the phrase book had betrayed me? Because Edwin looked confused. But Brigid was looking more perplexed by Edwin than by me. "His name is not Edwin."

"Sí," the man said to me in apparent agreement. "Me llamo Edwin."

I nodded my head at both Brigid/Brígida and Edwin/not-Edwin and left them to work it out. Brigid emerged from a short parley with the following somewhat frowning report: "All right, now he is Edwin." Apparently he'd been Dica back when she'd begun living with and studying his tiny forest-dwelling clan on and off in the Oriente.

"Huh? Which clan? In the where?"

"*Oriente* means east, the jungle, the Amazon." And apparently it was Edwin's clan that she'd spent the last four months with—whereas Edwin hadn't seen them at all in the year and a half since they'd moved further downriver and he'd left to make his living as a jungle guide. "And I have not seen Dica—or rather, I suppose, Edwin—"

"And why the switch?"

"He says he wanted a cannibal name."

I nodded at Edwin as if to confirm the reasonableness of this desire.

"Cannibal is what they call everyone who is not a Haponi."

"They're all vegetarians? The . . . Haponi people? Of the Oriente?"

She laughed. "No, they eat quite a lot of monkeys, capybaras, peccaries, tapirs, all these things."

At least I knew what monkeys were. "They eat monkeys and call us cannibals? Monkeys basically *are* humans. Look how hairy I am."

"I have noticed," Brigid said with heartbreaking neutrality.

"We're not cannibals. Exactly. All we want is to look nice and have cheap sources of energy. What are we?"

Meanwhile Edwin was shaking my hand a second time and telling me things in Spanish which seemed to include the words *hombre afortunado*.

"Huh?"

"He is congratulating you." She was laughing. "He is saying that the Oriente is excellent for a honeymoon!" She resumed talking to Edwin, who sent a look of sincere consolation my way. "I told him we are not so much as engaged, we have only just met." Then changeable Brigid went serious again in her mobile-featured face: "He is saying he has a fiancée in town nearby and he guides the tours to make enough money to marry her."

Edwin looked at me in this way that basically conveyed the pathos of his situation.

"He doesn't make enough. He is not a good salesman."

But it seemed untrue. Because now Edwin was addressing directly to me an admirably fervent pitch of some kind, and whatever it might be, he sounded so convinced—and convincing! "What's he saying?"

She seemed reluctant to translate, but I insisted.

"He wants us to go with him." She looked off to one side as if to appeal to someone not there. "He is telling you that five days are enough to go deeply. But—" She evidently began to break the news in Spanish that we were going on to Cuncalbamba. I saw the hopefulness start to drain from Edwin's face.

"No," I said. "Let's do it. Let's go to the Oriente." The name had a certain ring to it (as maybe the sound *Natasha* had at one point had); moreover a Knittelian notion of the profoundness of forests had rustled through my mind. "Can't Cuncalbamba wait?"

"But Dwight, *I* have only just escaped from this jungle. I want to go someplace . . . for fun."

"The jungle's not fun?" Edwin seemed so fun—in fact, "Fun!" he was saying now, repeating this reassuring English word. Besides, I had made the important if paradoxical discovery that I was so eager for time alone with Brigid that I wanted to postpone it. For a decade or more I'd gone from girl to girl with hardly a week in between; like a chain-smoker, I'd lit one new romance off the stub of another and rarely had time to just breathe. So for now it was nice to be Vaneetha-less and single, waiting to bust a move on medium-sized, mercurial, almond-eyed, and currently somewhat reluctant-looking Brigid until convinced by longer experience of Abulinix that I should or shouldn't do this thing.

With Edwin and me applying steady peer pressure—the look involved is exactly the same across cultures—finally she said, "Okay. You have a two-thirds majority. You want fun and he wants money."

"And also," I said, like the sensitive guy I might be, "I want to understand better where you're coming from."

"I don't come from anywhere."

THIRTEEN

But now let me do a kind of movie-style montage thing covering the first two days in the jungle and suggesting, the same way that movies do, when they do this, the excitement and emotional near-unanimity of the two main characters as they caper around and change locales, because once we were definitely going (and had made Edwin a split cash payment of two hundred dollars) she like me threw herself into our surprise excursion:

Dwight swallows serious fear of spiders and in a recklessly piloted van travels with Brigid down a washed-out road opposite which more waterfalls drop in white gashes from practically phosphorescent cliffs until past military checkpoints and the flyblown frontier town of Puyo the jungle begins, Brigid there translating Edwin for Dwight and displaying her own impressive command of flora and fauna, which categories include liana vines swung from Tarzan and Jane–style, caimans hiding in the water with loglike snouts, and leaf-cutter ants filing across logs while bearing on their backs pieces of leaves like sails. First night's camp is made near water along the high jungle basin, with the silver of the sky getting polished and tarnished in the flat river going by, then a sudden rain as abruptly stops, this

strong medicinal smell or muscular balsam afterwards
pouring out from the jungle at the travelers who sit
around the camp stove covered against mosquitoes
with bandannas over their mouths, Brigid looking in
the guttering candlelight like a trade-summit anarchist,
something that along with the presence of Edwin and
perhaps the overwhelming insect sound at night serves
to muffle or delay possible sexual tension between the
two principals, with their *mixed agonist-antagonist
profiles,* who nevertheless seem to keep warming to
each other as maybe generally people do in jungles,
waking in the steamy morning to slip with Edwin in
a dugout canoe down the river flanked by broken fans
of pima bamboo and later emerging on a gray bank of
gravelly sand only to plunge back in, deeper this time,
wearing Wellington boots and DEET and hearing
howler monkeys cry like *human babies* in the fresh
warm jungle dark that gets relieved at points by bright
red scooping slippers of heliconia flower and the similar red of some horse's cock of an enormous root dripping colorless sap, and then, more dramatically, in a
sudden clearing, by a waterfall shot yellow-gold with
decaying afternoon light as it pours from this forest
wall, an excellent site for stripping to underwear—
all that Edwin wears anyway—and diving in under the
surf and hard noise. Day two ends on a lookout ridge
with the river in sight and the silhouette of distant
ragged mountains etch-a-sketched a shade darker on
the pigeon-gray darkening sky. A short walk is taken
to camp, flashlights picking out curious eyes in the
trees—spider monkeys, Edwin claims via Brigid before
surprising Dwight and Brigid both by unstrapping a
shaft of bamboo from his pack and, with a single deft
blow, sending a poison-tipped dart flying off into the
night.

"Whoa. Did he just try to kill a monkey?"

Luckily Edwin had missed. So that our tasty dinner in fact consisted of patacones (or potato pancakes filled with a strange mild cheese) and funky-smelling papaya for dessert. I'd never liked papaya much at Gray's Papaya in New York, but was liking it a lot in the jungle, and attempted to smile at Edwin in such an eloquent way as to signify this tasty fact.

He nodded his head with judicious incomprehension, and he and Brigid resumed their conversation. Another monolingual person might have felt left out. But to me as I sat on the moss-covered log in the dark there was something exciting about the traded foreign voices and the constant chirr and throb of insect noise. Besides, it was a relief not to have to do any talking myself, since what I had to say wasn't anything easily reportable: for two days now I'd been feeling like the thin end of some enormous wedge of promise was beginning to enter me, and be driven slowly home. I even permitted myself to imagine that upon my return to North America I might travel through the United States and Canada as a well-paid but unimpeachably honest lecturer on behalf of Bristol-Myers Squibb, testifying in venues large and small to the efficacy of Abulinix. "Recently I found myself in the jungles of the Amazon," my inspirational talk would begin. Of course I didn't know how it would end; but to the credit of the drug, I wasn't worried in the least.

Eventually Edwin wished Brigid and me a buenas noches and walked off into the trees. The sound of his footsteps (he walked with a deliberate, soft, flat-footed tread) and the light from his headlamp were quickly submerged in the scissory hiss of the jungle and the moonless leaf-clogged dark.

A bit confused, I asked Bridge what was up.

Undecided between amusement and something else, she said, "He wants to sleep like a Haponi."

"But he is a Haponi," I observed as we repaired to the thatched hut.

Our headlamps revealed three hammocks hanging from rough-hewn ceiling beams, dangling a few feet apart above the floor of packed dirt. I dragged our packs inside.

Brigid sat down on her hammock, half under the mosquito netting.

"May I?" I asked, sidling in and sitting down next to her on the hammock so that our shoulders and arms were jostled together (I thought of a pair of dice shaken in the hand) and our heads briefly bumped.

She switched off her headlamp, like I did mine; and in the flawless jungle dark our voices seemed to acquire new intimacy or importance.

"I think that he wants to act the part of an Indian for me. It is not even allowed in the tourist zone to hunt monkeys."

"What's the blowgun for, then?"

"For show, for us. He was never good as a hunter." It seemed that until the age of seventeen or so Edwin had grown up in an Evangelical mission where the proselytizing Christians had discouraged not only animism, polygamy, and the consumption of hallucinogenic potions, but also hunting.

"Down with the Christians!" I shook my head. "Wrong on all the issues . . ."

She went on to say that Edwin had quit the mission when his mother died and two uncles, more traditional-style livers and much deeper in the forest, had come to reclaim him. "So he was at least seventeen before he uses a dart gun."

"And so is this why he left them, because he's not such a good hunter?"

She seemed a bit weary of recounting the situation: "You see, after the oil spill—very near here, by the way—there was such anger at the government, at the oil company, really at the modern world of this moment, that when this group of Haponi moved down the river they didn't want to traffic with this world anymore, not at all. So Edwin with his Spanish, whose role was to go to Puyo to trade—I suppose now he doesn't feel very useful. Also he has met this woman on the bus. In fact this was the topic of my dissertation—"

"Bus-induced romance?" Does anyone really want to hear the topic of someone's dissertation?

"If you want to know, my topic was the emergence among some of the Haponi of what you could call an *indigenous absolutism*. Where now they want to live absolutely in the former style. In fact it is not anymore the ones who are untouched by the market, the West, et cetera who live like an idea of the savage. Now it is those who *have* been touched, and some of course retreat, refuse, recoil—they become very deliberate about being indigenous. Even if they have forgotten."

"And Edwin thinks you want him to be more of an old-school Haponi?"

From a slight displacement of her shoulder I could tell when she nodded. "Naturally we are taught not to romanticize about cultures that we can't understand, not to speak for them—this is why your sister is studying America: that is the fashion now, to study oneself—but yes, of course I romanticize. And I think other anthropologists are also the same. They are all hoping for examples for a different life. And the Haponi *are* more spontaneous, their emotions are *not* so mixed as ours. It's not romantic, it's only true. Edwin is not a good example, but . . ."

"So in your thesis were you going to be pro–indigenous absolutism?"

"Officially neutral. Merely very ethnological. Secretly of course I was pro—but objectively I should be against this. Because ultimately they will need to accommodate. . . . To delay can only make it more difficult, no?"

"True," I noted from personal experience. "Well it does sound like interesting material. . . ."

"This was my trouble, someone else thought so too. And yet for months I am asking all the clan questions which it seems they are very familiar with somehow, and still, no, I don't see. Their answers seem all very packaged, or canned—and yet it took me several months finally to ask, 'Has another anthropologist been visiting you?' Of course yes, another anthropologist writing on precisely the same subject."

"Ouch. Redundancy. That hurts."

"And no one had divulged this at first because there was a man who wished for me to stay. For his part my admirer claimed not to understand why I should have to write something new. 'Isn't it true a second time, and as many times as anyone says it? Isn't the truth confirmed by saying it more often?' "

"Good point, actually."

"Really? Tell my advisor. Tell my committee."

"But your admirer is right. I mean, why do we need a bunch of new truths? You'd think there'd be plenty of old ones lying around unused."

"And which do you propose to use?"

I was considering kissing Brigid in lieu of a reply, when the beam of Edwin's light lanced into the hut.

He'd forgotten how long it took to thatch a structure together out of palm leaves. And a few minutes later, after an exchange of goodnights, we were all three dangling silently from the ceiling in the swinging cocoons of our separate hammocks and listening—or I was anyway—to the jungle's wet, dilated, rhythmic, chanting, serrated sound.

FOURTEEN

"So wait, again, *why* aren't you seeing anyone?"

I'd been lying there in my hammock for a while, too excited to sleep, when these words came back to me out of nowhere; and maybe this entire memoir, unbeknownst to itself, began its gestation or germination that night as I lay on my back in the dark, and remembered these words that Alice had said to me back at the end of last summer as we sea-kayaked around the bristling lower tip of Manhattan.

It had been a late summer Saturday, and we'd rented these sea kayaks like we'd been saying we would all summer. "I like preserving our self-image as athletic people," Alice had said as she fitted the nylon skirt around the sill and took her plastic paddle in hand. "How infrequently do you think we can do sports before we have to admit that we never do?"

We were paddling out around where the Hudson begins getting mixed up with the ocean when she asked me again why I wasn't seeing anyone. There were zero clouds, and the air seemed tall with clarity—it was that variety of day.

Alice's question surprised me because I thought I had just been *explaining* why. "Al, don't dad me. I just explained why."

Paddling along beside her, I had just been *explaining*

that most of what I ever did with a girlfriend was to talk,
and how when I talked to such a girlfriend there was
something unsatisfying about being the one who wound
up saying the things I invariably said. I never objected
in the same way to what I said to friends: friendship
seemed like an ideal forum for provisional conclusions
and marginal comments, and I assumed that the high
error quotient of most of these got forgiven by the fact
that I hadn't tied my friend's life to mine in a sort of
three-legged race, and wasn't therefore obliging him
to collude with my errors or to reject them, either of
which would have been painful. But when in an actual
romantico-sexual relationship I always wanted to be as
faithful and unique to the truth as to the young lady in
question, meaning that when talking to a girlfriend my
loyalty was really to the reservoir of truth left behind
uncontaminated by my words, instead of to anything I
said. This is what I'd been telling Alice, adding that in
order to actively boyfriend someone I wanted to add
love to the truth (truth which I already loved, if unre-
quitedly) rather than start with love and hope for the
eventual addition of truth.

It was the most elaborate speech I'd made since moving to New York, and Alice had seemed like she was
paying attention at the time. "When did you graduate
from college?" she'd said acidly when I was done.

"You *teach* college," I'd reminded her.

"Well so come out with the fucking 'truth' already.
Why not just say whatever you have to say to the poor
girl?"

"What poor girl?" This was several days pre-Vaneetha
and a day or two post-Nadine, utterly, totally forgotten
Nadine. "And I would but—"

"And the fact that you can't, the fact that you think
you have this special private reservoir of truth inside
you—I really don't see how this squares with your

I-agree-with-everybody-about-everything-ism. This is the one thing everybody *does* agree on. *Everybody* thinks they have their own special something inside. Only it happens to be so vague it can't be described. So everyone gets to keep their specialness all to themselves. So we all get to prefer ourselves to everyone else."

Now with my paddle I slapped a few splashes of water at Alice for her insta-forgetting of our whole conversation. "Do you still smoke weed? Because I just *explained*—"

"Not why aren't you seeing a girl. Why aren't you seeing a *shrink*? I've asked you this before. They have been known to help. Or they've been alleged to help."

"You really should meet Dan, Alice—that's what *I* keep saying." Alice and I sometimes would try to set each other up. "He's also very smart and cynical about things."

"I will have coffee with Dan if you will make an appointment with a shrink. Deal?"

I reminded her that in my capacity as an assistant communications technician subcontracted to Pfizer, I pulled down only around 26K a year and couldn't afford a psychiatrist. I didn't even have health insurance, despite what I'd told mom and dad, and whenever a cab bore down on me as I sauntered across the street I half hoped that if it landed a direct hit I would die rather than be maimed, lest our parents get cleaned out by hospital bills.

"So talk to mom and dad," Alice was saying.

"Oh that would be great therapy."

"No." She sighed deeply. "I mean about money. Ask them for money! For the shrink!"

"Oh. But no—because dad is bankrupt—"

"Formally."

"—and I'm not going to ask mom to subsidize my mental problems. Which then she'd have her suspicions of confirmed." So we just kayaked along in silence with wavelets quietly laving our bright, plastic-kazoo-like hulls.

I looked off to the glass shore of lower Manhattan. Its towers, especially the two tallest ones, were so bright and smooth that my mind seemed to squint and clutch at them without result. And the nearby water was equally dazzling, the whole lulled surface inlaid with blinding facets.

"I have an idea," Alice was saying. "*I* can play shrink. *I* could see you. We could do it twice a week. I'm serious. My schedule this semester isn't going to be that bad."

"But you're my—" I looked at her. "I don't know, Al. Some of my issues must be related to you."

"Trust me. We can deal with it. I've read tons of psychoanalysis. And I'm free—gratis."

"No way. Come and lie down on your couch? That wouldn't be just way too weird?"

"It'd be fun." She was smiling, which I liked. I always *had* liked Alice, always potentially too much. For example there was the incident which occurred one Christmas break at our old Lakeville house, when Alice gave me and a friend some acid with instructions to report back in a few hours. My friend—Ford, as it happened—soon got totally absorbed in the movie of Pink Floyd's *The Wall*—sorry, but true—with tears running down his face, refusing to be torn away. Whereas I feared absorption very much, and went to find Alice. She was sitting up reading in her four-poster bed. I wanted there not to be any evil brick wall between *us*, and since she was at that time a sex-positive individual opposed to all conventions, and had given me the acid herself, I figured she would endorse anything I thought or did while on it. Therefore I climbed onto her bed and tried to kiss her. "No, Dwight. You're very funny and smart and cute.

But I don't want to kiss you. The incest taboo is *that* strong."

"You'll lie on the couch," she was saying now, out on the water. "I'll smoke a fat cigar."

"I don't know, Al. I could imagine that for my problems to be cured by you might somehow compound them." Then again people often said that the best way out of your difficulties was to exacerbate them. *The worse, the better* was a slogan I seemed to remember Al quoting from somewhere. "At least you already know about my childhood," I allowed.

"Right. And this is typically one of the problems with analysis: how can the analyst evaluate the claims of the analysand? She has nothing to check them against. So, yes—"

"So you're saying only siblings should be each other's shrinks?"

"You have a tendency to generalize—that's another issue we'll discuss. We'll combine a cognitive approach with a more Freudian . . ."

"But aren't my issues your issues too? Something is wrong with us, Al. Clearly. I mean, the same thing—but as different for me as for you. What *is* it, do you think?"

"It's an overdetermined phenomenon. This is something we'll discuss. Part of it is that we belong to a social class and a generation where our parents live too long and remain too economically powerful."

"Is this going to be Communist therapy?"

"Neither mom nor dad shows any sign of declining, much less *dying*. Any fairy tale, the hero or heroine's parents are dead or as good as dead. Otherwise the fantasies can't come true."

"Dad drinks too much. That's declining. Mom—"

"They've been fucked up in the same way for years. They've really made a type of health out of being so fucked up."

"So should we kill them?" I asked. "And take the remaining money? Mom still has money."

"Which she gives to dad. This is also fucked up. But you love them."

"And you love *me*. That's another of our problems. We have this kind of unfulfilled incestuous—"

"Speak for yourself."

"Not that I'd ever propose actual *in*cest."

"This is about as close as you're going to get. Therapy from your sister?"

"See, you're trying to seduce me into doing it! *That's* what's fucked up."

"Unneutralized erotic transference is a common feature of the clinical situation."

"That's total malpractice, talking like that. I don't even know what that *means*."

Nevertheless we arranged for me to come by her apartment before work on weekdays. And then as if this agreement had been our destination all along, we turned around and headed back to shore. Back over Battery Park you could see a few kites with blunt rocking heads and wriggling tails straining like lost spermatozoa in the light.

"Another thing," she said. "We have to talk about this evil job you have."

"Tech support is not *evil*. It's beneath good and evil. This isn't really going to be Communist therapy, is it?"

"Beggars can't be choosers."

"That doesn't sound very progressive." And as we neared the shore I said, "What about you, Al, you seeing anyone? Like romantico-sexually? In that sense?" Alice was the one who'd coined the whole *romantico-sexual* term—the least romantic- or sexual-sounding term you could think of. But there was a labor organizer in Ft. Collins, Colorado, with whom she had, or at least *had* had, passionate IM-exchanges on apparently wide-ranging subjects. She'd even flown out to see him and come back with a roll of film proving his reasonably handsome and rugged existence. Yet last I'd checked the only framed pictures in her apartment were of mom and dad and the two dogs, and one of me.

"I miss Josh," Alice conceded. But the melancholy seemed to belong about equally to the missing him and the not-missing-him-more.

I sighed. "Dude, I miss *someone*."

FIFTEEN

Alice had opened the door dressed as herself in some seventies-ish striped silk pajama bottoms and this defunct indie band's tee shirt bearing the words MEET THE PERSON MOST RESPONSIBLE FOR YOUR SAFETY. But also she was smoking a big fat Freudian cigar. "These are hard to light," she said.

I just shook my head and went on in.

"Sit—or you can lie down—wherever you feel most comfortable. Of course I don't have the right kind of couch."

I sat down in her tan corduroy chair. "How it's going Al?"

"You can call me that instead of Dr. Wilmerding, but during our sessions we won't discuss *my* life. Or I won't anyway."

The chair was like a giant friendly person's lap and seemed too comfortable to face my torments in. I stood up and looked around. "You know how I love it here."

Dad had given Alice lots of money before losing so much of it himself, and along with this spacious prewar one-bedroom she had purchased some nice furniture and artworks, plus these soundproof double-paned windows that, hushing the city, made the dim environs with the warm lamps and the lazy fan, the plants and the green Middle Eastern rug, and then this red abstract painting that kind of throbbed in the gloom like a last mental sunset, feel like a semi-oasis somehow lodged in the metropolis. Outside you could see the sunlight just pouring it on, lighting up the surrounding walls of ocher brick and the neighbor's window box—but that was outside.

"Maybe we'll try the bedroom," I said. "A bed's kind of like a couch. But will it be revealing where I choose? Are you making notes about this?"

The little twin bed in the bedroom was covered in a pleasant and reassuringly girlish lavender bedspread. Yet directly above it was mounted the notorious, pouting *ibex* from Alice's and dad's last hunting trip. Of course I'd seen it before, but still . . . "Isn't that ibex troubling to any partners you might bring home, Al?" And it seemed like probably similarly troubling to the prospective lover—I thought as I sat down testing the bed—would be the propaganda poster from the former Eastern Germany, in which a grinning greedy capitalist, with dollar signs for pupils, reaches out from the sky to try and snatch up the smoke-belching factories of the generally pretty unappealing-looking workers' paradise, until his fingers are met by an enormous red hammer smashing down on them. The text underneath said *Unsere Antwort!* The meaning was *Our Answer!* and the feeling was of pain.

Alice sat beneath the slatted blinds in a chair upholstered in nylon like a winter parka. Blue smoke, the color of x-rays, leaked from her sarcastic mouth and got slowly riddled by undetectable air currents crumbling it away.

"I'm not going to ask you leading questions. You'll need to come up with our topics. In that way the ultimate cure, not that I expect you to believe in any such thing—but in that way the 'cure,' such as it is, will resemble the process itself. So what's on your mind, little brother?"

"Hmm. Well to start with, I do feel like I can be honest with you, Alice. That's nice. It's nice that you already know my arguably worst secret—I mean the mildly incestuous feelings that from what I've heard it usually takes a long time to uncover."

"Don't give me that—you don't *desire* me." She choked a little from unfamiliarity with being a cigar connoisseur. "The only reason you've been able to overcome the incest taboo mentally is that it's so firmly in place as an *actual* obstacle to your desire." She kind of burped and choked at once. "It's such a weak and easy fantasy for you to have, because actually you don't want it fulfilled. It's just that it's out there in the culture—it's a shoo-in for pathos and drama. It's a one-size-fits-all secret. Therefore fake. Look, the trouble is not that you and I or any siblings actually want to fuck one another. The trouble is that we don't—everything would be so easy if we did. We like each other, we know each other well, thank God we don't have to meet each other's parents. So why, then," she was asking rhetorically, "do you fantasize about me? Why—?"

"But I don't, I swear!"

Smoke ring, shrug. "The reason you have this idea is that I'm the one girl you actually got to know in the right way. It was gradual, it was inevitable—obviously we didn't have any choice in the matter. There wasn't all this deformingly distinctive and abrupt self-presentation that constitutes contemporary urban dating, where you always have to give your stunted personality the hard sell—the hooks, the slogans, the shtick. Where right away you always try to imply *Me, me, I belong to your demographic—and no one else ever will.*"

"Hey Alice, wait—"

"I mean, why do you think Nurse and Soldier are so popular with people like us?"

"You mean the band Nurse and Soldier?"

"Of course I mean the band. Go onto urge.com, look at the personals, everybody's like, 'Really into Nurse and Soldier.' That's how they describe themselves."

"But hold on—"

"Just bear with an adjunct professor for a second, would you? The characteristic feeling of Nurse and Soldier—like *I'm alone and full of dread and all I want is a tiny, tiny house to be safe in for a little while*—everyone feels that all the time. But it's a feeling you don't cop to. So when you do it's a guaranteed huge relief to find that someone else feels the same. The response is, 'Oh, you too?'—when actually all you've discovered is that this other person feels the one thing that they're bound to feel."

"Al, you listen to Nurse and Soldier. More than me I bet. You've got *bootlegs*."

"Nurse and Soldier are great. I listen to them constantly. But if I met some guy who felt the same way—meaningless. So we happen to share the basic feeling-tone of all anxious young white over-slash-undereducated people who happen to live in first-world cities? So what? And it's interesting, another thing—"

"Hey, who's the patient here? Aren't I the one supposed to have the issues?"

"Sorry. I think I feel a little high from the cigar—making me chatty." She got up and I heard the cigar sizzle out as it landed in the toilet.

When she returned she sat down with a notebook on her lap. "Ah yes, your problems . . . I bought a new journal to fill with them."

"That's a big journal. Is that a three-section notebook?"

She didn't reply. She looked at me inquisitively.

"All right, my problems . . ." But pretty soon I'd just been lying there with my eyes closed for several minutes thinking ineffectually about a whole host of issues each of which seemed indistinguishable from the others. Finally I said, "Mom and dad would think we were *so* crazy doing this."

In totally therapeutic tones she was like, "Do you often consider what your parents will think?"

"Um . . . No. But on the other hand I bet I'm aware at the back of my mind of a constant guilt owing to this failure to think about what they're thinking. Yeah . . . I think that's true. But also I feel like I'm just waiting for the big denunciation to come from them before I deal with it. Yeah. It kind of feels like nothing's happened yet in terms of parental judgment. Also—and I don't know if this is relevant but—"

"Go ahead, free-associate, that's the idea. More or less discredited, but still . . ."

"Okay, you know how I just said it feels like nothing's really happened so far? All right and then you have this poster from when Eastern Germany still existed—so that was a big deal, right? The Wall came down, whole world changed, now we're not going to die in a nuclear holocaust anymore. But it didn't really *feel* like anything happening—not to me. I feel like I have a certain resistance to events. They don't always seem to happen, even when they do."

"Well . . ."

"I know what you're saying, current events don't seem like they happen to anyone. But I mean also personal events. Mom and dad get divorced, I enter into romantico-sexual relationships, I get one job and then another, and yet—"

"We do have to talk about your job."

"No don't make me think about work when I'll actually *be* there in"—I looked at my watch—"in like half an hour. Wow. Psychoanalysis goes so quickly. No wonder it takes so long. But what I'm saying, Al, before I go, as the attempted major revelation of this particular session, is how I feel like I'm *event-proof*. That's one idea for a major problem I must have."

"I think I understand." And speaking in her authoritative professorial voice, she sounded like she really did. "Think about it, Dwight. Think about the Cold War, think about—"

"Free association alert! I just got one. Cold War equals mom and dad's marriage. Rival superpowers, mutually assured destruction, clashing policies . . . What do you think? Ah, I never free-associated before!" I started snapping my fingers, free-associating like crazy. "Cold war mom and dad day after golden pond olympic gold nostradamus HBO red dawn U2 . . ." I snapped my fingers three times, but no more associations came. "Fuck! It's not working. In fact when I do mom-and-dad all I really picture is mom. I don't even get dad so much. Damn. It was working so well."

"It's all right, we have enough for now. Think about the Cold War—as I was saying. Remember that during certain would-be formative years you and I both imagined that full-scale Armageddon might not be too far off. And therefore that—"

"But not me. I never thought it would happen. I think I thought people may not be very nice, but still, nuclear war? I think I figured even the Russians don't suck that much. Or then again if a few of them maybe drank too much vodka one night, down in one of those silos . . ."

"Right. So you acknowledge there was a serious question of whether we'd live to see twenty-five. Remember adults would ask us about what we wanted to be when we grew up? And didn't you always feel like you were humoring them, no matter what you said? And then," Alice went on, "how it came as a shock to discover midway through prep school, with the Wall coming down, that there really *was* something to prepare for after all. Yet you had no plans for adult life—none. We could never imagine growing up because the future could always be cancelled at any time. So beyond a certain narrow time frame our desires ran into a kind of horizon and had to stop. There was *no such thing* as the long term."

"Interesting . . ."

"And now, Dwight, now your desires have to find a place in a world which you never imagined you would live to see."

"They knew what they were doing when they made you an adjunct professor, didn't they? I'm impressed."

"So why do you sound sarcastic then?"

"Do I really? I don't know." I really didn't. And *did* I sound sarcastic or did she just hear it that way? Already I could feel the psychoanalytic situation sucking me into the whole mirror mirrors mirror problem, the bad infinity thing. "I love you, Al," I said because it was so bedrock true.

"But I want you to think about something. What institution also came to an end that, as you say, you happen to associate with mutually assured destruction?"

"I don't know. Destruction death grateful dead cosby show family ties summer vacation . . . Nah, not working."

"You doofus! *Mom and dad*—it's what you said yourself. That's what ended too, along with the Cold War. Ten years later. And you never once expected it." Suddenly her eyes filmed with tears. "And now," she said, voice cracking, "now . . ."

"Alice. Hey. Hey there." I nearly got up to hug her, before the patient-client relationship reasserted itself and I resumed my reclining position.

"I'm fine," she said. "They never belonged together

anyway. It's better. I'm fine. I even wish she still liked Dr. Hajar. *I* liked him." She sniffled. "He was funny." Alice was kind of abstractedly looking at nothing. Then she recovered. "Do you feel this helps at all, talking like this, Dwight?"

I reflected. "It's interesting. So that helps. I feel that anything that's interesting helps a great deal. And I come back tomorrow, right? So—"

She wore a look of misgiving as she stood up to see me out. "What would you think about coming in only twice a week? I'm sorry. Four times a week might get kind of intense."

"Sure, two's a good number, good even number. I hope you're okay, Al. About mom and dad. It doesn't really bother *me*, you know. People should probably get divorced more often. Then they wouldn't bother each other for so long. You know, more abortion, more divorce."

Alice had been arrested at the 2000 Republican Convention in Philadelphia, where in addition to other First Amendment crimes she had formed part of this large group chanting "More abortion! More divorce!" at the passing conventioneers. She'd ended up spending a night in jail without access to a lawyer or a bathroom.

"More toilet breaks!" she was saying now. "Which is a serious political problem, you know. Work in a maquila in Mexico, work in some EPZ in Vietnam, not enough toilet breaks."

"I'll look into it." I glanced at my fancy parental graduation-gift watch which ran on my own motion, so that you hardly had to wind it: "I've got work in five minutes."

"Till Wednesday," she said standing in her doorjamb. "In the meantime I want you to think about something else. I want you to think about what it's like for you to live in a consumer society in which tiny portions of desire are constantly being solicited from you and frittered away so that you can never save up enough passion to spend on any one thing."

"When am I not going to live in a consumer society?"

"Come on some fieldwork sometime." Before turning her attention to American garage-filling culture, Alice had lived for a while among the Akha people from Laos, where a bridegroom will be daubed with soot, mud and dung in order to give him a foretaste of married life. She much more favored the system of the Na people in China, among whom a lady is visited by whoever she likes at night and then raises her variously-sired children in a longhouse with her brother.

As I pulled open the elevator door I chanted out, "More abortion! More divorce!"

She stood to attention, gave me this crisp military salute, then slouched back inside her apartment in her pajamas and faded tee shirt. What would she *do* in there all day? Presumably she would read for a while, then leave to teach, then come back, reading or writing until it was late at night and she took some melatonin to fall asleep.

I walked out of Alice's building and started hustling to work. Along with the morningtime coolness there was also something new in the air: this slight kind of back-to-school tightness. The sunlight seemed faintly to smell of sharpened pencils, a sensation that comported very nicely with the feeling of renewed education you get from being psychoanalyzed. And along with back-to-school flavor there was a definite edge of anticipation in the air as well. Because going to school year after year—it really schools you, and so at every onset of fall I'd always feel a certain seasonal imminence of big games and difficult exams, new crushes, homeroom disasters. At the beginning of every school year and now into adult life I'd walk toward class or work in the morning and think *Something big is going to happen this year.* At some point during these nine months that will seem longer than a year, something is definitely going to take place. The statistical near certainty, combined with the utter vagueness, sent the same chill through me that was already in the air.

SIXTEEN

Readers may object to too many descriptions in this book of waking up. But then they will have to acknowledge that waking up is a very common if not always fully complete experience. The point is, on the third jungle morning, day eleven since I started on the Abulinix, I could feel something good drawing me awake, and when I opened my eyes it was with this birthday-boy or Christmas Day eagerness not always experienced by the full-grown even when on vacation.

And what I saw with opened eyes was Brigid lying inside her hammock under the veil of mosquito netting. She was lying there with her chin raised up and her hands pressed together (as you could tell from the shape) between her thighs. Either her eyelids were fluttering or else it was just the effect of light strained through mesh and wavering across her sharp pretty face with the high round cheeks and the—already, perceptibly—darkening complexion.

I put on a favorite tee shirt soft with much washing—A NUTTIER BAR FOR NUTTIER TIMES, it claimed on behalf of Mr. Goodbar—slid out from the mosquito net, laced up my boots, and after yanking from my pack my dog-eared copy of *The Uses of Freedom,* its pages slightly crimped with jungle damp, I went and stood outside in the warming sauna of the jungle morning and looked again at a favorite double-underscored passage:

> When at last we have reached our position of trembling certainty as to the nature of the world-request [die Weltbitte], then immediately we become aware of what has been for us the most perilous risk so far. We stood in the forest, and listened with intent—and discovered with disappointment that no sound was yet to be discerned in the air but the restlessness of wind. How tempted we were to make out an articulate sound! Instead we endured our difficult patience; we awaited the world-request. With difficult forbearance, we did not attempt to preempt it with our own demand. And now that we have arrived at last at our late certainty, we see that it was by our patience alone that we passed through a dangerous moment, the misuse of which would have led to years of frustration and continued exile.

What a great philosopher, saying shit like that! Thus after breakfast I just plodded patiently and optimistically behind Brigid and Edwin through the twitching jungly gloom. There was zero breeze—like the whole place held its breath. Meanwhile Edwin picked out routes along worn trails as the undergrowth thinned out, and the canopy got higher and denser, and everything became less claustrophobic, but also warmer, moister, obscurely more profound.

Edwin let me take the machete at one point and hack the trail clear. And he gave me the thumbs-up and a smile when following his directives I crushed some lemon ants between my fingers and licked the digits clean. Brigid also gamely partook, and likewise joined Edwin and me in painting the thick red nectar of an achiote plant across one another's faces in these fierce very savage-esque streaks.

"You look good as a savage," I told her.

"As you do," she returned in a curtsying tone.

"Of course Edwin looks best of all," I allowed.

I'd smeared myself with DEET, but nevertheless my legs and forearms were budding with weltlike mosquito bites erupting up through the excessive, matted hair. So in spite of all the luminous patience I was feeling on the inside I trudged along scratching at myself with one hand and with the other hand waving in lazy constant genuflections to ward off the mosquitoes. Edwin by contrast seemed unmolested by the bugs.

"Hey Bridge," I said over a lunch of more patecones. "Would you ask Edwin what he uses to keep los mosquitos away?"

"Dwight quiere saber something something los mosquitos."

To which Edwin replied, "Te mostraré something cuando something something, bien?"

Yet post-lunch we just continued hiking in our prima facie directionless way, wading on through the watery light and thick air—until, somewhere deep in the afternoon, Edwin turned to me and pointed out with his machete the thick cinnamon-colored roots of an unknown-type tree that did indeed somehow stand out a little from the rest. "Mira, aquí something something necesitas."

The tree stood about twice our height, and beneath its dome of heart-shaped waxy leaves were these strong-looking roots buckling up like octopus tentacles through the overgrown jungle floor. "Sí?" Edwin asked.

"Sí!" But to Brigid I was like, "Cómo?"

"He is telling you that this is the bobohuariza. It counteracts the mosquitoes—but it will make your hair fall off from wherever you use it."

Suddenly I went light-headed and dizzy. And when I tried to blink the feeling off, instead there came into my mind this rare unprecedented image in which I saw myself being handled by strange fingers reaching out of the dark. In my mind's eye the two sides of some dress shirt I was wearing popped open to reveal a hairless chest; loose pants were then pulled from my legs; and there my legs were, undisguised by hair and palely shining in some ambience-filled imaginary room. Was this the Abulinix making me see this—this—? This must be the Abulinix!

"Tell him I want as much as possible! Como quisiera," I said, "quisiera macho! Or I mean mucho!"

Omnicompetent Edwin took out of his rucksack a hand drill and this small plastic tap. I watched as the reservoir beneath the plastic tap started filling up with opaque yellow liquid.

Before long I'd stripped to my boxers and was basting myself all over with the coolish soothing stuff. Bridge offered to apply the unguent junk in the hairy center of my back, where I could never reach to. The touch of her warm intelligent hands made me squirm with romanticism even in the heat. And Edwin too was apparently having fun—laughing, calling me *loco*. The word was like a license, and I reached inside my boxers and began loco-ish-ly patting the goo all over my hairy but possibly not-even-all-that-uncallipygian buttocks.

"Edwin has never seen anyone so hairy as you!"

"Maybe no one ever will again," I said, sparing my pubes, scalp, and itchy face but otherwise covering myself completely. "Voilà!" I said at last, glistening. "Or mira!" I threw open my arms. But looking at smiling Brigid I feared I would spring an erection—until then I'd forgotten all about Abulinix's satyriasis side effect—and immediately I looked away.

Fortunately my dick remained well behaved as Edwin egged me on further. He encouraged me to fill my two water bottles with this incredible elixir of hairlessness, and then to machete off the other four roots of this incredible, in fact incredibly beautiful tree that I was—hmn, come to think of it—that probably I was in the process of killing.

"But Dwight really do you hate so much to be hairy?"

"Well it's just a question of what I'd more prefer. Others might prefer it too, huh?" I winked at her and resumed laboring in the dank heat, hacking away like some utter berserker as the Nalgene bottles filled with sap. Yet with knowledgeable, moral Brigid looking on I couldn't help thinking how unpleasant it would be to do this work for subsistence pay, as some casualized agricultural laborer, for eight or more hours every day.

"Edwin thinks you are interesting. He is saying that most of the English treat the Oriente like a museum. Maybe true," she allowed with a certain reluctant admiration that I was in such a good mood as to feel I might deserve, hacking away until I was finished, and sweaty, and tired. Then I stood up and began putting on my clothes, receiving a smattering of applause from my jungle companions. And using the tamshi vines which Edwin had handed me for twine, I bundled up the thick roots and then carried them off lashed to my pack as we proceeded through the rest of this remarkable day.

Around sunset we reached a scenic oversight perched on some cliff's edge. There it was—the same river we'd first paddled down, unraveling uphill like the past. And also on view was the Oriente spreading all around, and off in the distance the famous Andes, just like the mints, but with a sideways drift of smoke trailing from one volcano. Edwin went off to make dinner, and I very nearly sashed one arm around Brigid's neat, tight waist.

"No question about the bobohuariza," I said instead. "It definitely works." Fallen-out hair already lined the insides of my pants and shirt like some shedding short-haired dog shared them with me. And the change worked by this special sap had also functioned as a symbol of more interior change, because the main event of the past few hours was that I could feel the mild sure sensation of the Abulinix colonizing my system and lightly mastering it. The choice, made in a flash, to be rid of all the hair south of my neck, was seeming to have been the drug's first annunciatory effect—and that was also how it had seemed at the time! I reveled in the sensation of feeling the same way about something both later on and while it occurred. . . .

Brigid seemed like the sort of person who needs larger questions resolved before submitting to be kissed, therefore I proceeded to lay out the big idea that had popped into my brain: "Okay so I'm unemployed and you're having issues about your studies."

"I have no more studies!"

"Still, what I propose is we keep some of the bobo-huariza, we take it to a lab in the States, we have it analyzed, then we patent a synthetic version. We have some giant cosmetics firm market it as the incredible depilatory it truly is, and we make our fortune."

She shook her head at my ingeniousness.

"Then," I said, "if you find new work that's meaningful, great—and if not, don't work. Didn't you say you admire the Haponi capacity to be lazy? And meanwhile I can enjoy access to the stuff just by going to the drugstore."

"I wasn't warned you are so vain."

"But all my other motives are so, so good. We'll split the money two ways. Maybe with your share you could create some Belgian foundation to, you know, counteract and undermine the sort of—what?—neoliberalism?—anyway the sort of capitalism that you don't like so much."

"And you like it so much?"

"I don't know, my knowledge is in the process of aris-ing. And as long as I don't have to have a job I can just learn things all day long. But so what do you think? I mean, bikini lines—gone."

"You become more strange by the hour."

"But this is so not about me. You may have noticed there's a war against hairiness going on among the hir-sute peoples of the more western or northern world— who also happen to be the big spenders. And we've found the silver bullet! I mean it's obvious to me that in the future all the women are bald and the men have flowing hair—but only on the head! Brigid, I feel very lucky about this."

"But really this is your idea? To market the n'importe quoi, the bobohuariza? I have to confess what I think—"

"Think what you want. Really. You may have noticed that I'm something of a cipher who could probably be halfway molded to your wishes."

"But what has affected you this way? You are behav-ing so bizarrely."

"I know I'm acting a little differently. True. But we can never really schedule the important things that hap-pen to us, do you think? Let me admit something to you, Bridge. Lately I have been suffering from this *chronic indecision* or—"

"Ah, you too."

"—or abulia. But today, for whatever reason"— Abulinix made me decide not to mention Abulinix— "today has felt like a total breakthrough day. Today it has occurred to me that if all of a sudden I chose to be rid of my body hair; and if the certainty has also emerged in me that tech support is the wrong way to go, and a right way is going to be found, very possibly through selling the bobohuariza; and if now I know that even to have mistakenly gone after Natasha was absolutely necessary, since how would I arrive where I needed to be except through a detour? and if furthermore I've detected that many of my thoughts and feelings have become swift and super-sure and that's a big part of what happiness is . . ." I felt like the Abulinix was making my consciousness so acute that life would just describe itself to me as it took place, and merely to open my mouth would render me the tribune of articulate events.

"Yes?"

But here it was hard to go on. "Well, then," I said, thinking that it was a wonder drug after all, and presuming that if prolonged use didn't cause nervous disorders, or a dangerously accelerated heart rate, or some other health consequence, then my life might be saved (while it lasted).

"Yes? If, if, if—then what?"

Fervently I clasped Brigid's hand. My touch may have been ambiguous—"Quoi?" she said—with all the ambiguity of the future, but there was also the sureness in it of believing the future can be met head-on and converted into past time without too many leftover regrets. I figured, and tried to transmit this figuring to her through my palm, that whatever we turned out mutually wanting would be just the right thing, to which this touch would end up having made a good prelude. Meanwhile decide things, I told myself, but only the ones you can, and using honest developing feeling as your sole single principle, decisively divide the objects of decision from the objects of a sure and careful patience. So just go from moment to moment like someone picking his way from rock to rock across a stream.

"Ah, Bridge." I was filled with gratitude toward the revolutionary pharmaceutical giants of our age. And even Pfizer, for firing me! Because in any other period of human history what could have been done with me, with my condition? I squeezed Brigid's hand.

"I care for you as well," she said, weakly squeezing back. "Mais tu es complètement fou. Un fou. Do you know what I am saying? You are fully crazy, really."

"I *was* crazy," I acknowledged.

SEVENTEEN

Edwin looked at us, chuckled, and said that he was going to give another shot to constructing a palm-leaf structure. I hoped this announcement might indicate so much sexual tension bristling between Brigid and me that Edwin (with the special psychobiological acuity of a premodern man) sensed the intensity of our need to be left to our own devices.

However when we retired to our hut Brigid seemed in no mood.

"I'm sorry," I said as she established herself on her hammock in a definitely noli me tangere sort of way. "I forgot about Edwin. We'll split the money three ways. I should have thought of that before. Think of the wedding the guy could have."

"You happen to chance upon the bobohuariza and now you want to take it away and then maybe take out a patent? I am sorry, but no, you cannot do this." She'd taken off her boots and slipped beneath her net. "It would be the history of South America repeated all over again." She shook her head and her headlamp made the gesture especially dramatic. "It would be just as with the rubber tree—"

"What? What's the problem?" And did rubber really grow on trees?

She'd shut her headlamp off—now it was utter, utter

jungle dark—and was asking me whether I knew the rubber tree also came from the Amazon.

"Everything comes from somewhere," I said, slinging my ass onto my own hammock and beginning to pull off my Wellington boots while Brigid explained that in 1870 some English dude had smuggled a few rubber-tree seeds out of Brazil, with the result that before you knew it rubber plantations had sprung up in *British* Malaya. "So that by the middle of the twentieth century Brazil, Ecuador, Peru, home to the rubber tree, now they are mostly purchasing all their rubbers from abroad."

Stupidly I laughed.

"Yes, so ironic and cruel that it *is* quite funny—to take away the wealth of the place and then sell it back at a high cost. But it will be the same black comedy if you take the bobohuariza and sell it as hair remover to the rich blanco ladies of Quito and Lima and New York."

For a moment I just sat there on my hammock listening to the jungle.

"Well how about if we share the profits then?" I suggested. "With the Ecuadorians?" No response—and it seemed like the jungle got louder the longer you listened, like some huge insect riot where their demands went increasingly unmet. The sound had begun to fringe the edges of my good mood and freak me out a little. I had to say something: "So what's up with the Ecuadorians anyway? I mean, where's the initiative of these people if they have to wait around for someone like me to show up before anyone even *thinks* of becoming the local bobohuariza tycoon?"

"An interesting mystery. But also it is very interesting about you, that you come from New England."

"How do you say non sequitur in French? It's not interesting at all."

"Don't you think so? Because New England is very rich and that's where America first began, yes?"

"Yeah. Sure."

"And there in New England with your wealth you also have freedom, relatively speaking, yes?"

"Yeah."

"And yet in *South* America as you notice the people are quite poor and lack genuine freedom with their economies, and have not a lot of cosmetics companies?"

"Sure." But she was making me feel like one of those dumb-assed yes-men in Plato's dialogues who just keep on going *Yes, Socrates, right Socrates* until they've been led unwarily by their own dull answers into serious extremities of contradiction.

"And why do you think the cosmetics companies are there and not here?"

"You know Brigid you can seem pretty didactic sometimes."

"Only sometimes? For me an advance."

I lay slung in the hammock listening to the surround-sound eruption of humid white noise. "Oh, go ahead," I said. At least she had a nice voice.

And now she was saying that it was kind of strange on the face of it that New England and then all the US would get to be so rich while South America remained so basically poor, something that seemed very natural to me—or at least it did until Brigid pointed out that South America had always been loaded with natural resources, whereas New England was pretty singularly impoverished in those terms.

"All right." But the darkness of the hut, tucked inside the massive spinning night, was making me feel a little disoriented and uncertain.

"Maybe this arrangement of wealth doesn't seem very strange to us, but—" And here she reached back into history and referenced the incredible mineral wealth of South America circa its conquest, the super-fertile coastal soils, and then the fact (which I'd never believed before or believed the opposite of—had simply just never considered) that South America had also had this comparatively large, concentrated, and therefore readily-enslaved Indian population. "In New England by contrast you had nothing for Europe to want—no silver, no gold. And your climate was very like England's, while here and of course in the Caribbean one could cultivate sugar, cotton, coffee, tobacco, indigo. And what is the result of this, I think?"

"Oh you don't even think it, you just *know*."

"Bof—okay. Well I *know* or I *believe* that for the mother countries, it was therefore possible to let *go* of New England, let *go* of North America. Because you were redundant, you can see?" And now in the superdark cabana Brigid pitched or spun the argument that America had been able to win real as well as notional independence from the old European metropolis, and ultimately escape the neocolonial predicament of things down here, because its early industries were identical rather than complementary to Europe's. So New England had established its own manufactories and created and relied on local markets and thus eventually built up some real economic independence consisting of powerful producers and strong consumers, a project that had also been attempted in Ecuador and elsewhere after the Second World War, and abandoned since the debt crisis of the eighties. "It's depressing for South America to be still the same as always—raw materials, cheap labor."

"That is depressing," I said, feeling somewhat glum myself, like the Abulinix might not work after all. And yet I found it was really *doing* something to me to imagine the original American Wilmerdings happening onto the meagerness of New England nature as in fact a piece of luck. To think of anything is just a step away from imagining it otherwise, and now that I thought of my particular American family, and the portion of lucky accident that seemed to have fallen onto our lives to get mistaken for grace, I became a little unreal to myself. Their luck had become my luck, and what did I do with my luck? It seemed like I just sat in it, waiting for more.

"Brigid?" I said.

"Yes? What?" The pouting semi-impudent way she said this, like some bored girl unhappy at being indoors, reminded me suddenly of Alice. I'd been about to congratulate or else console Brigid for all the things she knew, but now I found I was thinking about Alice, so similarly lucky to me, yet more favored by nature in the brains department. Alice must have been thinking along essentially Brigid-esque lines for years, but it wasn't clear whether this had done her much good. Her sad or grim politics got more and more sophisticated with every rung of education, until finally they landed her a sweet job complete with health insurance—but they also seemed to have exacted a serious revenge against her, according to which she considered all the good things about her, from the straight teeth and stocked brains all the way down to the long legs in the fancy knee-high boots, to be just some side effects of *class* or whatever. And this seemed not unrelated to her reluctance to go to nice restaurants, or ever have a boyfriend, or even a girlfriend. Or really even to be very happy at all.

"You know, Brigid," I found myself saying, "you're a kind of impersonal person, you know that? You're like a brain on wheels. Which I'm not saying is *bad*—but I wonder if it ever gets in the way of some of the more personal relationships you might like to have."

I could hear the vicious smile in her voice: "Maybe I am simply not like the personal people which you are so happy to know in New York that when you are lonely and at a loose end you come here to Natasha—about whom you know *nothing*. Instead you find me. I am sorry."

"Hey . . ." I dangled one arm outside my netting, in case a physical rapprochement might be made and some more hand-holding be enjoyed.

"I am sorry if you don't enjoy me as much as your tree. But who are you, that you find a strange tree in the Amazon and you **act as** if this is your invention? You behave as if you **are Adam** and it was planted there especially for you."

"You're talking Adam from the Bible."

"Evidently not the tree of knowledge that you have smeared yourself with."

"Um, hello? The tree of knowledge is the one you're supposed to avoid? If you read past the first five pages—"

"I don't want to discuss theology with you. I could show you what it has done to Ecuador and even to Edwin to rely on this economy of raw materials."

"You can show me whatever you want. But I'm not going to be an ideologue, all right?"

"So it is bizarre for you that I believe in something? What do you believe in then, besides a hairless future for the Western world?"

"I believe in things, Brigid. I believe in my*self*."

"And your self that you believe in, what does *it* believe in?"

Around this time I seemed to feel something tickle my dangling hand—a brush of coarse fur seemed to slip across my fingertips. I hoped to God it wasn't a spider and yanked my hand back under the net. "How about love?" I hurriedly said, tucking the net under my sleep sack and sealing myself off. "Love I believe in. But then I admit that love is like family, which I acknowledge it can lead to, and which likewise seems to be a fairly painful institution. Hmm . . . Well, let's see . . . Other convictions and beliefs. Sex—enjoyable. TV—diverting. Sleep—refreshing. Free trade—on balance a good thing. You see how I could go on. And life in general, Brigid, I would have to say is maybe a very mixed blessing—but I do believe the blessing part is there." I thought a little. "So I'm very anti-death, as a conviction. Therefore anti-spider."

I'd never touched a tarantula before. But that was really what it felt like I had touched.

"I don't like death either. In Ecuador the first cause of death is children's diarrhea."

"Well obviously I'm against *that*. And don't think I don't have any political convictions. I'm a Democrat, definitely. I'd vote for any of them."

"Oh good night to you. We'll discuss your creeds in the morning."

It was true that the Democrats seemed like a pretty lame finale.

I lay there listening to the Oriente. It hissed and hissed like some big leak in the humungous withering beach ball of the damaged earth. The spider or spiders had really changed the tone of this toneless sound. "I don't know about this jungle, Bridge. I mean didn't humanity, in order to be human—didn't we decide to get out of a place like this? You know, head down to the nice soft savannah instead? Maybe deforestation isn't so bad if we get rid of all the places like this. I'm sorry, but so what if the world gets a little hotter. You could turn the whole disoriente into a golf course. What do you think?"

"What do *you* think? You don't think any of this. Bonne nuit," she said unpleasantly. "Fais de doux rêves."

"You don't believe in anything either," I pointed out. "Anthropology? Indigenous absolutism? Belgium? What are you doing next?"

And now I just lay there with my eyes shut in order not to glimpse a roaming or stalled patch of pure blackness suspended on the netting a few inches from my face. I couldn't decide whether to apologize to Brigid or what. My arachnophobia had rarely seemed so severe, or my abulia either.

Maybe ten minutes had passed when I noticed these weird little rhythmical sighs she was making, complete with heavy breathing. Until then I'd figured she was asleep. I couldn't believe it! I listened to the suspicious stifled sounds, then heard a telltale whimper. Apparently she was one of those perverted girls who get turned on by having a fight! At this juncture our mutual loneliness seemed basically consummated and, filled with indignation, I resorted to my own genitalia and started doing what I could. Alas my dick felt difficult to convince of any abstract lust, and nothing was working until I hit upon an image of naked dark Brigid walking ahead of me up some spiral staircase. This pleasant picture was curiously succeeded by the memory of Vaneetha undoing her white Oxford shirt beneath the mirror-faceted party globe spinning slowly on a cord dropped from the Chambers St. ceiling, and now Natasha climbed on the merry-go-round of pornographic imagery and rode by naked as could be, smiling her Joker's smile. But here was Brigid again, turning around at the top of the stairs—

"What—may I ask you what are you doing there?" Real-life Brigid had interrupted my fantasy, in which tiny propellers were spinning on her two pasties.

At length my dick had obeyed and now I was—"I'm jerking off," I said.

"What are you doing?"

"I'm masturbating—I'm manually stimulating my penis in pursuit of orgasm?" I stalled out in my exertions. "What are *you* doing?"

"I was crying a little—if you want to know it." You could hear in her ragged voice it was true.

"Oh . . ." Feeling extremely uncouth, I put my penis away. I might have thrown it away if I could.

"I had so looked forward to you, Dwight. I had such an *idea* of you."

I didn't say anything. Then I said, "Well I had some ideas too. About Natasha. But Natasha doesn't know me, and I don't know her. So I'm sorry about any ideas she gave you but—"

"But what has happened to you today?"

"*Nothing,*" I said. Yet while this statement was strictly and even somewhat harrowingly accurate—all at once in a surge of shame I gave up on Brigid, the bobohuariza, and Abulinix—it was also true that the nonoccurrence felt like one of my bigger life-events to date.

"Nor to me," Brigid said with some sort of a sad/angry snort and sniffle combination. "True, you are nothing. Return to your pleasure, go ahead. I hope you are imagining the sight of many hairless people in orgy together?"

EIGHTEEN

Eventually Brigid fell asleep for real. Somehow even pitch black goes dimmer with the subtraction of one consciousness, and you can tell.

I had no intention of touching my penis then or ever again. Yet among the pornographic images I'd entertained, one of them was planted in an actual historical sequence of real and undeniable events, and now with my hands at my side I helplessly watched a certain episode from my past play through my mind like some small-hours rerun on TV.

Vaneetha was standing near the doorway, saying that while Ford's birthday party hadn't made for much of a date, at least it had helped to make up for the *dreadful* one endured the weekend before with a young man of the same caste whom her parents regarded as a decent marriage prospect. "I'll have to bow to them eventually. But I think I may have several years of holding out. And your parents? Do they also want you to find someone from the, er—"

"No articulated policy. Actually I think mom is very pro-miscegenation. Because she's like look at the WASPs. Alcoholism, listlessness."

"You might end up with anyone."

"Except you." Involuntarily I sighed with relief and she laughed.

Yet it *was* a relief that, as well as things were going— with several vodka gimlets behind me, the fantastic sensation of improved mental health which I'd derived from beginning psychoanalysis that morning with Alice, and now this lovely woman before me—marriage was already ruled out, and I could proceed more or less anxiety-free.

"This nice Indian boy," Vaneetha was saying, "didn't even have a favorite French film when I asked." Her enunciation remained impressively elocutionary despite a slight drink blur at the edges. "I'm curious—what would you say is your favorite French film?"

"My F.F.F.? Hmm . . ." I told her that at some point I had seen a movie in which all these beaming brightly-attired people, singing French words, had danced around with twirling Technicolor umbrellas. Then I remembered the title: *Les Parapluies de Cherbourg*. I couldn't tell if her expression commented on my pronunciation or my choice, nor were the possibilities logically incompatible. "Well it just seemed to be this colorful utopia of cheerful nonsense," I said. "So I loved it. I know I might suffer a lot in later life. So in the meantime I try to avoid art having to do with suffering. Or the human condition."

This caused her to choke on her wine, then snort. "I'll see you soon then?" she said brightly.

"Cool." I bent forward to drop a kiss on her cheek, as is widely done in New York—but she shrank away and was like, "I *con't* kiss you."

"Don't worry, was only going to be a cheek thing. I wasn't going in for the kill."

"I should have told you. I have something of a boy-friend. In Boston."

"Right on," I said, and then *she* grabbed *me* and started Frenching. Naturally I Frenched back in kind.

Politeness would have demanded it even if desire hadn't caught up and clamored as well.

Before long Dan had appeared beside us asking whether we wanted to participate in the big roll. I translated: "He means do we want to do Ecstasy with—what—with five or six other people? It *is* Ford's birthday," I added by way of peer pressure. And after some mumbled unfollowable deliberations Vaneetha surprised me by saying, "All right! I never do anything spontaneous. I have all my sick days still."

In the living room Sanch and Ford and Ford's girlfriend Kat were sliding the couches together in order to facilitate what Kat was forecasting would become one big cuddle-puddle. Meanwhile Dan climbed unsteadily on top of our card table to take down the homeroom-style clock nailed to the wall. "Don't need to know the time."

"Do you know about Baudelaire?" Vaneetha asked. "He's said to have torn the hands from a clock and scrawled across its face *It's always later than you think*."

"Hope this girl isn't too smart for you, Dwight," Ford said. And then with an incredible aura of inevitability he went off to fetch his old St. Jerome's–era lava lamp.

A spatter of light flakes shed by the party globe was carouseling up and down across the walls as we all six sat down and arranged ourselves in a row on the melded pair of couches. Vaneetha and I sat facing each other in the middle. The music consisted at this point of a propellery sound spinning underneath warm electronic washes of tone. "Who are these guys?" I asked anyone. "Because I'm getting into this."

"Sounds like warm milk," Sanch said.

"That a band?"

"No I mean it actually aurally sounds like the audio equivalent of milk from a mammal that temperature-wise is warm." The astutely synesthetic observation elicited a murmur of consensus from the room. And pretty soon Ford said, "Is anyone feeling the . . . ?" He looked around for confirmation.

"Yeah," I volunteered. And I *was* feeling some sweatiness of the palms and queasiness of the stomach, as well as a certain sizzling fizz of expiring context at the rear of my brain.

"You're feeling the yeah?" Ford said.

By now the unanimous collective feeling seemed to be that we were all rolling pretty hard by now. Kat stood up and spread her arms. "I *need* to do some yoga. Everyone let's follow me in some sun salutations." I stood up along with the others on the squishy rolling cushions of the couches as Kat hopped onto the floor and we formed a forward-facing row of five with our hands dangling to our sides.

"Funny about America," Vaneetha said. "In India it's more often the men . . ."

"That makes sense." I didn't know what she was talking about—but it did seem like men sometimes did do some things more frequently than non-men.

I spread my palms outward, and in imitation of everyone else raised up my arms into a neat spiritual point above my head. Then we all pressed our palms outward and brought our arms down trailing glowing combs of light. This was repeated several times.

"That's the only segment we have room for," Kat said. "But doesn't everyone's chest feel so, so much bigger now? Isn't that so great?" Everyone kind of heartily said yeah and we all sat back down again.

"Kat's a hippy," Sanch announced.

Ford: "Hippies were good. Except how they dress."

"And *think*," Dan added.

Kat: "We're all so smart here. Think of it—millions of years of evolution have evolved us to exactly where we are now."

"One step forward, two steps back," Dan said.

"So good *you're* here," Kat said to Vaneetha.

Vaneetha smiled a smile on which some dentist some-where must have made some serious money.

Kat: "It's not nice always being the only girl around. Can we all just look at our new friend Vaneetha and think how lovely she is?" There were some more very earnest yeahs, and then in an action that may or may not have been connected to any of the foregoing Sanch started unbuttoning his shirt. "Show us your tits!" Ford shouted.

"Not mine!" Vaneetha sounded alarmed.

Ford: "Sanch's is the tits I was talking about."

Sanch tossed his head back, threw open his shirt, cupped his beanbag-shaped male breasts and jiggled them at us. Ford and I were laughing but Kat said, "I think they're the most *beautiful* tits."

"Thank you," Sanch said. "I've been waiting for that remark since I became obese."

Ford: "Yeah man, every spring break, Sanch just walks around San Padre Island hoping somebody'll compli-ment his tits." Sanch had never been anywhere at all on the spring-break exhibitionism circuit. Still he was say-ing, "Mine is the tragedy of the frat boy. We frat boys go around demanding that women show us *their* breasts but it's our breasts that we want the world—to want to see. This is why so many of us get sex-reassignment surgeries."

Kat: "Come on, we're rolling. Let's all be honest with each other. You Chambers St. fuckers *never* mean what you say."

Ford: "What about Dwight?"

"Good *question*," Kat said.

"Show us *your* tits, Dwight!" Sanch said.

Ford: "Vaneetha, have you seen Dwight's hairy blond

chest? He's like a European ape. He's a total freak of nature."

"Dwight looks frightened," Kat said—and this did make me feel alarmed. "Hey everybody," she said. "Let's just talk about how great Dwight is." Everyone agreed how I was really great—except Vaneetha, which was all right since she was the one who looked the most sincere about it anyway. Nevertheless Kat went on: "What are your deep-seated worries? You can tell us, Dwight."

"No, I'm feeling good. And I feel especially good because I just started seeing a psychoanalyst today. So as for worries . . ."

Dan: "You can afford that?"

"My sister's helping out." It seemed to violate the whole sharing spirit of the room to be misleading everyone, and I felt bad toward Kat. Yet chemically I was feeling very, very good. Moreover, one of my feet was touching Vaneetha's thigh through her mauve-colored, possibly rayon, yet somehow crepelike skirt.

"But Dwight tell us what terrifies you," Kat was saying while she on one side of me and Dan on the other had started unbuttoning my blue Brooks Brothers shirt.

Sanch: "Probably his worst fear is that a bunch of people will take off all his clothes and sit around asking him questions." And it was true, I was afraid that the friendly inquisition would continue—and equally afraid it would not.

Then Kat evidently forgot about inquiring into my fears; I watched as the topic vanished from her mind. She said, "I *need* someone to lick my eyeball. Have you ever licked an eyeball, Sanch?" She'd pulled her eyelids wide with her fingers. "Wanna?"

"Not my first choice, but all right." Sanch clambered over us with his shaking belly and leaned above Kat to lick her cornea. Next thing you knew an eyeball-licking craze had swept the crowd and more clothes were being

shed and Vaneetha was saying, "I *love* New York City.
It always surprises me!" At least two voices called out,
"We love Vaneetha!" and Ford said, "Dwight got lucky."
And I did feel pretty lucky, since Vaneetha seemed so
brave, to have thrown herself into all this, and now to
be going so far as to unbutton her own shirt as Kat and
Dan attempted to pull off mine.

Kat, laughing: "Look at Dwight's eyes! Everybody
look at Dwight go bug-eyed while he waits for Vaneetha's . . ." She was wearing nothing on top now but
a black lace bra, and as she reached around to unclasp
the back she paused and looked into my eyes.

"Dwight," Ford said, "what do you think you're
going to see?"

Dan: "Hold on, Vaneetha, hold on. I want Dwight to
do something. Dwight, are you willing to be a prophet?"

I would have looked at him in confusion if I'd been
able to tear my eyes away from Vaneetha's imminent
chest. I felt so stupidly happy I could hardly believe either the stupidity or the happiness.

"I want you to gaze into Vaneetha's breasts and—"

Kat: "Yeah, Dwight, tell us what you see—"

Dan: "Dwight, you are about to have before you two
crystal balls. We want you to tell us what you see in
them."

"It's all right, we're all mammals here," Vaneetha re-
assured me as I watched her left breast emerge from one
cup of the bra. "Please tell me I won't remember this!"
she said.

Ford: "This is your job, Dwight. You've got to look
into the future that no one will remember. You're our
prophet."

"I see happiness." Everyone laughed. "But I don't see
my place of work—I can't see Pfizer at the same time as
I see this—this—"

"He's going to quit his job," Kat said.

"Right," I said. "There's one prophecy. We're all going to quit our jobs."

Dan: "And become soft-core pornographers?"

I did feel that women's breasts were objects of an undepletable fascination. But even in the fugue of Ecstasy it was also clear that I wasn't the first to notice this, and my discovery wouldn't be parlayable into any particular career. "Hmn . . . what *do* I see? I see like a radio-tower beacon, a radio-tower beacon and it's flashing a secret message."

Vaneetha: "It's called a nipple."

"It's sending out waves of very happy information, very good news."

Sanch: "What news?"

"It's some tender news. More good, less bad—that's what I'm prophesying for the foreseeable future."

The other breast popped out.

"Double tenderness for all the world! Mutual constant consoling tenderness and satisfying unemployment for everyone!"

Dan: "Dwight is a prophet of tenderness!"

"Families taking Ecstasy together!" I said. "Everyone sort of being gay! Or lesbian! Free public psychoanalysis for everyone! Lavish state-funded group therapy in the nude! Very colorful umbrellas and no more rain!"

Everyone was laughing—although Dan was laughing his evil laugh. Still I couldn't stop myself: "An end to the Cold War! Or that's already happened. But I mean a permanent future that we can rely on! Warm milk and guaranteed tender safety for all honest mammals willing to work a twenty-hour week!"

So then we all sat around holding hands with boys kissing girls, and girls kissing girls, and boys occasionally kissing boys, and everyone saying there was going to be more tenderness in the world starting right now and spreading out from this room. Especially if we installed a webcam. Global tenderness would radiate from us in waves, and no one (except maybe Dan, who was reticent on this question) could understand why we couldn't kiss just as promiscuously every day, and as sincerely hold hands.

"More good, less bad!" reiterated Sanch, who was completely naked now and had started distributing hard candy suckers for us all to suck on.

"Waves of crashing tenderness," Ford announced, standing up to strip off his boxers and then displaying himself slowly in rotation like a verticalized lamb shank in some falafel joint.

Kat: "Tenderness in the world! Especially the Middle East!"

"Yeah," Sanch said. Then a silence of bliss-scoured consciousness sort of fell across the group even as tiny grains of reality seemed to start gathering in the corners of the room. An hour might have passed as we listened to the ambisexual Scandinavian voice from the stereo singing in a made-up plaintive language over scattered break beats, computerized indigestion, and swelling synthesized strings. The end of the album seemed to prompt or else just acknowledge the whole group's coming-down dissolution, and with morning leaking into the room the others began slinking off to their cubicles. I stood up and led Vaneetha out onto the fire escape.

In the grit-speckled lavender-ish dawn we sat on the cold painted iron and shared one of Dan's last cigarettes. (He was quitting one more time.)

"You smoke?" Vaneetha said.

I shook my head. "Never."

"I don't either. Nasty habit." She laughed and shivered and took another drag.

"You must be cold."

"Not until I admit I am. I'm so pleased with this evening, Dwight. You and your friends are precisely the reason my parents didn't want me to come to New York. New York . . ." she said, and there standing guard above us were the twin Zen sentries of the WTC. Down below a couple of cabs patrolled for fares, and across the street some cast-iron classical pilasters dropped beneath the snoozing Z's of the fire escapes. Generally the whole mongrel romance of the city was in place. I was like, "So about the *Bhagavad Gita*."

The nice eyebrows went straight up.

"I'm interested in this nonattachment-to-the-fruits-of-one's-actions idea. Wouldn't it be true that if you didn't worry about the fruits . . ."

"Yes?"

"Then the actions would be easier to carry out?"

A smile seemed to her to be answer enough; and then we repaired to my bedroom, where like the uninhibited prepubescents of some future race of more enlightened beings, we lay around petting one another without climax until finally it was time for Vaneetha to go to work.

"What? No sick day?"

"I really should. I'll see you soon?" she asked.

"Get up." This was Dan, standing above me, rocking my shoulder.

"Don't wake me up!" I said. "Aren't none of us going to work again?"

"I'm not saying work. I'm saying get up."

He pulled the comforter off the bed and told me to follow him. The lava lamp sent up another psychedelic burp as we walked across the filthy wooden floor that was strewn with bright sucker wrappers like flowers torn from some cellophane trees.

I ducked out the window and followed Dan up the fire escape. The morning air felt residually sensual as it mingled around my hairy legs, and also I liked the snug half-prehensile feel of climbing barefoot up the painted rungs. Yet I had a developing feeling that something bad must be going on. For instance it seemed like there might be an unusually high number of sirens going by.

"Come on," Dan said.

"Is this going to be a bad thing?" So why hurry then? Why not loiter a little? Still I reached the roof—Sanch and Ford and Kat were already there in various states of fascination and undress—and turned around. A huge gout of smoke was pouring from a lateral tear in one of the towers, six blocks away; and suddenly, beneath the massive buildings, under the tall sheer sky, I felt obscene and small, like a fly batting at the bottom of a TV screen.

"What happened? Bomb?"

"Supposedly a *plane*," Sanch said.

Ford: "I mean, go back to flight school, dude."

"At least there's two of them," I said. In a leftover effort at optimism I was trying to look on the bright side. "With any other big building, there's usually only one, so—" Then I saw some white projectile streaking in from the southwest. "Hey! Another plane!" I was delighted. "They've sent it to rescue the other—or it must be coming to help all the . . ."

NINETEEN

I woke up and learned to my dismay that I was still in the Oriente. Dully I pulled on yesterday's ripe-smelling tee shirt, pushed the mosquito netting aside, looked around for spiders, and emerged, feeling a certain dazzled, shaky day after–type sadness, from the hut. I offered Edwin and Brigid the apologetic smile of the disgraced bobohuariza magnate, adding, for Brigid's more particular benefit, the sheepish shrug of the convicted sex offender.

I spent the morning trekking behind them through the silvery syrup of the jungle light, underneath the huge straight trees dripping with last night's rain.

I felt shamed into modesty by the ignorant enthusiasms of the day before, also somehow by the unhurt quality of my minor life. The merely personal content of this life, happening to be its only content, had somehow seemed to thin out like something spilled on the floor, and all I wanted was to get out of the disoriente, go back home, and slide on with my own little version of the nonreprehensible American way of life, and not make other claims. Or I don't know what I wanted. But I figured as soon as we got out of the jungle I would ditch Brigid, take a bus back to Quito, maybe bring along some bobohuariza, just leave Ecuador ASAP. The Abulinixes might or might not be duds, but in any case I had arrived at a major life decision, which was that I really didn't give any particular fuck what happened to me once I got back to America, as long as I *did* make it back and got some new job there as unsatisfying as the last one. (Weird how quickly sadness had turned to anger. . . .) As long as I could sit in a comfortable chair, in a private home fumigated against spiders, watching some quality programming on TV, as long as I had some non-Ecuadorian food and upholstered furniture, fresh laundry and regular access to a hot shower, if I had shaving cream and razors, and shampoo and conditioner in a jungle-free environment—that was going to be fine with me. And since it wouldn't be fine with my kids, who would feel ashamed of dad's lifestyle, I wouldn't have them. Little fuckers.

"Are you all right?" Brigid turned around to say when she heard me sniffle.

"I think I'm just having a bad reaction to the Larium." After all, that was possible. "It's nothing."

Eventually the three of us stopped for lunch at some random epitome of nowhere. Edwin sat down on a log a little ways off and set about roasting more beetle larvae, while Brigid stood looking at me—as I wished she wouldn't when I was sweaty, welt-covered, and tearful, hair falling off my arms and legs like I had some dread disease—with such unnerving frank regard that I couldn't tell what she saw.

"By the way," I said, "there are some pretty sound reasons to masturbate, you know—if you're a man. There are scientific, supposedly lowers the risk of . . ." I put out my palms to say what can you do.

"But what is causing you to suffer like this?"

"Nothing. Nothing's wrong. I just think that when we get out of the jungle I don't think I'll mind going back to New York. Where really nothing *is* wrong."

Skipping the detail of the Abulinix, I revealed to

Brigid how I'd come all this way to set about changing my life, but in the end had resolved that my life was just fine as it was. "I didn't want to tell you that at first. I wanted to surprise you with my new decisive ways. No one trusts a convert."

"But a convert to what do you mean?"

"I don't know. To action! I was tired of doing just maintenance on my life. You know, put on clothes, do laundry. Eat food, brush teeth. Excrete waste. Go to work. Have or seek girlfriend—"

"You did have a girlfriend?"

"New York is a really tragically unfair city—there's such a surplus of attractive women that frequently they end up with people like me! And in addition to maintaining a romantic entanglement of some kind, generally I'd try and keep up my friendships. And—"

"But what about Alice? You enjoy her."

"Listen, a mediocre person can only be so close with other people."

"But who is so mediocre? You are quite unique. You are even very strange."

"What I'm *trying* to say"—I felt a little annoyed with Brigid that I wasn't arriving at the point—"is that I was eager to change or be converted or whatever. But my tastes, my interests, my relationships and beliefs are all really mediocre and typical, okay? And so as of today what I've decided with utter decisiveness is just to resign myself to mediocrity and being totally clichéd." She looked a lot more concerned than I felt. "No, it's not so sad. Right now I'm twenty-eight. If a young twenty-eight. But it's going to be ugly if at forty-two there's still this like holy grail I'm hoping to trip over—"

"I lose you."

"Well, I'm well lost okay? Even if I get rid of my hair, off of my body I mean, I'm still only *kind of* good-looking." I was hurt she didn't contradict me. "I'm arguably intelligent in my own secret way, but not really very." Still nothing. "Furthermore I'm misinformed, as you constantly inform me."

"You have made a study of philosophy."

"You want to know what my *study of philosophy* is? It's one enormous elaboration of increasingly total ignorance. You know what Otto Knittel said? He was like, 'Philosophizing ultimately means nothing other than being a beginner.' He actually said that." I shook my head.

"I like it."

"No." I met her eyes. "For a long time, Bridge, I've been thinking of myself as just this beginner who's some kind of novice at life. But the fact is that I've developed a system of mediocre habit as if I'd been working on it for like *two hundred years*. And it's in that rut of never learning or changing, but always feeling like you're about to—that's where I live, and that's the rut where I've decisively decided I am now content to go on living." Jolted with feeling I said, "And can you guess what the result of all this will be?"

"You will go on a shooting attack with a gun?"

"No." I was suddenly calm. "I'll become just as happy as I've always been tempted to be." An image or vision came to me and I said, "I plan on becoming a motivational speaker traveling across the United States." My eyes filled with tears at the prospect. "I plan to go around preaching the gospel of mediocrity to already mediocre men. I want to tell them that the new heaven and earth will never arrive until we finally give up on them and accept our *florid total mediocrity*"—I imagined the packed halls of overweight mediocrities, bald and nodding, their eyes shiny with tears—"into the least little ventricle of our average American heart! Or hearts. Our hearts of darknesses!"

"You are joking? Maybe train to be a comedian instead."

"No, I seriously plan to become the satisfied denizen of my somewhat flabby and already declining body, which if I'm lucky an imperfect but loving woman, chosen by me entirely at random"—I thought with a pang of Vaneetha—"will nevertheless manage to caress with actual if unreliable passion. And with this vaguely-pictured woman I plan on settling down into the paradise of being average. My job, when I find one, may not especially grease the wheels of neoliberal capitalism and contribute *remarkably* to the immiseration and environmental despoliation of huge tracts of the globe"—I looked around me, imagining it with satisfaction as a smoking waste—"but nor am I going to be some kind of gum in the works or clog in the wheels. Or whatever." The thrill of mediocrity appeared to have supplied me with a certain semi-eloquence: "And on the holy day of Sunday, I plan to drink too much coffee, look at the paper, and run some errands. I'll go with my wife to an overcrowded museum or watch the game on TV. Before my death from prostate cancer we'll have sex if nobody's too tired."

"But—Dwight, do you have a fever?"

"All I'm saying is that all along my mediocrity has been just what I needed to accept, to embrace, in order to have a healthy, happy—"

"Not particularly happy!"

"Right, just an okay sort of life, all right? A new sort of just fine, merely okay or actually pretty good but never very special . . . yes. Okay?" So I wound up, having apparently gone insane. But Brigid seemed unmoved. She was wearing a pained look, about one part amused to three parts disappointed. Well, intelligent, ethical Brigid, damnably attractive and a good singer, fluent or close in three modern languages—she wasn't my target demographic anyway.

I imagined pounding on the lectern before the assembled men. *Our life sucks only because we wish it didn't. Meanwhile we immorally betray the world's laboring and unemployed poor people in the nation of Ecuador and elsewhere by our failure to enjoy the fruits and nuts of our privileged consumer lifestyle. We have to be happy with this arrangement, so that someone can be.* Then I saw myself returning to the front row to thunderous applause, and letting fall across my features (if anyone cared to notice) the serene mild look of the Buddha as he is depicted in certain statues of porous sandstone (such as mom had a nice coffee table book of).

"I think that you are right," Brigid was saying, "that it is very mediocre to be so verbose. Good. But what is best is that you have recognized that you are not actually such the beginner as you suppose. You thought you were very open to whatever can happen. But the reason you have remained so open is that nothing can enter you. So this is not actually to be *open*. Very good that you should see this. Nothing can happen to you. You are that type."

I started to protest—"The real thing about mediocrity is you're misunderstood even worse than a genius"—but Edwin had returned with our food. We ate our lunch in silence, and for me at least the fun of eating beetle larvae had gone out along with the novelty. In fact I felt that earlier I'd mistaken the novelty *for* the fun.

Post-lunch we persisted on our march, going vaguely uphill and following trails more abandoned and overgrown than the other ones we'd taken. We ducked under branches, kicked through fronds, pressed past grasping tendrils, and definitely I couldn't see the tall forest for the equally tall trees. And even the trees . . . Some identified themselves to me as rubber trees, and others as mahoganies and ceibas—but mostly they were just trees, totally as various as they were nameless. I plodded on among them listening to Brigid and Edwin talk to each other in the incomprehensible parlance of Spanish. Their words signified nothing more to me than the occasional whistle of a bird, or the table-saw buzz of a cicada, or the odd creaking laughter of an invisible monkey. And in fact as the day wore on my own words in my mind began to seem as alien to me as the babble of all outer nature; and somewhere deep in the afternoon, with the fluent silver light shifting to bronze, and the shadows beginning to heap on top of one another, I tripped over the concealed root of some unknown-type tree—not a bobohuariza or anything I knew—and stumbled into a kind of wordlessness or true mental nothing. I felt it would violate the endlessly multiplied zero of the natural world to think a single thought or say another word—much less become a traveling motivational speaker. My mind had gone green and empty, and I was feeling futureless and frightened, when we spilled out onto what somehow seemed to be a road.

The sudden appearance of a ten-foot-wide line of stubbly earth, shooting clean into either distance with the jungle wall on both sides, seemed to save my sanity and restore order and logic to things. However there weren't any tire tracks on this "road."

"What is this?" I asked Brigid. I had a strange sensation of suspiciousness, like somehow I might know.

Tersely she said, "A seismic exploration. That's what to call it."

The words had a weird, familiar ring—and vaguely a feeling of sitting down to dinner in the Lakeville house filtered back through me. Possibly had I actually listened to certain after-dinner debate-a-thons at which Alice and dad had gone at it on the extractive industries?

"Perhaps I shouldn't take you to where we are going."

"Is it closer to the exit where we're going?"

"It has that virtue, yes."

"So let's go then." I was being jerkish, hostile, too aggressive—and maybe one effect of Abulinix (if it had one) was to disorder the patient's limbic system so that the famous fight-or-flight response upon which all mammals rely got confused into a single unattractive impulse to fight with the person you are fleeing.

"Don't tell me," I said. "The oil companies cut these seismic exploration lines to test for oil. Or maybe they pay the people they're displacing starvation wages to do it for them?"

No response, and the three of us continued walking single file down the cut with the sun dropping at our backs and the mosquitoes coming out from the trees in doubled numbers like the fact of sunset particularly annoyed them.

Around this point I noticed the dark and then darkening soil laid bare by the cut: it failed to reflect the dwindling light in even the modest way of regular dirt. And its matte finish became more and more visible as the forest wall declined on both sides into jungly hedges and tropical shrubbery, and the ground cover got more sparse. Soon the jungle had turned into a mixed population of dead or dying trees, and living ones with their leaves thrashing in the picked-up dusk-hour breeze. Maybe a mile or two in the distance I saw an enormous tip of flame reaching up into the sky just above the tree line, and I got the almost-strange or even uncanny feeling that I knew what this might be.

Edwin led us off the stack cut and we followed him uphill through a quieter forest than before. I had the unreasonable sensation that I was going deaf. And then to our side was some sort of leaf-studded swimming pool of black crude waste. A few enormous green leaves were stuck motionless on its fearsomely still surface like a parody of lotuses or lily pads floating on some lake. This was not where I wanted to go on vacation.

"And there, in the distance, through the semi-denuded trees," I said like a chipper cicerone, "tourists will be interested to note a high tower of flame reaching high into the air. You can all take out your binoculars and cameras now because that's an oil separation station along the oil pipeline. Welcome to the source of the Nile."

"I am sorry, you are not in a good mentality to see this."

"Now are you going to tell me how Ecuador is trapped in a spiral of dwindling commodity prices where it takes increasing amounts of their oil as well as shrimp and flowers to import the same amount of manufactured goods? Because I know that. My father is—or was—a high-level commodities dude, whereas my sister is an old-time leftist of some kind, and I have sat around some dinner tables in my time, and I have heard some things"—the terms themselves were coming back—"about the plight of the commodities-based national economy and its declining terms of trade. So I don't know that there was such a need to drag me here."

"I can see you learned something at your father's—"

"He's of the opinion, by the way," I said to her apologetically, "that I'm an obedient *dog*."

I was suffering from some serious mental-health concerns and a generalized sylviphobia or forest fear when Edwin—nice, pleasant Edwin!—turned to Brigid and addressed her like I had in distinctly hostile-sounding tones.

"What's he saying?" Suddenly I was flush with sympathy for Brigid, and completely in emotional disarray. "Oh Brigid," I said helplessly.

"A very free translation would be that Edwin too thinks I am a sadomasochist to bring us here—"

"I never said you were a *sado*masochist."

"—he says that I must like to injure him and myself to have made us return here." Her tone was sharp and brisk as usual, but from behind I could see her shoulders slump forward in frankly a heart-prodding way—and I considered the sad possibility that *she* was considering the sad possibility that Edwin might have supplied her with an accurate psychological diagnosis.

"You're not a sadist *or* a masochist," I assured her. "You're a very nice person. So am I. Usually. So I'll try to be nicer now."

But she didn't turn around, and so it was from her posture alone, plus my one-week knowledge of this strange or at any rate foreign woman, that I deduced the dejected look slapped across her expressive face.

Pretty soon we'd come to higher, uncontaminated ground, where, in the dregs of the grapefruit-colored light, with uncomfortably large bats patrolling the air, you could make out an abandoned hut to one side of what must have at one period been a clearing. The tree-less chunk of space was thick with new-ish ferny growth, so that the jungle reached to touch you from all sides in a fashion guaranteed to remind the human person of his native fear of an unknown touch in the dark.

Edwin placed the lantern on the ground and began pacing the perimeter of its light, swinging the machete. He hacked away at the ferns or fern-ish verdure with slow, deliberate, brutal strokes, meanwhile talking to Brigid.

Eventually I said, "Why's he saying nada nada?"

"Nothing is here, nothing is left."

"Tell Edwin I think he's a very good guide. And maybe we can pay him an oil spill–related bonus? He doesn't usually take people here."

"He doesn't usually take them anywhere. You know he has not enough business! That is why we came at all."

By now Edwin had stood up and stopped hacking away. He was talking to Brigid in tones of a certain shakiness.

"He is saying perhaps he should follow them down the river."

I found him sympathetically reminiscent of something too basic and also vague to be identified.

Brigid looked at me, blinding me with her headlamp. "I am sorry to everyone that I did this! I am sorry to bring us here. I mustn't always do these things."

"Come on, don't make a meaning out of it. Today is only today. You don't do *these things*."

But without a word she'd walked off into the woods. There were several possibilities for why this might be, and I was unable to estimate how long she would be gone. The reason I wondered was that while I had painfully little idea what to do about Brigid, vis-à-vis Edwin I had come up with a plan I felt most comfortable executing just between man and man.

I flipped in a hurry through my Spanish phrasebook/dictionary, looking for the words. And possibly Abulinix worked after all, since now I was very deliberately shaking half my supply into my hand, stuffing the pills in my pocket, and presently going up to Edwin with the prescription bottle in hand. With a certain stealthy gesture—like a drug dealer in the Washington Square Park of bygone years—I folded the bottle into his cool, flat, somewhat stub-fingered hand.

His eyes shone a little, but whether this was just the common human moistness wasn't something I could tell. In any case I said, "Estes te puede aider. Maybe. Uh, these can help you. What is Spanish for maybe? Any-

way, tiene una para día. Solamente uno. But each day.
Todo los días, okay?"

Probably if he remained in Baños I could get his address somehow and send him some more if they worked,
and he wanted. Although if the way they worked was to
make him go back down the river, then he was out of
luck medication-wise. In any case I could hear more
than see it as he took one Abulinix, chewed it up—not
the recommended procedure—and swallowed it dry. Then
somewhat violently—almost somewhat sarcastically I
felt—he knocked his forehead into mine.

I shook his hand in the most general fashion.

When the rain began to pour Brigid and I took shelter
under the rasping thatched roof of the hut. Standing between the leaks that were drilling the ground at our feet,
I switched on my headlamp and looked around. At first
when my eyes registered all the poised dark blotches
covering the wall, I figured there were so many of them
that they must be patches of moss or I don't know what.
But then with a feeling of slowed-down time and horrific
lucidity I determined that the spots were in fact enormous spiders, and some were on the move.

"Brigid," I said. "There are spiders all . . . over . . .
the . . . They're everywhere in here."

I'm not sure if outside of movies I'd ever heard someone literally gasp in horror before.

I grabbed her hand and pulled her from the hut.

Brigid and Edwin and I trekked all night through and
out of the jungle, until eventually we stood without talking by the side of the road in the dawn. After a while a
courteous gap-toothed fruit seller slowed down to pick
us up and in his truck we hitchhiked back to Edwin's
van. Seated on fragrant crates of guava, lemons, grape-
fruit, papaya, guanabana, and oranges, we listed around
curves, jounced violently over washboards, and said basically nothing to each other as we watched the red dirt

road unspool behind us or else looked out the slats of
the truck bed at the trees and more trees, the occasional
chicken, pig, mule, guy on a bike, barefoot schoolkid,
raw garden plot, or hut raised on stilts, TV set bawling
inside.

TWENTY

The wool-upholstered modernist couch in Alice's living room had been so forbidding-looking, the night before, when we'd gotten to her apartment after such a long day of hanging out with mom at Dr. Hajar's place and watching the footage on CNN, that she'd said I might as well sleep on her bed. I'd flopped down on top of her comforter with my clothes on, had fallen asleep on a plumb line and slept deeply all night, like nothing had happened; and now I had opened my eyes and was looking at Alice—her mouth went tight for a second with the idea of a smile—in the early gray light of the following day.

"There's you at least," she said.

"Exactly. I mean about you." Looking into her kind blue bloodshot eyes, the big tenderness-based sensation of two nights before revived somewhat, and pushing forward my neck I kissed Alice lightly, with a laugh, on her actual lips.

Next thing I knew I was on the floor—and my head hurt from hitting the wooden chest beside the bed.

"Ow," I said. "Ouch!"

Alice had turned on the green-shaded banker's lamp by her bedside. "What is wrong with you? Who raised you?"

"I'm sorry, Al."

"No, go!"

I got up to my feet. "Come on. Kissing's just a physical sensation—come on!" Nevertheless I had started looking for my shoes. "I'm sure there are cultures where it's totally fine to kiss your . . . And it's not like, you know, second or third base was on the way. I was just—"

I sat in her fancy Aeron desk chair and started lacing up my shoes.

"You're just too weird to deal with."

"One kiss was going to be all. The other night on Chambers St. we all took a bunch of Ecstasy and everybody kissed everyone else! So it's not like . . ."

"Oh, just a slow Monday night before the country is attacked, so you and your Chambers St. buddies find some girls and take a bunch of E. 'Hey dude it's Monday night, dude!' Yesterday must've been a really fun day for you. I thought you seemed more out of it than usual."

I was standing up shod and groggy, ready and reluctant to go. "Look I'm sorry Alice—let me try and explain something."

"I'd like to see that."

"Nothing is normal to me. See? In human life . . ."

"What are you saying, you're immune to acculturation? Fine. I guess it's partly my fault—we've been too close. Go kiss somebody else."

"Just as long as you know that my *tongue*, for example, would never have been involved. . . ."

"Thanks. Think of me as banishing you for your general estrangement from all human customs rather than for any specific perverted act, okay?"

"I *am* sorry."

"Thursday's off. Psychotherapy's off. I can't believe I thought—"

"It was useful while it lasted."

"Not very."

"All right. Good night. Or I mean have a nice day."

I went into the bathroom, pretending to use it for its sanctioned purpose, and actually looking into the mirror instead. Alice possessed one of those illuminated cosmetic mirrors that, flipped to one side, allow you to study up close the precise eccentric course of a nose hair straggling out your left nostril, or to determine exactly how much urban grime (even on a day of normal smokiness and no ash) has been slugged into your pores. I leaned into the mirror looking into my questionable eyes and porous complexion, and like the exact reverse of God when He could see His Spirit on the face of the deep, I felt my features kind of blending back with chaos, and I had to resort to some words. "What is your problem?" I watched my magnified lips form the shapes. Then I flipped the mirror over, and on my way out flushed the toilet.

Turning around in the living room I said, "Al, I'm never going to get over you, you know."

She bolted up furiously in bed. "What do you think it means to be in a family? We're the people we never get over. Now go!"

Entering digits into a pay phone on the corner, inhaling the tang of pulverized industrial materials in the air, watching the morning unroll down Sixth Ave., and punching myself repeatedly in the thigh, I called Vaneetha Trivedi.

"I'm . . . glad to hear from you. Even if you are waking me up—at God, what time is it? Are you all right? You didn't know anyone?"

"Not so far. You?"

"I don't actually know too many people in New York—I've realized. Do you have anything to do just now? Or would you like to come over for some breakfast?"

I went down into the subway—amazed that it was still running despite the carnage downtown, and that I continued living my life, doing everything I did, despite the confusion involved, like it was somehow regular and automatic—and got on a train to Brooklyn. In less than thirty minutes I had rolled off naked Vaneetha and was lying beside her, naked myself, in her big white bed. I had taken the express.

Part Three

We said goodbye to Edwin in the dim shop decorated with photos of rare jungle animals we hadn't had the luck to see. Also there was a picture of a watchful hairy spider which Edwin presented me as a mock gift. I asked Brigid to thank him for everything else instead and wish him good luck. Heading out toward the street I called back a fond and useless "Adiós."

Brigid stepped out of the shop with her sunglasses on. "He seems rather shaky."

"Are *you* okay?"

"He made a promise to update me on his decision. And you—back to Quito?"

"What about you?"

She shrugged in her Brigidesque fashion. "I would like to go on to Cuncalbamba—if only to remain on vacation from my future for a while."

The trouble with going on living would seem to be the mortifying implication that somehow you approve of yourself—and I'd started to wonder if instead of waiting for the prostate cancer (or car accident, or large-scale terrorist attack) I should take things more into my own hands and set about making firm plans to kill myself. However this was a question I wanted to postpone dealing with more conclusively until I got back to New York.

"Cuncalbamba?" I said. "I'm there."

"After twenty-four hours on the bus maybe you are there."

It was more like twenty-seven and I should probably say now, unless I should have already, that travel in Ecuador can't really be recommended in good conscience to anyone who dislikes buses or hates listening to endless loops of the same vallenatos and cumbias (words I would here translate freely as *crazy mountain bus music*) or who resents having to hold on his lap a squalling child, handsome of face but with a shitty diaper, loaned to him by a peasant woman; and if you're inclined to take umbrage at a bus driver's willingness to stop for anyone who flags him down, then it's also the wrong country for you.

Yet at last we came over the final pass and began to drop down into the Cuncalbamba valley. The bus crested a hill, its engine sighed, and we began to descend into a glowing green valley along the swinging curves of a potholed road. The shoulder of the road was planted at random intervals with rude home-style crosses apparently commemorating roadside fatalities and these, being white, stood out particularly against the hazy vista of graduated hills in the dimming light of this or any afternoon. "Your life is still passing before your eyes?" Brigid asked.

Back in Baños, I'd told her about my memories but hadn't said which ones they were. Basically I hadn't said anything at all.

"Or will you tell me what you have been thinking of? I am sure it's not so fascinating that it must remain a secret."

I figured at this point I didn't have much to lose by the truth, and went ahead and admitted that my inappropriate feelings for Alice would seem to have ruined me for love.

She scoffed: "Nothing so obvious could be true."

I confessed furthermore that the memory of the abject circumstantiality and total contingency behind my relationship with Vaneetha led me now to mistrust what I had previously been inclined to consider my "impulses."

"But this is nonsense—you are the most impulsive person!"

Moving right along, I informed Brigid that I'd had the misfortune of taking lots of Ecstacy in the early hours of 9/11; that I'd submitted therefore to an orgy of reckless optimism, soon disproved; and that this had caused me to doubt the truth-revealing features of drugs in general.

"I can hear from how you say it that you don't believe it. But really you ingested these drugs on September the Eleventh? Not a good idea."

"Well we didn't know what was going to happen—or we would have given our E to the terrorists!"

She looked at me with either admiration or dismay.

"Well just to sum up, I've come to doubt the wisdom of my behavior in general. I can never decide what to do, so I just end up doing it—or something else instead."

"I don't understand."

"Honestly that's just as well," I said, and vaguely wished to have lived a different life.

At least all the hype about Cuncalbamba looked true. We climbed off the bus on the early side of dusk and went to find a room in the beautiful hillside pensión/spa that Brigid's guidebook apparently praised. They had only one habitación left: this stuccoed cottage, yellow-orange on the inside like a peach, and boasting a perfectly matrimonial-looking queen-sized bed, as well as a finer-quality couch than we'd enjoyed on Chambers St. The cost was thirty-five dollars a night—thirty-five dollars in quasi-bankrupt and increasingly sad-seeming Ecuador—and the sum should convey some idea of the luxury. I'd never been to a *spa* before and wondered if this would become something for me and mom to bond over.

I went out onto the porch and settled into a plastic deck chair. The Valley of Longevity . . . That was what the guidebook called it, since its inhabitants were supposed to be these mestizo Methuselahs cradled over the course of their absurdly long lives in the permanent equatorial summer of this gentle, fertile valley where on most days the high averaged out at seventy-eight. I kicked my feet up, cowpuncher-style, onto a wooden railing and took in the view of the valley. I heaved a sigh and rocked back in my chair, watching the spreading, forward-folded hills get filtered into definition by a falling saffron-esque light. Now Brigid came out in a fresh tee shirt, her harem pants, flip-flops, and sat down too. The light went gold, then coppery, then more like roseate— with all these stalled clouds a lurid coal red on the undersides—and we just sat there as the sky powered through the spectrum with as much sunset grandeur as I'd ever seen mustered in one place. There was this last long throb of violet light, then—bang—night, stars, crickets.

"Wow. That was some coucher du soleil there, Bridge. *I* feel like I could grow old here." I was trying to be more nice and less sullen, while alive.

"I have empathy," Brigid said. I looked at her. "I feel the same? Oh I am sick that my English is no better. It constantly improves if you will talk to me. Otherwise—"

"On peut parler le français, si tu veux. Je comprends— plus ou moins."

"Beaucoup moins que plus! You are nothing in French. And in English you have no strong wish to be clear."

"I like *your* English, Bridge. 'I have empathy'? I'm serious, that's a nice expression. It deserves a wide currency."

Down on the terrace we ate some great organic food—a main dish of nothing but quinoa and carrots, but somehow spiced to be good. Maybe Episcopalian vegetarianism really was the thing, or so I considered as we sat munching among the usual suspects: the American, German, Israeli, Scandinavian, Norwegian, British and French backpackers who apparently haunt all the cheap idylls of underdevelopment and paradises of neoliberal neglect. Next to me was a suntanned and boyish young Israeli lady with her hair cut short and a dusting of freckles across her nose. I asked what was fun to do around here.

"Drugs," came the firm unhesitating answer.

"Really? I like drugs." So maybe I'd just been maligning drugs to Bridge—but whatever.

"There is a drug here called the San Pedro cactus. You drink a boiled juice of it and then you vomit. But don't worry—afterwards you become insane."

"Hey, Bridge, you hear that?" I thought it might be nice to try *one* more drug. Then to the Israeli girl I said, "I'm on a potent drug right now. It's meant to cure your chronic indecision, although to be honest—"

"This should be very popular in Israel."

"So where do you guys live in Israel? You live in the part of Israel that's Israel or the part that's not so much?"

"Does this drug make you very inquisitive?"

"Yes," I said. "I guess it does. So what did you guys do in the army?" I was entertaining the last-ditch idea that conscription into some force might do me some good. They must have a whole regimen of calisthenics and mental training.

Brigid elbowed me sharply in the ribs.

"Brigid is from Belgium," I told everyone in order to

encourage a shared curiosity among nations. However this seemed the wrong line too. I felt bad about my mysterious gaffe(s), and tried to make up for them by inviting Amira and the others to happy hour at the bar. It was reported that there you could get two drinks for the already scandalously cheap price of one, and I began to tell the Israelis how they all ought to take Abulinix, if decisions ever gave them trouble, and not only for that reason, but also because it was a potentiator with regard to alcohol. "Basically at happy hour I'm going to be getting *four drinks for the price of one*."

"We don't like drinking," Amira's male companion said. "We're more into drugs."

"Sor-*ry*," I said later on as Brigid and I sat swaying together on a porch swing in the dark. "I was only being friendly. I don't even know what's going on over there in Israel and the other parts. I wash my hands of the whole thing."

"You wash your hands of everything."

"Look I've *known* people who've known things about the Middle East—and it was never any good."

Brigid ignored this concern—and as we sat together on the swing, sipping doublefistedly from our four mojitos, there followed from her what I really hope was an exhaustive account of the traded crimes of Palestinians and Israelis, as well as American connivance in the mess. And when I asked whether Belgium was so wonderful in comparison, she was ready with tales of the evil Belgian adventure in the Congo, and a handy analysis of the not-very-helpful Belgian division of Hutu and Tutsi into separate administrative castes in Rwanda.

"You're a real student of atrocity, aren't you? This is the most beautiful place I've ever been—and it hurts and pollutes my mind to know all this stuff which I couldn't have done anything about. Sorry if our presence here was paid for by a bunch of atrocity coupons, but I mean . . . What good does it do if we have all this knowledge and no power? That's poison. Don't you think? And who wants to drink poison? Except Socrates, of course." And maybe me too. (I sipped at my mojito.)

"But what do you mean when you talk? Perhaps this drug you are taking disrupts your mind."

"What I mean is this. So you're interested in human happiness. Good for you, Brigid. But you're kind of human too. So your happiness also figures in the basic global tally. And it doesn't seem to make you very happy to consider all the massacres and thefts and frauds ever done, am I right? Or am I right?"

"Tu es nul!" She stepped violently off of the swing and left it lurching askew in the dark.

"I'll sleep on the couch," I offered.

"I can't tell you how little I care what you do. I have been *with* you for a week and while sometimes you are very productive of bizarre things to say, have you ever mentioned this drug to me? But then to tell a stranger?"

"I was *embarrassed.*"

"This is a drug for making decisions with? If I were to swallow this drug I would decide to hit you. So you will masturbate in front of me but you won't tell me about the drug in your mind?"

A blaze of embarrassment more existential than onanistic went through me, and I couldn't talk at all.

"Oh don't be so arrogantly ashamed. Don't you think I masturbate as well?"

I sipped from the right then sipped from the left mojito, just to do something with my mouth besides talking. Eventually I said, "How do you enjoy masturbating?"

She made a sound of exasperation. "Frankly I find it rather second-rate." And then she was walking up the stone steps, going from terrace to terrace until she was gone, and formulating by her absence as much as by her presence a number of questions, starting with: to run after or not to run after?

In my experience when a person doesn't know what to do with himself, he will check his email. So with a blank and troubled mind I strolled into the office of the pensión, and stood in line waiting for the one super-slow email connection. When it was my five-minute turn I logged on and found my inbox mostly choked with of-fers for penis enlargement and longer lines of credit—but also there was something from Vaneetha.

FROM: lakti17@hotmail.com
TO: wilmerdingansich@mail.fignet.com
SUBJECT: [none]

You may wonder how I'm feeling. But you're not coherent enough that I feel anything much.

On our first date remember we discussed karma. Now I wonder: what is the karma produced by meaningless actions? An interesting question-- perhaps you have simply placed more nonsense into circulation.

But would you like the pop psychology post-mortem? Here is what I tell my friends: "He was a screen. I projected hopes. It was right after 9/11. The night before had been so blissful and I suppose I always imagined something like that might be recovered." And in fairness--to me, not you--I will acknowledge your better-than-average looks, your infectious enthusiasm (the appropriate cliché?), and I will say that you gave the impression--it took some

time to wither--of being quite responsive and
attentive. You also seemed so American. I believe
this made me feel more at home here.

Do enjoy the best nation in the world.

No reply necessary. -- V

The world has probably never been so hospitable to ill-
considered words as since the invention of email. So I
wrote:

Thank you, Vaneetha, denouncing me as the
nonsense I am. What you say is true.

Just before I left America another credible
denunciation was leveled at me and at this moment
I am synthesizing my fathers constructive criticism
with yours to conclude that I am or have been a
DOG whose master has been nonsense.
jhsdlkjhfksadhflkasjhdflkjsh!!!! is what I say,
frothing at the mouth. Ijshedfkjhsdkjfhskdjhfk!!!

Plus your email is helpful in another way. I see you
as liberated from me and this makes me feel better. I
can imagine that I would feel like this a lot if I could
date many wonderful women (not to compare them
with you--you're incomparable!) and then leave
them, feeling that in this I had done them a good
turn. Isnt it nice to be rid of me? I nearly feel that
way myself. --D

PS Natasha not here, btw.

PPS hjkhkjhaslkdfhlaksedjfhlkasdfk

PPPS Sorry if I'm being a jerk but it is a nice-guy
fallacy that you should keep being nice into breaking
up--then the woman might persist in imagining you
are a decent person whom it is hurtful to have lost.

Next I wrote to Dan:

FROM: wilmerdingansich@mail.fignet.com
TO: dan_rorschach@defunct.com
SUBJECT: [none]

Not much time but some questions.

a) How are you?

b) Could serious involuntary memories be included
in the package of side effects, do you think?

c) How about--speaking just hypothetically, and out
of impartial curiosity--thoughts of suicide?

d) Would any trial participants have reported a
marked increase of taciturn and/or jerk-like behavior
in themselves, especially with regards to women, if
they are men, at the same time that no other
decisions have been made by these male participants?

Would write more about the good time I'm having
but my minutes are almost up.

Maybe it was some reckless desire to bring things to a
head between us that led Brigid to seek out the big-time
autochthonous hallucinogen Amira had recommended.
In any case when I got back to our cottage, this pair of
South Americans, somehow obviously non-Ecuadorian,
just these generally very sketchy-looking dudes—they

were standing negotiating with Brigid while two hippy-
ish gringo girls beamed in, beads and all, straight from a
Phish show, sat giggling on the couch.

I nodded at everyone and told them buenas tardes.
Brigid glanced my way as if to ask a question and I looked
at her like *Whatever you want*. Eventually it was my job
to hand over our money. Forty dollars. Gouged—but we
didn't protest.

The Chilean guy in the bodhisattva tee shirt stuffed
the bills in his pocket while his henchperson handed
over a big two-liter bottle filled with this turbid semi-
Coke-colored water chocked with floating particulate
bits.

"A tea made from the leaves. He says it is best to
drink it in the morning so you can experience the whole
day."

The Chilean raised his eyebrows and twirled his index
finger in a circle to the side of his temple. In sequence he
looked at me, then the liquid, then Brigid, rolling his
eyes and grinning a lascivious grin.

"I'm glad you trust those sketchy people," I said to
her afterwards. "I don't."

"*No*—I thought the same. At least *Dwight* trusts
them. You are the one to let me buy it. Before I was only
asking questions."

"It's cool." I didn't care about anything anymore.
"You don't believe, but you believe the other person be-
lieves. I think that's a model for how everything works
out in the end. So I'm sure we'll be fine."

TWENTY-TWO

About nine hours later we were vomiting. And as Brigid and I took turns retching over the toilet, my previous theory of the joys of evacuation had come to seem wrong-headed.

"Mon Dieu. C'est affreuse. Combien des heures est-ce que cela peut—" She hacked, coughed, retched, and then just moaned.

My entire life was marching itself before my mind's eye as a leering Halloween parade of continual mistake-making. I stared into the face of my first cringed-at shot of Popov vodka, then into the frowning visage of my first inhalation of brain-warping pot smoke—or who knew what originally fucked me up? Maybe it was puberty that did it, as I began to see the world sometimes through lustful excitation, then sometimes through post-coital disappointment or après-onanistic resignation, and never in the same level way. Not to mention that I had been raised in a two-parent household, as is so wrongly recommended by both major political parties, when it so clearly induces a lifelong schizophrenia. Yet the crowning error of my life must have been to go on Abulinix. And the shining jewel in the dunce's crown must have been then to swill this emetic San Pedro drink that was making me need to vomit again.

I crawled back to the toilet, and puked.

A botched life, was my conclusion as I watched the last of the morning's orange juice, chocked with food bits, wind counterclockwise, the wrong way, down the flushing toilet. I crawled back to the feverishly undulating couch, and there determined that when, after twelve or more hellish hours, I had at last recovered from this evil drug, I would finally set about firmer plans to kill myself. I'd write a suicide email to my parents and cc it to Alice. And in this email I could mention Abulinix. The bad press might keep the drug off the market, and maybe with my dying keystrokes I would have accomplished a minor social good.

Plus I felt that suicide would bring me some closure.

Very, very slowly, Brigid was thrashing back and forth on the bed. It was like she was toiling in syrup-thick air to hide one of her three dimensions. She punctuated these remote efforts with moans. "Bof—" she kept saying, or crying.

"I'm sorry," I said.

"Oui, oui. Je suis tout à fait d'accord." She got up again, so slowly it seemed like time itself was low on batteries, to wade a few steps into the bathroom and there lethargically dry-heave above the toilet. She sounded like a sick enormous bird whose calls of distress are played at too few rpm.

When she didn't come back out, I stood up with my feet a little too far out in front of themselves, and went to see what was going on. There was Brigid kneeling on the tiles with her head collapsed and dark hair spilling over her face, looking like some last-gasp pilgrim crumpled down with ruinous piety on the final, most meaningless floor, and I felt very bad for her, very sad for this sad person.

Then she sprung up. I staggered back. "You are sensing the difference now?" she asked, looking around with a dawning smile. "So it is not bad, in fact. Ah ha!

What a change from one minute to the next!" She pulled her sweater off, so that she was in just a tee shirt and painter's pants. Her breasts slid around intelligently beneath cotton, and I saw that she was equipped with working sun-glazed forelimbs.

"Huh." I sat down on the bed and tried to be a good person, glad whenever the amount of suffering in a room is cut by half.

Bridge took my hand. "You are still quite miserable."

"It's okay. I—" My ego was jumping up and down impaling itself on its own emptiness and I began to stutter like a skipping CD: "I—I—"

"But come with me."

I was taken to a chair by the window. I looked sideways at her face gazing out through the glass. And from the fairly, in fact extremely beatific expression on this face, I garnered a new impression of things. What a change from one moment! It was true. But I was afraid that the awful parade of successive errors would recruit this perception too, and I said to my happy impression, "Stay! Stay!" clutching Brigid's warm dark arm in the cool dark room.

"I am not going anywhere," she said, baring her teeth at me in that friendly way that humans have.

"Wait—do that again with your teeth?" I smiled at her without the word for it, and she caught on, matching me tooth for tooth.

At last I looked out the window. Beads of dew hung from the still spears of grass, looking as delicately placed as if somebody'd gone around setting them there with an eyedropper. Wow, was my reaction, and also to the fact that beyond the little prospect of short grass the valley swooped out into path-scored and crop-checkered hillsides, sinking down and parting away into the distance, where the miniature town popped into view glinting like some scale model done in tin and balsa wood.

"Thank . . . God! Thank God Himself for windows!"

"And for doors," she said, her next action being to throw into my daypack her sweater, two water bottles, and two plump tomates de árbol. My mind was not so destroyed that I didn't remember how my sunglasses were already in there, along with my notebook of to-do lists.

I was glad to leave the vomitorium behind as we proceeded semi-unsteadily down the stone steps to the main terrace. Up in the impressive sky two flat-bottomed cumulus clouds prowed through the stately air, their shadows slipping across the hillsides like swimmers' shadows gliding silently across the floors of pools.

After some distended length of time Bridge and I came to our porch swing again. We sat down together. The speakers mounted in the trees above the crocuses and violets, the gentians and dragony orchids, were playing a song that I recognized deeply. *Making love,* went the chorus (backup singers: *making love*), *out of nothing* (backup singers: *out of nothing*) *at all. Making love . . .* The flowers bent and rocked delicately in time with the beat.

"What . . . a great . . . song." Evidently Air Supply were visionaries suggesting, in simple harmonies, how nihilism might be overcome by baseless love! I hadn't realized the world was so abundant with easy genius, and felt the band had suffered outrageous critical neglect. We sat rocking in the swing until halfway throughout the group's next masterpiece—"Every Woman in the World," but Bridge replied, "I don't want to be *every*"— then headed off into the rest of the day.

Amira spotted us as we passed the swimming pool and gave a sly thumbs-up. I was right back at her with both thumbs. Many mostly naked Germans and Israelis, giddy/solemn on Ecstasy, were splashing around in the moiré doodlings of the watered light.

"What a really nice scene," I said, thinking also that it would have been more nice sixty years ago.

We went walking together vaguely westward down a road of brick-red dirt. The idea was to climb up into the hills, then look around and come back down.

"That's all?" I asked. "That's the whole goal?"

"The goal I suggest . . . Others may be added."

"Just go up and come down? There and back? That's the whole point of our journey?"

"Yes, we *move*." Grasshoppers crackled like loose electricity in the roadside grass, and glare was slapped down thickly on the still, nitid leaves of the absurdly tropical, tropical-type trees. We walked past groves of coffee plants, and it was amazing to me that the glossy berries, a glamorous red, ended up back in America as nervous black water in your guts. On the porch of a tin-roofed shack the berries—or beans, I mean—were laid out drying, and like subaudible sirens they radiated little diminishing waves of vibration in the air.

"I'm experiencing this really Van Gogh sort of eyesight. Are you? Where everything throbs in these bright slashing waves?"

The only break from constant perception was to talk. But then you can veer off in so many directions talking a language that you know! It was terrifying, especially if like me you were gullible, and believed whatever you heard yourself say.

I said, "On these sorts of days, Brigid, I feel like I'm on my way out into the open with you." I was feeling like *existence's alert awareness of itself*, and Otto Knittel's half-comprehended philosophy lay under my thoughts like a watermark beneath notes scrawled on creamy paper.

"These sort of days! What sorts are these, when there is only the one? Only today are we taking this very strange, this very powerful . . ."

Unconsciously I'd come to walk ahead of her, and had stopped before a ravine or arroyo leading off and up to our right. With a doorman's welcoming gesture I swung my arm out onto an aisle of shifting leaves with a vaulting of sky at the top.

"Really—into here? You are sure?"

I took her hand, and tugged.

"Hold the other hand. That one you have held before."

So I took up the left one, and led her. And even as we entered the narrow arroyo I felt like my mind was becoming a wider aperture, with experiences of ever-wider bore forcing themselves through me. A decision had been made—we were going in. I couldn't pinpoint the rationale of this decision, but the thing was done, an action undertaken, and I felt that maybe from now on I could follow my *will* through my life like a hound on the trail of a delicious scent. "Just trust me, Bridge. I trust you."

"Hence I don't trust you!" She too was alert to something—alert for the moment in the way of a rabbit's ear, cocked and rotating, ready for flight—and everyone, I saw, was indeed a soft instrument, however calibrated, registering the world.

Stopping her in the dirt track of the arroyo, I hugged or embraced this Brigid person, woman, girl, certainly by now a friend; and mouth near her pink ear, with its sparse blond velvet at the bottom of the lobe's inner rim, quietly I said: "I trust you because you're smart and just and knowledgeable. Sorry to use such basic English, but I think you're just so *good*. And I trust myself because I'm so right about you."

We moved apart and she said, "Why don't you ever touch me before?"

"I did too."

"Scarcely once you touched me. Ah—I can't speak English."

"Well also I feel like you can see through me—"

"But I can't. No."

"—and my transparency offends me, and I would think it would you." Was that English, those words? "So I wasn't sure if I was so attractive to you. But I'm just here now to say with whatever words that you're free to propose using me for your good ends in almost any way, if you want. There's a high likelihood I'll go along."

"This is your next decision? I decide how best to use you? Do you reach all your vital conclusions while on drugs?"

"I've never done *this* drug before. The Abulinix–San Pedro combo? Come to think of it—" I began walking up the ravine again, picking up a long smooth stick and taking it at once for a staff. "It's revolutionary, probably." I turned around. She looked anxious. "And maybe you'll feel better if under the influence of these two drugs I sign up for justice right now? With you? Global justice?"

"But how do you subscribe? Inscribe? Or rather, sign up, yes. Ah, I can't talk."

"Here." I slung the backpack by one strap around to my chest and fished out my notebook of to-do lists. *Justice!* I wrote, a little unsteadily. "There," I said. "Justice! Only there should be a verb, there should be—"

"Serve justice?"

"Okay," and I wrote this. "See."

"So easy? Then, *recognize*—" she gently commanded me.

"Those should probably be reversed, I mean first recognize then serve—"

She shrugged. "Do what you can."

"I write that down?"

"You may, yes."

I said as I wrote: *"Do . . . what . . . you . . . can . . . and . . . write . . . it . . . down."*

"What else?" A convenient rock presented itself to me, and I sat down, looking up into Brigid's flushed face, a rosiness afloat on her dark-ish cheeks, and her gaze wide with candor in the pupil-blotted eyes.

She said—she laughed—and I wrote, *"Care for Brigid."*

"Sure. Done. But . . ." Slowly I wrote the words down.

". . . and give your enthusiasm into her. Or rather, to her. Give it to her."

I formed the weird-looking letters of my native tongue. "Give me a second there with that one."

"Stand up now."

I wrote and then did it, inelegantly, like some backwards-ass cub reporter of these unfolding current events.

"Kiss—or—no—"

I'd turned a page and was looking at the blank ruled notepad. I waited. "What are you saying? Because say it and it's done."

"I intended to say my name, Brigid." I looked up at her. "But then I had an idea of Eden."

This was a heavy word, very threatening. "Eden like as in the garden of?"

"And then I understood that in an Eden there is no third person, not a him or a her to address. There is only one other so you address the person simply as *you*. You say 'you.' There we have the pair only. Only you and I, I and you."

I was like, "Whoa . . ."

"Well the surroundings make me think of Eden." It was like she was apologizing.

"But you wanted me to kiss you," I reminded her.

"But naturally then with Eden I thought, *a fruit.*"

We had the tomates de árbol in the bag but I hoped this wasn't what she meant. I pulled her close to me, all trembly and excited, except—"Except," I said, "I guess the lesson of Eden, which of course it wouldn't be very human of us if we learned it—but in theory we're not supposed to eat whatever fruit we're talking about, right?"

"I have conceived a fruit for you. Tout à coup." She smiled. "A fruit I would like for Dwight—would like for *you* to eat."

"Hmn." She was the fruit? Or what was up? I wondered this until a butterfly fell and lighted, along with Brigid's and my intention, on the blue cotton of her tee shirt. "Una mariposa," she said, naming the creature with its dark veined wings, bands of pale-ish jade at their edges, and also red dots like Hindu-type bindis in the centers of the raised and lowered, delicate, breathing, cantilevered things.

"Later I tell you of the fruit," Bridge said, taking *my* hand now and scaring off the butterfly.

Several long moments, swelling as they did so, went past and popped.

I began writing in my to-do list as I walked along: *Form a plan.*

This was to get her to kiss me.

Think, I wrote, as she dropped behind me.

Be brave enough to lead her—then I crossed out *her* and wrote *you.* Then I heard her say "Look," and was writing that word down when something crumbled and clung across my face.

TWENTY-THREE

I did a crazy little dance or frightened tarantella as I kicked and slapped myself all over. "Bridge," I screamed, "is there one? Is there? On me?"

She was looking at me with such an open mouth that I felt bitten already. "Aaagh!" I screamed.

"For a moment I thought, 'He is mad—finally he is utterly mad.' " She started laughing really hard. "But—but—" She could hardly talk for laughing so hard. "But there is nothing on you to fear."

I was plucking spider web off my face. "Swear to honest God?"

She was able to stop laughing for a second. "I swear to the truth. There is nothing."

In my terror bad visions had passed through my mind. I'd glimpsed myself playing hackysack in hell, I'd imagined Alice in a Halloween costume—black dress, bare arms and breasts, with six bouncing artificial legs trailing behind her on a black-crepe-covered cart—and I had seen dad being electrocuted in a desk chair while mom sat in the next cubicle manipulating a parrot puppet by strings. New York, New York was at the center of the universe and we all lived downtown.

"You go first now," I said. "You're not so arachnophobic as me."

Brigid was trying to wipe the giggles off her face. "But

I am—how do you say this?" She pointed confusingly at her crotch. Which looked wet. "I am incontinent!" She was laughing hysterically and wiping away tears from her eyes. "I am ashamed. But you are so funny!" Gigglingly she untied her boots then slipped off her underwear and pants. "I am very sorry." She smiled as she handed me her clothes, and I stared at her half-nakedness.

"Dude, this is getting weird." But somehow like it wasn't all *that* weird I removed the tomates de árbol from their ziplock bag and replaced them with Brigid's damp things. She had already grabbed the water bottle away and was spritzing herself off between the legs.

"I am sorry." She was still laughing.

"That's cool. Who wears pants in Eden, right?"

"Yes so now you take yours off, so that I may wear them, okay? I will let you keep your undershorts."

"Thanks." I stepped out of my pants and handed them to her as she'd asked.

"Regarde le sans-culotte!"

The breeze infiltrated my boxers as I picked up the dropped staff and started up the path again. I was looking for any glint of spider cord and carrying my staff held out before me like some altar boy's candle or caveman's torch. Thus I felt in touch with ancient types of hope and dread.

"I am sorry that I peed on myself," Brigid said.

"Nah, come on, it's an icebreaker. But what was this designer fruit you were going to engineer for me?" I hoped it might be the kind of fruit to counteract any tendencies to freaking out I was feeling as I led her up the ravine.

"Continually I am thinking today of Eden or paradise or utopia, I don't know why. For me that is the effect of this drug. Besides that I sweat and have peed in my clothing! Continually I am thinking of whatever would be the most happy thing."

"Okay."

"And I am thinking that once everyone is admitted into paradise—"

"I always thought of paradise as being very selective."

"This is my fantasy—so, for me, yes, everyone is allowed. No borders."

"Bad people too? Mediocrities?"

"Yes, bad people particularly. All mediocrities. Because it must be everyone. This is my idea, to invite everyone." She turned and looked at me straight on. "But would you be afraid to be *me*?"

"Wait—to be? To be you? I mean yeah, if that's the question—yeah, I'd be kind of afraid." She looked sad at this news (and also beautiful, not that that was either here nor there). "Sorry, Bridge, but for me to be you—I don't even know why we're talking about this—but being you wouldn't just mean being this beautiful smart cool woman, which I'm sure must have its perks. It would also mean *thinking your thoughts*. Which it seems like a pretty dark world . . . Anyway what happened to the fruit part?"

"I am imagining a paradise in which there is no lack of time. I would like for everyone to have so plentifully much time, and everyone such an excellent memory, that eventually, over time, everyone will have *been* everyone else. Do you see? In the length of history everyone will have been all the other people in the world. And then for once finally we will treat each other well. You and I will treat each other perfectly."

"That *would* take a long time."

"Forever, I admit. But don't you think that at last the people would—if one at a time they had *been* all of us, at one time—?"

"I'm sure it would help."

"No!" She punched me on the shoulder. "React to

me! Think, or feel—don't *guess* at it! If you ever had been *me,* you would react to me, not always guess."

Our discussion fell away as the ravine or path or arroyo constricted to allow only single-file traffic. Bridge led the way without any stick, thinking about paradise but putting herself in what seemed like harm's way. Maybe it would have been better to have taken the drug in some environment less hostile than nature, where not to mention spiders there is nowhere to sit down, and you have no stereo to listen to. Nevertheless as I walked stooped over behind Brigid through the narrowing tunnel of leaves I allowed myself to contemplate her soul-cycle of a paradise. I was wondering what all the other citizens of paradise would make of having once been *me,* Dwight B. Wilmerding. Would they feel that I/we kept trying out women, drugs, and philosophies because I/we loved to begin things but hated to proceed? And then, recognizing that the flavor of stale beginnings threatened to overtake my/our entire life, would they, when they were temporarily being Brigid instead of me—Brigid who was crouching right before me, with her ideal ass strangely concealed by my own pants—wouldn't they then turn around to address a saving gesture towards me, doing just the exact thing I needed done? I didn't know what this was, and hoped Brigid would perform the gesture on her own. Then if I were ever her, and in a similar position vis-à-vis a me-like person, I would do him or her the same good turn.

Brigid revolved around on her heel. "I can't go any farther. Look. You are unfortunately right, there is a very big spider before us."

Over her lowered shoulder I saw the obscenely spread-legged spider, heavy-looking in the sac, posted at the center of its glistening web. A blind or ignorant butterfly, with Tiffany glass wings, flitted past, and had, as I watched, an extremely close call.

I sighed, and with a sensation of giving up like when I'd learned Natasha was gone and realized I'd come to this country for no reason, I said, "Time to go home."

"Oui, c'est juste, mais . . ."

"Mais what, Bridge? That's a serious spider there."

"Can't you see through the leaves? You see that beyond a few meters there is grass there and then it becomes more open, more . . . Truly open really."

"Hmn. I guess maybe we could just walk through the trees and circumvent the . . . I mean somebody, in addition to the rain, must have cleared this path we're on. Not without effort but . . ."

"No. Not without machete."

It was true that the growth looked pretty impenetrable. "Fuck spiders," I said. "We ought to kill them all." But this seemed to be thinking like a spider and I didn't want to descend to their level. Instead with a sudden scheme I opened the backpack and ripped out of my notebook an ancient to-do list. I read this particular page—

1½ cups canned tomatoes
½ cup green beans
1 red pepper
pine nuts
basil
couscous [apparently I'd been planning a meal for Dan]

health coverage?
VT options?
toilet paper

contact:
  Vaneetha
  mom
  dad?

—then hocked a fat loogie into the paper to give it a moister semblance of life.

Now with the crumpled spitwad in my hand gravely I looked at Brigid: "You see what I'm thinking?"

Gravely she nodded yes.

"When I run screaming up the path, you follow suit. Got it?" Apparently I was on the brink of a brave deed. Thank God for Abulinix! And San Pedro too! (Unless they were about to get me killed.)

Brigid said, "Yet first . . ."

"Yeah?" I'd husbanded my courage and didn't want it running out on me. But before you knew it we were kneeling in the dirt, holding each other's faces and kissing full on the mouth. The lips and two tongues involved felt nimble, thick, and rude, and who was doing what to whom quickly became moot, and wet. Unless I was wrong this was the best kissing I'd done, with that one time in Fourth Form, in the Old Chapel, with Stephanie Pettigrew, a close—or actually a very fast receding—second.

"Wow." I was gasping. "The French must have learned that shit from the Belgians."

"This adventure would never happen in Belgium!"

We kissed again, and it did seem like we had the chemistry going.

Finally I stood up as much as the tropically bosky growth allowed and steeled my nerves for an assault on the web. "If I die you'll tell everyone in the whole justice movement that they've lost a brave soldier in the cause, right?"

"Yes, everyone, I will set up a memorial website."

"Don't say web. Please don't use that word."

"Never again."

"Can you tell how serious we're being here Bridge?"

"No." Tears filmed her eyes as she smiled a tight smile. "I cannot tell."

"All right then." I counted to three, and then for good measure to four, before throwing the big spitwad to one corner of the spider's web and watching as the idiot monster scrambled after the thing. "Aaagh!" I cried and ran screaming through the web and up the narrow path until I had crashed with swimming arms through many sets of branches and at least one more web and in this violent process been able to think, with terror-sped logic, that I feared spiders not only as hairy, parasitic, stealthy, patient, easily deceived, and genuinely, actually, unmetaphorically poisonous, but also because they were hairy like the crotches of human beings and hairy like I myself had so recently been and, moreover, they had eight limbs like coupling pairs of humans have, so that when I emerged—shouting and karate-chopping with my hands—into the empty space and grassy zone which Brigid had predicted and foreseen, I stopped, sighed, and knelt down on the grass, kissing the soft earth as if I'd braved some warp-speed course of psychoanalysis and might now become sane: luxuriously, triumphantly, ultimately sane.

Brigid collapsed into my scratched-up hairless arms. "Oh but please say there is nothing on me either. J'ai peur!" I began to pat and inspect her all over just as she did me. Soon it seemed like she was making particularly certain my groin region was all right. Meanwhile I checked and rechecked her breasts as if suspecting spiders to be fully as tit-crazed as the worst of lechers.

Someone started laughing—it may have been me. Either way I joined in, and we began rolling around on the tasseled purple grass of the very accommodating hillside. I loved kissing Brigid; it felt like a better use of my mouth than even to say the wisest things. "Mnhm, nhm, nhm," I said, kissing, until she'd pushed me onto my back and was looming over me: "How is it that you wait until now? You are such a bad prude. I wondered even if I am not good-looking to you."

"You know it's not the looks. You're so hot that for a while I was afraid it might influence my opinion of you."

"I don't have very large breasts," she said philosophically.

"No, but you've got the ass. And the face. It's pretty much the face that's really the thing. And the brains. Behind the face. But the ass is a factor. But mostly it's something else about you, I'm not sure we have a word for it anymore. Or yet."

"Why do I like you? I like you so much. I want to speak English more colloquially like you. But also I would like to make more sense than you." She was looking down at me and shaking her head. "So why until now did you never *bust a move*?"

"You gotta understand, Bridge. It's not so easy to go from having abulia to deciding—to deciding—I can hardly even say it, see?"

"For once be clear." She yanked me up and pulled off my shirt. "What can't you say? Of what are you afraid?" She scampered her hands spiderishly across my all-but-hairless chest.

"No . . . no . . ." With an enormous effort of will I said, "It's just that I'm afraid of becoming—becoming a—a—"

"Mais qu'est-ce que tu veux dire enfin?" She was laughing. "Ça va, d'accord? N'importe quoi que tu dis, ça va. Avec moi."

It seemed to me that for many years to come I would feel the light of this particular day like a clean sword going through me. "I'm afraid of being a—I'm terrified of becoming a socialist!"

Brigid looked at me and I watched her blinking. "Really you should only fear to be so strange."

"The thoughts you have to think!" I said. "The things you have to know!"

"But even I am not a socialist exactly."

"Come on, have the balls to say so, you are too, I can tell! Alice—my sister—she's one, so I can tell. I'm actually much smarter about this kind of thing than we'll ever know. So—"

"Okay." She put a hand to her plump-lipped mischievous mouth. "There is something I must tell you at the last. You will be angry that I waited. But please think of the other things you have also waited for."

"What? You're not"—I rose up on my elbows to kiss her—"you're not a Communist are you?" Kiss. "Because I can deal with socialism maybe, but . . ." Kiss. "Or you aren't an anarchist, I hope, because"—kiss—"I don't know, I mean I have *some* black clothes, but they're not"—kiss—"torn and dirty. And I have some dirty and torn clothes, but they're not black, so—" I wanted to kiss her all I could before learning that she wished to smash the State. "Don't you think the State will always have a role to play?"

Bridge had gone looking for something in her wallet and I feared she was on the verge of taking out a twenty and explaining to me the hidden meaning of money. But then I saw she was displaying between her thumb and index finger one of those passport-sized photos taken by a coin-operated booth; and in it you could see—if you could believe it—Alice and me! This was back somewhere in the eighties, maybe at the Millerton Mall, and Alice, grinning in the mouth, looked sad in the eyes, while I was sporting that strange expectant dog's look I'd seen on dad's wall some eight completely unbelievable days before.

Brigid was holding the picture in front of her heart and smiling. I was sure I hadn't brought my own lost copy for her to filch; I didn't see how she could have downloaded it, much less *printed* it, off of my mind, or

even off the world wide web; and meanwhile in my
bewilderment I suspected that at the ten-year reunion
people were going to have to be told by the nurse ac-
companying me that I was our Form's designated drug
casualty.

"Do you see the plot?" Brigid asked.

"No." I put my hands over my eyes and closed my
eyes behind my hands. "Bonne nuit." I took leave of
even pretending to be compos mentis. I would have
to retire gibbering and broken to my teenage bedroom
in the Lakeville house, the ward of my dad. Someone
would come to feed me with a spoon. "Mom!"

Bridge's lips were suddenly on mine with eloquent
kisses—a nice surprise. Usually sane people can't relate
very well to society's more broken-minded individuals
and therefore refuse to kiss them.

"I am sorry, but Alice has only tricked you for your
good. Already she thought we were complementary to
each other, she said to me, Brigid, he is just what—what
you require."

I chalked up my incomprehension to insanity and just
let her talk.

"For a while if you can believe it Alice was—
ridiculous to say, but she was acting as my psychoanalyst. I don't know, I want so much to be believed, this
is something we learned together—"

"I'll believe anything," I said.

"This is what Alice says, he will believe you. Dwight
will. *You,*" she said to me.

"How are you like channeling Alice?" Was everyone
psychic but me?

"Of course there are some men who think more or
less the same as I do. But in spite of their claims really
they don't like for a woman to be like me. I am disagree-
able, severe, maybe strong-headed. Or else these men
are no fun. Mais—ouvre tes yeux."

I consented to these few words I could parse, and looked up into her wide eyes almost eclipsed by the pupils. Brigid straddled me with her knees to either side of my chest and, taking my right hand, she placed it below her ribs, near the valvey heart. I felt they should send in fleets of such women to all the asylums.

"Or simply I don't *like* these other men. And many men who are leftists, really they are not quite good-looking, I don't know why this is, an anthropologist should study it. But you—you are almost like Alice would say." She looked truly happy about whatever this meant. "Ever since the moment in the airport I have the sensation that *you take me, you accept me.* So it was very unusual that you didn't touch me. Usually only after sex does the question come of whether to accept one another. Which—finally—no, I never have. And yet to *you*—it seems to me . . ."

"Yeah?" I asked.

Slowly she said, "It seems to *me* that it seems to *you* that I am like a piece of nature. Simply you take me like a bush or a snake or a bird—"

I was laughing, just kind of cosmically shaking my ruined head.

"—or like a waterfall or a pig or a swan—"

"I *love* you Brigid." Oops: was I not supposed to say that yet? "But I'm insane!"

"But you love me? Now I don't think you are insane."

"But Alice—Alice—how is Alice—how—"

"She gave the picture for proof. Don't you believe me? I was her student in New York. She advised my thesis—also advised me to end it. Don't you see?"

My astonishment somehow stayed level as my sanity returned. Reaching inside my boxers and fondling and stroking me for a moment, then fortunately forgetting about it, since this was my *sister* she was talking about,

Brigid explained that as soon as Alice heard how I might come to Ecuador to see Natasha—"A very pleasant woman," Brigid interrupted herself. "Now I think we are friends"—she, this was Alice, had come up with the idea of putting me together with her, this was Brigid, who was in Ecuador already and had just abandoned her doomed dissertation. "And it was not so difficult for Natasha to accord with this, because frankly she was alarmed that you should really visit. Of course there were inconveniences, such as we must pack up Natasha's apartment so you will believe she has left, and you mustn't suspect—oh, yes, I am very sorry, there was no abortion, Natasha is not pregnant, not that I know. But I couldn't let you rush to the airport. Perhaps there is not even a flight to Holland that day. At any rate, Alice insisted that you are a very trusting person, very ready to believe, and you don't know Spanish. You *do* have a fantastic woman for your sister."

"Treacherous too." I could hardly believe it.

Brigid ministered to me a little and then semi-shame-facedly smiled. "You are not too angry?"

Above us there were soft cornices of chalky soil mirroring the ones on the opposite side of the valley. And flowing beneath the pale cornices or cliffs was all this tassely grass, green nearby but getting more and more purplish the farther it spread away. Brigid touched me in the time-honored style as all the bending grass brushed as one in loose obedience to the breeze's course. "Ah," I said, lying down on my back. The sun was flaying all sorts of light from Bridge's dark, dark hair; and off to the right of her head I caught sight of the tilting plane of a hawk on an updraft. He was really sailing, or she was. So apparently I was the object of a friendly conspiracy of remarkable women. The discovery had me feeling pretty blessed, and I sat up and began slipping Brigid out of her shirt. "No, I'm not mad." Her bra seemed as unnecessary as eye patches over perfectly healthy eyes, and I took it off too. The bare shuddering breasts made me laugh, and Brigid said, "But you must promise you will be less silly when you age."

"I promise. I'll be somber. Later." I distinctly felt I would be.

For the time being however I alternated blessing-style kisses on the top of her head with some intense Belgian-style lip action, and lots of lambent tonguing of the alert budding nipples. Brigid was making the first of those awesome female sounds that can eventually portend a crisis of pleasure. Yet out of respect to Mademoiselle or Señorita Brigid Lerman I want at this point to execute a temporary narrative fade-out and just content the reader with the suggestion that for two curious and mutually attracted young socialists without a condom between them to swap oral sex 69-style on the soft grass of a picturesque equatorial hillside while they more or less peak on an intensely sensitizing drug trip can really boost their relations to a great new stage, especially when, in an epileptic fit of an orgasm, the woman finally comes above the young man who, as it happens, is ejaculating like a garden hose, and I'd definitely recommend these activities.

Afterwards we lay down beside ourselves on the grass. Omne animal post coitum triste est? No way! Now that I was a socialist fucking made me joyous, and I wanted to do it again right away.

"So that was the fruit, huh? Now I'm on to you, Bridge. You're the fruit!"

She looked a little triste, maybe, at the mention of the fruit with its overtones of expulsion from nice places. Nevertheless I busted out our tomates de árbol. I wanted to eat one while my hard-on revived, and offered her the other. I figured actual fruit might replace the more troublesome symbolical kind and include no penalty for eating it then. Using my Swiss Army knife I peeled the tomate de árbol until it was nothing but facets of wet flesh, then I sank my teeth in.

"These damn tree tomatoes are so fucking good. They're like the marriage of peach and apple—but superior to either. Can't *this* be our fruit? I promise I won't try to patent it." The stuff seemed to smack in its sweet grain of our anomalous romance.

"In fact I had thought of a different fruit—a very difficult, a dangerous—"

"All right." Now that I was a brave person I supposed I had to be one all the time. "Tell me about this dangerous fruit. I eat what you eat. Mi casa, su casa or whatever."

Around this time I felt the first tug of sunset and noticed a certain taint of gold decay slipping a few parts per thousand into the still-strong light.

"A fruit. Or it could be a drug. Ça m'est égal." I didn't know those words. "But what I imagined before is a fruit which simply to eat will cause an enormous change in the world. You eat it, yes, and it tastes very great, but then a change takes place."

"That's exactly the behavior that'll get you expelled!"

She shrugged—pretty recklessly, in my opinion. "When you eat from this fruit then whenever you put your hand on a product, a commodity, an article, then, at the moment of your touch, how this commodity came into your hands becomes plainly evident to you. Now there is no more mystification of labor, no more of a world in which the object arrives by magic—scrubbed, clean, no past, all of its history washed away. Do you see? Once we eat this fruit or drug—"

As now we'd done—that was the alarming part.

"—now whenever we touch something that was grown or made we will sense how it was grown or made."

It was terrible, it was wonderful, I had met someone as philosophical as me.

"We will feel it," she was saying of the drug which we could perhaps dump into America's water supply, "like a shock from the door handle. And of course if there was pain involved in the making of the product, the provision of a service, we will feel this. Of course it would be a difficult world to bear with this drug. And so then—changes."

"But I feel so bad for all the poor consumers."

"But you say you are a socialist."

"I guess I did say that." I reflected. "But all the people in the West—in the North—in the rich countries—everyone will start wearing gloves whenever they touch anything."

I had the other tomate de árbol in my hand. Gently I started peeling it. "Ah fuck, how will we ever be happy again, Brigid? I was afraid of this happening." I sliced the skin off the fruit in red-yellow-green scabs. But this was only on autopilot and beneath or through the careless actions of my hands I was looking at something else. It was like flying over water and then when you looked down to the ocean the skim of mirror was yanked off, so that the water became transparent, and there the sea was, filled with what you knew had always been there: the rubbery gardens and drowned mountains, the creatures from plankton up to nekton, the swimming bodies and the unburied skeletons, and now you—or I—I saw it all at once. And so in this fucked-up San Pedrified way the entire world system of neoliberal capitalism disclosed itself to me, and I felt somewhat grim.

I looked at Brigid, who was saying, "I want you to be

happy. But I also want you to be with me in your mind. That is why I invented the fruit. Which doesn't exist! Isn't this so strange?"

Now I was tearful too, feeling definitely a little apprehensive about the hard study of political economy that I would have to do to confirm my undeniable intuition. But I wanted to go ahead anyway, not only for sake of truth, but also because Brigid struck me as a very attractive being even in the ways that she wasn't yet. And where she wasn't yet beautiful, maybe she would become more so once her life was more consistently brightened by my consistently more enlightened company. "Here." I'd cut the fruit in segments and was offering her some.

"But you have cut yourself."

It was true—blood from my index stained the mango-colored flesh. Nevertheless she took the sullied piece from my hand and ate it. "I hope you don't have AIDS," she said before sucking the blood off my thumb.

Things were maybe getting cheesy. But at least they possessed the dignity of taking place.

I pulled Brigid up to her feet. And then we were walking back laterally across the hillside, following a ditch that we had reason to believe would convey us back to the pensión/spa.

"It would feel wrong—" I began.

"To go back the same way? I agree."

It remained necessary to watch out for spiders. But for me the creatures had returned to their mere nature and I forgave them for what they couldn't help being. Humans like me were different, I reasoned: they could help almost anything.

We walked along in silence, hand in hand when we could manage, until at length we came to a path that descended toward the hostel. Moving down it single file, we also seemed to come down in our minds, the drug subsiding in time with the light, and at last at the end of the path we were standing before the grounds of the spa, some of the cottages already lit up against the duskiness falling everywhere.

I turned around and kissed Brigid again, and the moist operation definitely had an us-two-kissing-each-other-in-a-quickly-darkening-world kind of feeling—an accurate feeling, given the condition of the sky.

I stepped semi-symbolically out of what felt still like the narrow path, onto the grassy lawn of the spa. "I guess this is hour one of my new life—hour one, year zero."

"Don't say this."

"What? Come on, Day One! Year Zero!"

Then she told me how the Khmer Rouge after taking Phnom Penh in 1975 had declared Year Zero and begun to massacre and starve their fellow Cambodians to the tune of one or two million people. "Be careful with your socialism," she told me as we walked down toward the cottages.

"Point taken," I assured her.

Amira was coming up the stone path in a bathing suit with a towel slung across her shoulders. "Oh," she said with this big complicitous smile. "You must be insane by now. Isn't it so intense!"

"It was very good," Brigid said, "—except for spiders."

"I became a socialist," I announced.

"*Democratic* socialist," Bridge reminded me.

"That's right. A democratic socialist. We would never sink to coercion."

"Ah yes," Amira said. "We also were happy, crazy, tripping super-hard. Then someone, he mentions the Palesteenyans. So for a few minutes we all have a bad trip."

She shrugged in the more usual, less Brigidesque way of the gesture. "Not a good idea to talk politics on this drug."

"No it's cool," I said. "We're democratic socialists, so we can handle it."

TWENTY-FOUR

I woke up sober as ever, afraid that nothing would have stuck. But when I wandered out onto the balcony in my boxers I could somehow tell that yesterday was portable and therefore here to stay.

I looked around me at the mist burning off of the valley, and I did one of those awesome sun salutations the yoga people do. Some poppies planted along the terrace were tipping a little in the slight morning breeze, indeed the whole pale sky seemed to be tolling weakly like a little bell, yet I did feel sober as ever. I turned around and looked through the door to where Brigid was sitting up naked in bed. "Democratic socialism!" I shouted. "Only more democratic, and more socialistic, than ever before!"

"What have I done?" She pulled the sheets over her head and lay back down. But I knew she was kidding, and she knew I wasn't really.

Various sex acts were performed while I had her regale me with tales of neocolonial dependency, the ruthlessness of metropolitan power, and the corruption of local elites. "You're kidding!" I would interject. "Really?!" I'd ejaculate. "Those evil fuckers!" I'd snarl.

Lying still beside her an old question recurred to me. "How come businesses have no trouble with the unions in Colombia?"

"Easy—because the trade unionists are often murdered by paramilitaries. But now"—she curled into me—"now I don't want to talk about politics. We have to talk about everything else."

Everything else was the principal subject of conversation as we walked into the town of Cuncalbamba itself, talking the whole way.

We both needed to check our email and went to the local emailería. The first thing I looked at was an email from Alice. But all it was was this sarcastic bulletin forwarded from the Sackett Street Coalition for Global Justice:

Important, long-overdue changes in the judicial system and surveillance culture of the United States are taking place. While for the most part these changes have been made without public consultation, many good citizens would nevertheless like to help out Attorney General Ashcroft's Department of Justice in any way possible. One quick and easy way is to cc all of your emails to our protector. The Attorney General may then peruse your communications for any indication that any of you are in need of being detained without charges, without a trial, and without access to legal counsel. It may be that such steps are overdue.

Please cc all electronic communications to the address supplied below.

So to Alice and the Attorney General I wrote:

FROM: wilmerdingansich@mail.fignet.com
TO: big.al@muggletonia.net
CC: ashcroft@justice.gov

One of these days, Alice-- But actually I am not angry and never really was, with you or anyone. But now this has changed! I am VERY ANGRY not with you but with the architects of neoliberal globalization and neoconservative reaction and I want to do something about this. What to do I'm still working on but nevertheless I have settled various things and will inform you of even more of them on my return.

Meanwhile I'm flattered that you cared enough to launch your conspiracy. So thanks. Its a secret unrecognized dream of everybody, dont you think?-- that some fantastic conspiracy will be arranged against us so that the otherwise senselessness of life can be temporarily defeated by deceitful love?

I dont know what will happen with me and Bridge. It seems wrong having too much hope or anxiety in advance of data yet to come. Also it could be I would make a weird husband if chosen as one. But we're glad to know each other, so--actually I'm not going to be able to thank you enough so I won't try.

How about you? What are you doing? Reading? (I mean I know you are right now but . . .) The other day with concern I envisioned you as lonely. Always, Dwight

And before dealing with the rest of my inbox I dashed off the following communiqué to the enormous Listserv of fellow Formmates, plus the Attorney General:

Hello St. Jerome's Form of 1992!!! And with a special shout-out to Attorney Ashcroft!

Just a reminder that the countdown continues, at
T minus five days. Soon we will be reunited and it
will feel so good.

Hope you have all worked up a good tolerance for
alcohol and if need be booked rooms. The rest can
pass out near the dam or finally act upon age-old
crushes and fall into bed with--not with me. I am
taken. Want to hear more? Or learn of my exciting
trip to tropical yet mountainous Ecuador? Or would
you like to know of a great new mind-curing drug
soon to be available from your doctor, if you have
benefits, and health insurance, and *have* a doctor?
Or else live in Canada?

I havent done much since seeing most of you--and
yet important things have happened even to me. So if
even I am so fascinating, think what others must be,
and please come.

D. Wilmerding, Form Agent

And to dad and mom in their separate accounts, and as
always Attorney General Ashcroft, I wrote:

Dear mom and dad, divorced now but forever united
in my mind,

I write to you from Cuncalbamba Ecuador with
good news which I hope will strike you that way.

I have met a girl and amazingly, but too complicated
to explain, this girl or at 30 really a full-fledged
woman, also Belgian, albeit originally Argentine, is a
friend of Alice's. Alice is a devious person as we
know. So it will surprise you less if I say that Brigid,

the girl/woman, has convinced me to become a
socialist! But dont worry, the democratic kind.
(We're anti-violence, although I guess we're not
above the occasional ruse.)

Since you will want to know how this happened
and I am a bad liar I admit that my conversion
experience took place while we were *fucked up*
as you (dad) and I say on a physically more or
less harmless but powerfully deranging local
hallucinogen.

Yet I am happy to tell you though that my insights
withstand sobriety.

You (esp. mom) will also be happy to know that--
except at my upcoming reunion where peer pressure
is bound to prevail--I plan from now on to live a
reasonably abstemious life. I also plan to help bring
about another possible world, and in this I somehow
hope to make enough money to afford necessities as
well as sometimes new CDs that no one I know has
a copy of to burn me. Therefore any monetary help
you (plural) can give will be met with great but
probably insufficient thanks.

Meanwhile rest assured that I have no intention of
waging class warfare against *you* (dad), who are
just one of many rightwing voters, therefore
negligible as such. Whereas you are my one and only
father and thus bulk correspondingly large to me in
the father dept.

How are the dogs, dad? Are you unfathomably
lonely as I sometimes suspect? And mom with your
birds--you? Myself I am very happy to have gone on

Abulinix, the indecision-curing drug which I confessed about to you, dad, and which, mom, sorry, in my shame, I never breathed a word--but the thing is, it works! it really does! and presumptuous as it may be to say so, both of you might benefit from taking some when to all appearances you live your post-marital lives in suspension (read: indecision) and would love to be helped out of that, and sharpened, shaped-- Anyway go on this stuff and youll see what I mean and can never quite say.

I want at this time to thank you both for your laissez-faire parenting style which hasnt at all times seemed ideal to me, but now I realize that for you (plural) to have criticized me more often would only have made me defensive, and I probably would have been even *slower* in coming around.

Dad, so you know, I think about you and the dogs very often and--though you are my father and therefore semi-enemy, owing to human nature--I do this with outstanding love. Mom, I bear the same love to you, or more, though it is tempered with respect since you are a person with standards and have disapproved of me up to now, understandably.

Much love from your own son, cured by Abulinix at 28, and somehow glad of his life in this fairly terrible world,

Dwight Bell Wilmerding

PS Sorry that both children are leftists. Medicine is so advanced these days that why not have some more?

I have already said I was somewhat well-known in my North American life, and won't list all the emails in my inbox. But for the purposes of this winding-down story it's obligatory to reproduce one more, the last one I read that day:

FROM: dan_rorschach@defunct.com
TO: wilmerdingansich@mail.fignet.com
SUBJECT: re [none]

Suicidal ideation? That's not good, Dwight.

I hope you're reading this and not dead. I promise that if you are dead I will throw your memory a big party such as we used to have in the 1997–2001 period.

MEANWHILE: DO NOT KILL YOURSELF! You're right about Abulinix. Thoughts of suicide, not to speak of acts, have been found to be fairly frequent in experimental subjects. I guess to be or not to be *is* the question. No one had counted on this. But apparently the decision to end it all is the first important decision some people make. Naturally also the last.

But the strange thing in light of your suicidal ideation, is that YOU ARE NOT ON ABULINIX! I'm sorry. Really. Really sorry. I just found out the other day.

The batch I stole your bottle from--all placebos. It didnt say so on the labels for obvious reasons. You could only tell from the Rx #. I wasnt thinking. Didnt check.

I feel bad about your bad time. I know you arranged
this trip in part--in whole?--because for whatever
reason you wanted the Big Effect to happen in
Ecuador. (You'll have to tell me how it's been there,
with Natasha. Here it has sucked, btw. I continue
to study with fascination the diverse hydraulics of
things sucking.)

Anyway its possible that you've been thinking of
offing yourself because you expected the Big Effect
and obviously it didnt come. Again, sorry. I might be
able to get you on a legit trial when you come back.
Which is when?

Mild anxiety over your welfare,

Dan

PS I take it the placebo hasn't caused you to realize
you are gay.

I sent off a note to the effect that I was alive and well
and heterosexual, if perhaps a little bi-curious, and swiveled around in the chair. "On y va?" Brigid said. She'd
finished emailing and had paid the attendant. I stood up
and looked at him, a stoop-shouldered student type,
thin in the cheeks and lips, but romantic in the eyes and
the swept-back hair. "Cuánto?" I asked, and handed him
a small sheaf of filthy cotton-soft singles. Then I went
out to the street with my change.

Across the street was the empty town square with its
sad dry fountain. Brigid had grabbed my hand. She was
asking me what the matter was. An old man in a straw
hat and dirty suit sat on a bench picking his teeth and
watching us with as mild a form of interest as is any interest at all.

I looked at Brigid. "You know what a placebo is?"

"Yes, for a control of the experiment?"

I nodded.

"So? Yes? Dwight, are you all right?"

"I am, actually." I could see in her eyes that she could hear that I was. "I'm fine."

In the Elizabeth St. boutique we found a nice sundress that would respect Brigid's semi-hippy-ism at the same time as it stamped her with fashionality. I handed over my VISA to the saleswoman and to Bridge was like, "They don't make this stuff in sweatshops do they? Seems way too expensive."

"Dwight, how do you have this money to spend?" This was Dan, who I'd brought along with us.

"I don't know, I figure racking up a lot of credit-card debt will put me in an even better position to understand the terrible indebtedness of the whole global south, not to mention the American consumer. Plus I want the whole reunion fantasy. The well-dressed beautiful fiancée, the fancy new car . . ." Of course we were borrowing the Audi from dad.

"So in Ecuador you had a midlife crisis," Dan said. "Dwight, people don't do this anymore. You don't fly to Latin America, take psychedelic drugs, and find sexual liberation with some suntanned goddess of international socialism. Excuse me," he said to Brigid. Then back to me: "Now is not thirty-five years ago."

"We're not gonna quit until they quit, Dan," I told him.

"Until who quits?"

"The bad guys," I said. "And isn't it confusing how

neoliberals and neoconservatives—they're often the very same people, did you know this? I feel like there needs to be a new terminology for things."

"Like socialism, for instance? There's a new word."

"Dwight," Brigid said, "has explained his concept to me. He is to dress in old tee shirts and ragged shorts, and this will imply that I only love him the more for his personal magnetism. Since he is a slob and a socialist."

"I taught her the word *slob*," I boasted.

In our AM spending spree we had also picked up a bargain bin copy of Air Supply's *Greatest Hits,* and it was with special anticipatory glee that I imagined rolling onto the leafy campus of St. Jerome's and blaring out the windows "Making Love Out of Nothing at All" as Brigid with her nice mezzo voice chimed on in. Meanwhile I taunted the state troopers as we zoomed through Connecticut and Massachusetts, and finally into New Hampshire with its impressive ridges of bared granite rising to either side of the road.

"I'm probably going to be called on to give a speech," I told Brigid, shifting down into fourth. "Maybe you could help me think of one."

"Be brief," she suggested.

I pulled the to-do list notebook out of my pocket, swerved briefly, accidentally, onto the shoulder of the road, and handed it to her.

"Brevity," I said. "Write that. Hmn. What else?"

"What do you think is important to have happened in the last ten years?"

"I don't know, the creation, following the fall of the Soviet Union, of an unprecedented opportunity to regulate the world by law and justice? Which was spoiled by the global hegemony and frequent lawlessness of the US? And of course I should mention the badly flawed Washington-led model of global economics and the rise of the internet. How about that? I'm not going to deal with the terrorism issue. I don't know what to do about that."

"I think there is nothing to do but to kill them."

"Huh," I said.

"But what has happened to *you* in ten years? Besides me?"

"I feel like you're enough. But you're right. Let's be vague. Write down WORK AND LOVE. I feel it would be nice for an individual to have found one of those, in ten years."

With Bridge as navigatrix, I followed green signs to the hopefully named city of Comity, and then came at last onto Duck Pond Road. Ever since I was a kid it had always impressed me how through the narrowing operations of travel, and from out of so many possible destinations, places of such incredible specificity will realize themselves right in front of you, but there it was, the campus of St. Jerome's, looming up in red brick. Of course all of this happens much faster in a late model Audi.

"Hit track five," I yelled as we slowed, and the great melting song of universal cheese poured from the top-flight stereo as we nosed through the parking lot looking for a spot. Brigid sang like a dying opera star the backup words *out of nothing at all,* and we attracted the anxious gazes of beardless youth as well as several milling alumni. I got out, shut the solid expensive white door, and saw that approaching me was old Andrew Mulland of Oak Park parentage—these days a sporting-events promoter in San Francisco. "Dude," he said, "Wilmerding," as we each laid our arms across the other's shoulders, "those were some crazy tunes you were blasting. Nice car, man."

"Air Supply is underrated. Meet Brigid."

"How's it going, Brigid."

"Very well, thank you." She was looking around at the bright grass, the colonial and neo-Gothic style buildings, the white-painted fences—and it really *was* pretty absurd to have educated children such as me in an institution such as this. "You went to a remarkable school."

Mulland was like, "I guess so if they let Wilmerding in."

"They let you in too, man. Don't forget that."

"When they let me *in* I was fine."

Greeting people, shaking hands, introducing Brigid, patting shoulders, smiling all the way, and even kissing several babies, I proceeded like a presidential hopeful down the paths of red brick, across the manicured youth preserve of the grounds, and ultimately conveyed us toward the Upper School. Our reconstituted Form was supposed to meet for supper in the Lower Dining Room, where all our names would have been carved on a wall, and where we would eat terrible cafeteria food in the old style, but chased down now—legally, even—with liquor and beer.

"You're a good sport," I said to Brigid as I caught my breath between greetings.

"I am good arm candy? For one day."

St. Jerome's looked as miraculously undisturbed as a crime scene. Everything was the same as before: the stern warmth of red brick, and all the old towering pines, the large blue ponds still lit at dusk, and that weird high note of adolescence constantly threaded into the circulating breeze.

Stark bald Arthur Ribble (currently a head and neck doctor in the Bay Area) stopped me near Connerly House and asked me about Ecuador. I told him that South America's first popular uprising had occurred in Quito in 1809.

When asked about my trip by Luisa Calder (now a video artist in New York) I said: "In the jungle the water was green, the moss was green. The orchids were green, the parrots were green. Like, every tree was green. I definitely took away a strong impression of greenness but—"

"You're just the same aren't you?"

"—but think of all the different shades of the same color. You could definitely make some video art about *that*."

The dim Lower Dining Room was loud with whispered or shouted recognitions. Everyone seemed genuinely glad to see everybody else: if someone looked great that was a pleasure, and if they looked worse than you—so much the better. With one hand I clasped Brigid's wrist, and with the other shook hands with old Formmates. Then with a serene air of inevitability I noticed someone who stood out a little from all the rest. She was looking at me from one corner of the room with her deep cartoon crescent of a smile brightly on display. Natasha van der Weyden! I rushed over to her and we intensely hugged.

"I decided," she said, "to come after all. I want to hear this story! Alice tells me everything happened exactly as she planned. Hello Brigid."

The two of them neatly shook hands.

"Oh come on. Embrace! Hug!"

They willingly obeyed—although I hadn't exactly asked for Natasha to peck Brigid on the lips and then whisper things into her ear.

"Hey Natash," I said. "Thanks for your role in the conspiracy."

She pulled away from Brigid and said, "I always liked Alice."

"Me too. Less now. But also more. In a way."

"Should I try to understand him?" she asked Brigid.

"Don't start to try!" Brigid said. "It takes more than a week."

As dinner was served I took my assigned place at the dark round table, staring at Natasha across the room.

Recent and ongoing experience had stripped off the old nimbus my fantasies had conferred, and I felt a twinge of wistfulness as she departed from the realm of pure ideas and resumed her rightful place as—even to me—a real person in this only world.

We'd been served some roast beef sodden with its own stale blood. I sliced the cut into squares without any thought of eating them. Then with one hand I sipped cold milk, and with the other downed some of the Wild Turkey someone had brought.

Before long a chant had gone up: "Speech! Speech!"

I joined in. "Speech! Speech!" Then roommate Ford, Formmate Ford, good old Ford—Ford was drilling at my shoulder with his finger, saying, "Dude! Dude!" ("Speech! Speech!" was all I heard.) "Wilmerding! Dude! Dwight!"

I looked at him.

"Speech means you. You're supposed to give the speech. After that we do toasts."

So I stood up as if learned in some ancient practice, when in actual fact it was my first time, and knocked the blade of my butter knife three times ringingly against the tall glass that I'd emptied of perhaps overmuch Wild Turkey. Bridge slipped the notebook into my empty hand.

"A-hem." I cleared my throat and raised my voice above the din. "A-hem." I took in the quietened room. The large quantum of consciousness out there, pictured in the watching eyes, was really something to behold; and it alarmed me that as soon as I said a single word it would multiply like crazy and crop up understood in the minds of approximately eighty-five people. There were also fortysome no-shows, and three Formmates whose absences were the result, respectively, of suicide, cancer, and a motorcycle crash on a rain-slick road in eastern Oregon.

"Brevity," I said. "That's what it says in my notes here. After all, brevity is the spice of life. And I guess, when these last ten years have passed in the blink of an eye, it's only appropriate that I should speak briefly, and not detain you any more than I already will."

From behind me I heard a feminine whisper. "Look, he has no hair on his legs. Look at his arms. He used to be the hairiest—"

"A-hem. When I came to you as Third Former or 'new boy' I was, in those days, like every one of you, a relatively hairless individual. Yet increasingly I grew hairier. Right . . . Yes. Okay. And indeed by the time of the collapse of the Soviet Union—which don't get me wrong, that was a good thing—by this I had become the extremely hairy man I was fated for almost ten years to remain."

"This is your brain on drugs," someone grumbled.

"My point is, Vic"—I looked at Victor Murphy, the grumbler—"we can do with our brains whatever we want. You see, if a person as hairy as me is capable of rubbing himself all over with the sap of the bobo-huariza tree, to be found in the jungles of Ecuador, and becoming hairless as a baby; or if, for example, star athletes such as McMeekin who I see is here tonight—"

"Cheers!" someone yelled.

"McMeekin!"

"—if Sean McMeekin, that is, is capable of becoming an Olympic-class rower and therefore making his heart fifty percent larger than normal size; and if, indeed, some of you who were honestly kind of unattractive last time I saw you, have now become really fairly good-looking—"

There was some laughter at this.

"—you see, what I mean is that if we can change in all these really drastic physical ways, as clearly we have, then how much easier it must be to change our *minds*." It wasn't quite the applause line I'd expected. "Over many years," I confessed anyway, "I tried not to change *my* mind. Yet it was changing all the time. And that, my fellow Formmates, was the way in which it never really changed. My mental promiscuity was finally a form of virginity."

Someone snorted. "What?"

"Wil-mer-ding! Wil-mer-ding!" Ford and someone else had begun beating on their table with forks and knives in their fists.

"But I mean to be brief. Life is brief. And youth briefer than life. Except for some people. Lots of people actually, especially in the third world, where lots of people die very young. For us, however, youth has been appallingly expanded, in our remarkable time, when there are more people alive on the planet today than have ever even existed before, and when therefore the things we do have a special new importance, and also, by the same token, each individual possesses a special new irrelevance, because of the same numbers—anyway, for us, during this time, youth has expanded to dimensions apparently without historical precedent. And I would like, in passing, to thank our Formmate Elaine Weddleton, who could not be here today, because she is a labor organizer in D.C. and waging the good fight against people such as ourselves and particularly our unkillable parents."

"Power to the people!" someone yelled out.

Someone else: "What the fuck?"

Yet another: "Who has a cane?"

And another: "I have a tomato."

Still another: "Wilmerding is a child of God!"

"Thank you," I yelled, climbing up onto the table, on which I was now standing. "So all I mean to say is that youth, brief youth, long-lasting youth, is for contemplating choices with your ever-changing mind. And yet the time has surely come for choices to be made. And many of you have made them. I hope you've made the right ones. Which kind of I doubt in some cases you have. Some of you are probably demonstrating in your daily lives the dubious fitness to rule of America's ruling class. To me that sounds like bad work and no love. I see my notes here say WORK AND LOVE. Um, yeah, and I have found both of these in the woman here with me, Brigid Lerman, who is both a Belgian drug-company heiress and my fiancée"—I looked down at this beautiful woman who was laughing and shaking her head— "though she denies being either. Anyway, I have chosen to be *her* fiancé, and a worker on the garden path of global justice. And this happened more or less at the same time I lost my hair. On my body. Just to come full circle. As you may have noticed that I did. Finally I guess the one single thing I would ask of you, as your Form Agent, in closing—"

"Who elected him?"

"—I would ask that you all think of what change, analogous in happiness, and with a psychological concomitant, to losing your hair, if you really feel you're really too hairy, might happen to *you* to make *you* satisfied with *your* decisions. Because it seems to me that we, in this room, for reasons of cruel and unusual socioeconomic conditions, have an especially big range of decisions we could make, and so there is a particular burden. So without further ado—"

"Too much ado!"

"Speech! More speech!" I could hear loyal Ford yelling.

"I would only say, in overdue conclusion, that the weird thing about freedom to choose would seem to be that no one knows what to do with it unless they give it to others. Which I think was a large factor in the horrible confusion that until recently I selflessly took it upon myself to exemplify. Until the bobohuariza, and the love, and the democratic socialism."

"What?"

"On behalf of which ideology I mean to say that only when other people have the same freedom which we have devoted ourselves to squandering—only then will we really finally know what we should have done with ours in the first place. So let us remain faithful to those privileged kids we were by seeking to honor and cancel our condition by making it general throughout the world."

"Wilmerding is insane!"

"He's *inane* . . ."

"He's a child of God!" Who was the person saying that?

"He's exactly the same."

"He's totally changed."

"Make him shut the fuck up!"

I clambered off from the table, while a few people apprehensively clapped. Others had taken up my name as a chant: "Dwight Bell Wilmerding! Dwight Bell Wilmerding!" And still others were trying to drown this chant out with the more familiar "U-S-A! U-S-A! U-S-A!"

Before sitting down I raised my voice a final time and addressed the crowd: "I want to conclude with some vacuous statement we can all agree on. Whether or not we are jingoistic shouters who respond to the promise of democratic socialism with patriotic non sequiturs. Well anyway, thank you all for coming! You're all beautiful! Maybe not morally. But mostly so well groomed!"

People starting cheering, clinking glasses, or else muttering darkly against me.

"Thank *you*, Dwight!"

"And thank *you*." I pointed to Martin Groman, who had thanked me, and was a screenwriter in LA, "and you, and you, and you!" I began pointing wildly all around. "Thank you for coming! Thank you for listening! Thank you for having elected me ten years ago!

That's what you get for democracy. Good night!" I bowed, with maybe two-fifths of the room applauding as a flung tomato sailed by.

The tomato nicked my chin as I sat down on Brigid's lap, and at that moment an idea shot into my mind like it was already there, and as surely as I felt Brigid's thighs through her dress I felt that I should write this book. I wanted to write a memoir that would do a better job than my reunion address of convincing susceptible and unformed young people to campaign for those better economic arrangements and that fairer disbursal of freedom which, for the sake of efficient reference and inevitable misunderstanding, I had taken to calling *democratic socialism*. Furthermore I wanted readers to keep an open mind about foreigners and visit Latin America. And then by the late end of the night I'd added another hope.

So that—or this—is the book that I have now written after several weeks of intense effort expended mostly at night, sitting here at my desk in this cold furnished apartment that I rent on a hillside in Cochabamba, Bolivia, a city of some four hundred thousand souls where a few months ago I also began my work on behalf of Bolivian—why not?—economic rights. I'm trying to complete the book by tomorrow, dawn of the summer solstice—up in the North the year's shortest day—since without arbitrary goals, fervently chosen, I don't know what I'd do with myself.

Right now it's totally dark here except for the desk lamp and, as it's early in the morning, practically as quiet as your breathing. In half an hour or so the sun will come up and the dogs of Cochabamba will bark like they've never seen it before. Meanwhile I feel alone as if lost, though I'm not lost and am in fact pretty happy, albeit in a painful pining way, given that Brigid isn't here.

Bridge is living in Buenos Aires these days, working as

a stringer for a French newspaper. The economic collapse is ongoing, and I guess she couldn't stay away.

Meanwhile I console myself with the thought that at least I still have in my head the vision we combined to see in Ecuador, in which commodities disclose their history to the touch and in one huge epidemic of empathy we start repairing the world. Yet said vision remains so far from realization that I could figure out no immediate way of conscripting myself into its troops. Therefore because I wanted all the same to have some larger purpose practiced through me, and was eager to return to South America, I took up a suggestion of Brigid's—namely, that with her help I sucker the director and only other employee of the Bolivian Action Node, here in Cochabamba, into hiring me as an assistant, a position once held by Brigid.

Ely is the director of the Bolivian Action Node. He too is a gringo, or sort of—he is Canadian, saying *aboot* for *about*. He also has two dogs, a baby, a wife, all of them cute and pleasant, and a serious commitment to our work here, which in a minute I'll describe. Ely's Spanish sounds excellent, the more of it that I learn, and he's got some Quechua too. As his assistant I sweep the office and fetch his lunch and coffee with a frantic alacrity. However my main task is writing press releases on the—as of December 2002—worsening situation down here. Fortunately I am allowed to compose these in what he tells me is idiosyncratic English.

The news is not great. People have been cultivating coca in the nearby Chapare region since they showed up approximately eight thousand years ago. Locally they chew the dried leaves—particularly the tin miners, since it suppresses appetite and thirst and possibly makes them feel somewhat better about their poverty and likely deaths, if not from injuries sustained underground, then from silicosis of the lungs (occupational hazard) before reaching twenty-nine. That is my age now, and I can testify that it does creep up. Anyway: the American government doesn't want the coca grown and has got the Bolivian one to crack down. Helping out in this process is the Expeditionary Task Force, whose members draw their salaries from the local US embassy and then go out to burn down farmers' coca.

The farmers have been protesting this. Many of them have amenably tried growing legal crops like pineapple and passion fruit and so forth. But infrastructure here is so sub-Ecuadorian that the campesinos can't get their produce to market before everything spoils. They prefer coca because it's resistant to rotting and disease and fetches enough bolivianos that mostly you can feed your family. (This isn't the place, unless everywhere is, to discuss the mixture of unstable commodity prices and first-world agricultural protectionism that characterizes the current order of things.) Lately the rotting fruits have been dumped along the roadsides in protest against the shutting down of one of the until-now legal coca markets and just generally against the whole policy—under which you can grow what doesn't pay, and can't grow what does—of the national government and its American patron.

The Expeditionary Task Force has sometimes beaten or shot and killed farmers. Most of the protesters received into hospitals have been discovered to be suffering from malnutrition. The big question is whether the government will keep shutting down coca markets, sparking more carnage, or what.

My job is to publicize this and et cetera. Meanwhile I let myself hope that to publish this memoir on the growth of my mind may bring these issues more notice than our press releases attract. But I don't mean to bring you down as a reader, and one main effort of my life is to try not to spoil my own mood. Currently the party line I give myself, and do in part believe, is that what's happiest is just to be alive and sensitive when it comes to feeling the world, and if what your senses, honed beyond usefulness, end up registering is so much suffering out there that you become light-headed with it at times—well, those senses can still be used for extracting pleasures from fruits, nuts, beverages of all kinds, words on a page, a loved mammal in your arms, music (including sad kinds), and anyway this is only the tip of a list anyone could assemble. I know my list is basic but maybe to utter banalities is a type of solidarity in these lonelifying times?

Don't imagine, though, that I have no wish to be a better and more erudite spokesman for things. I do! But what is the premise or promise of democracy except the full intellectual competence of even the confused and half-baked mind? Any movement failing to recruit ignoramuses or turning its nose up at fools can never succeed. Democracy is the better route, and everyone likes it, except usually those claiming to. So: democratic socialism! (Democracy and socialism being reinforcing tendencies.) That's my idea, and in having it I inherit problems that have been piling up for centuries. Though I can't deal with these problems, that is what I do, and only now that my problems aren't exclusively my own do I really feel, in a last-minute twist, that they are.

Not that I don't have doubts. Have Ely and I helped at all? Or will policy go on being made in Washington and La Paz the same as if we didn't exist? And not that I'm not also somewhat embarrassed by my existence. For instance which of the formless souls that Plato talks about milling around in the afterlife would ever say, on reflection, that what it, this soul, would like most of all, is to take up residence in the hairy body of Dwight B. Wilmerding (having no more bobohuariza, his hair has come back in force), given that someday he will live as I

live, work as I work, writing at night in this headlong
way, in the dusty city of Cochabamba, where I've just
now heard the first rooster starting up?

Most mornings I'm asleep now. Then I get up and
stretch and yawn and drink café con leche, sometimes
feeling as good as if I'll never sicken or die. The feeling
is often different when at night I go out on the balcony
and look up at the stars—*way* more of them down here
than in the northern hemisphere.

Definitely I miss her. I feel I would like to corrupt her
pure spirit with my own . . . I even toy seriously with the
thought of children. But then the relationship between
inputs and outcomes would seem to be particularly un-
predictable where parents and their kids are concerned
(an impression mom and dad have both recently if sepa-
rately conveyed). Plus Brigid is hesitant, needing to
know me better, etc. Therefore I transcribe portions of
the journal I'm keeping, and post them to her via email:

November 28, 2002
Dogs barking. Annoying me. Yet this is the 3rd
world. So dogs bark. Get used to this.
  (1 PM) Fucking dogs.

December 1, 2002
Hot December, a first for me. Dreamed last night of
taking off pants in public. Somehow not ashamed.
Others follow suit.
  Hard time wrapping my mind around Kondratiev
periodicity, aka the long waves of capitalist
expansion. Formerly mentally dealt with shorter
increments.

December 3, 2002
Patience and mortality—how to reconcile?

December 4, 2002

Number of injured unknown. Serious foreboding it seems in the market, on the streets.

   What I'm doing: right thing, but for wrong reasons? But what do I know about reasons?

   Evening spent reading. Lonesome. Also flatulent. Too flatulent to marry?

December 5, 2002

Began memoir today. How fast I write! As easy as talking.

December 15, 2002

Pornographic/utopian thoughts of Brigid. We should live together slowly, making most of time even while world speeds up and distances collapse. Snowballing conviction.

Brigid likes being sent these notes—"I am becoming addicted somewhat," she wrote from Buenos Aires the other day—but so far her answer to me hasn't changed since the night of the reunion.

After toasts got proposed and scattered goodbyes said, after email addresses were exchanged and compliments made and wishes for future life expressed, and once I'd been avoided or embraced or just ignored by my departing Formmates—going off to motels or hotels or tents pitched on the Freaky Fields—some of us went to hang out near the dam by Long Pond. Everyone was skinny-dipping and a fat joint was circling round. Long-haired Earth First!er Ramsay Fondaras was playing old Dead tunes on his acoustic guitar, and—with one arm around Natasha's wet shoulder and the other draped over Brigid's—I joined in, singing, "Sometimes the light's all shinin on me—" I tapped my foot three times. "Other times I can barely—see—"

"What do the two of you plan to do now?" Natasha asked after a while.

Brigid shrugged. "We live the good life."

Ford was there too. "But what do socialists *do* for a living?"

"Not *that* good life," I said, "the other one. The more like ethical one." Still, that was a good question Ford had asked—one that had been weighing on my mind.

"Both," Bridge was saying. "Both these good lives." She looked at me and laughed at us. "Very likely, don't you think?"

She stood up naked and walked away toward the dam in this very classical-seeming, moonlight-marbled, statue-come-to-life sort of way. I got up stepping out of my clothes and followed her, watching from behind as she balanced on the concrete ledge of the dam and then sprang from her toes, diving into the water and going invisible except for the clear globes of breath that peeled away and broke on the surface in a wake of wet sparks. Her head popped up slick as a seal's, and she beckoned me in with a sweeping arm. So I dived or dove in after her, and plunged hard in the form-fitting cold.

When I came to the surface Brigid had swum off to the other side of the water. So I followed her there doing the butterfly stroke until, wanting to savor my approach, I instead took up the dog paddle and dawdled through the water.

Sitting on the reedy bank she kicked a splash at me. "Je t'aime, Dwight. Vraiment—c'est vrai. C'est absurde mais . . ."

I hauled myself onto the shore and finding myself on bended knee I said, "Will you marry me then? I want to marry you. Seriously. There's a place in town that sells rings."

She smiled a smile rigged up with mockery and delight.

"Listen," I said. "If you don't know what to want you'll never get it."

"What logic! I like it."

"Then follow the logic. Come on."

"No—I always like your logic because I cannot. Dwight, we have to think of what we will do with ourselves."

"We'll become professional revolutionaries."

"But this was the great mistake of the Third International."

"True," I supposed. "Don't want to repeat that shit again."

"We need to make our own mistakes."

"So marry me then."

Sad and delighted, skeptical and full of longing, and just generally very Brigid—that was how she looked when she said, "I'd like to. But not now. Maybe not ever. Really I don't know."

ACKNOWLEDGMENTS

The phrases "Philosophizing ultimately means nothing other than being a beginner" and "existence's alert awareness of itself," attributed here to the philosopher Otto Knittel, are in fact the property of Martin Heidegger. As for the fictional band Nurse and Soldier, the author is grateful to Erica Fletcher and Rob Thacher for allowing him to make use of the name of their real band.

ABOUT THE AUTHOR

BENJAMIN KUNKEL grew up in Colorado. He has written for *Dissent, The Nation,* and *The New York Review of Books,* and is a founding editor of *n+1* magazine. This is his first book.